DEADLIER THAN BEAUTY

A SCI-FI CRIME THRILLER

RAOUL EDMUND

For more information, please go to **RaoulEdmund.com**

Printed in the United States of America

Printed & Distributed by BookBaby in Pennsauken, NJ

First Printing, 2019

ISBN: 978-1-54398-646-4 (print)
ISBN: 978-1-54398-647-1 (ebook)

To my sister, Rosanne, who encouraged me to write.

CONTENTS

CHAPTER 1

CHICKENSHIT AND LEMONS. THE AIR REEKED OF IT. THEY rolled up the windows but it was already too late. Cromag shut off the siren and got out of the car. Bennett did the same. They looked out over an ocean of gridlocked cars. Here they were, at an accident scene evolving into a major clusterfuck, and they couldn't do a damn thing. They were stuck. Not the best place for two cops responding to an urgent call.

Just five minutes ago, they'd been cruising the 101 Freeway. It was a nice day. Not just nice for October, but *nice*. No clouds, mid-seventies. Traffic was light heading into the Valley. Cromag had started to daydream about the beach, and Bennett had angled his face in the open window to snag some rays.

Suddenly, like a thunderstorm rolling in over the mountains, their reverie had been shattered. The dispatch radio had come to life, crackling: "All units. Reporting a 273D at 1155 De Garmo Street, Pacoima…"

"Wow, perfect timing," Cromag said. Ordinarily, being homicide detectives, they would've let the beat cops handle a domestic violence call—but they were so close to the scene. And it was a nice day anyway, right? Cromag looked over at Bennett. "Let's check it out."

They exited on Paxton and snaked into an open lane. Cromag plunged his foot to the floor and the car's big Hemi woke up. The speedometer jumped like it had been goosed. The torque pinned them to their seats. Cromag smiled, looked over at his partner and said, "Light 'em up."

Bennett switched on the lights and siren, and the show was on. They roared down Paxton, as cars scrambled to get out of their way. Cromag was enjoying this. Their usual car, which was in the yard for maintenance, was just plain *boring* compared to this muscle-bound Interceptor. Their everyday ride was low-profile—no lights or siren—and definitely anemic under the hood. An under-powered excuse for a cop car, compared to this beast. Cromag loved driving it. It brought him back to the days when he was a rookie, newly-sprouted from the academy and greener than broccoli. So long ago.

The cars they passed became a blur. They were a quarter-mile from the intersection of Paxton and Glenoaks when everything suddenly changed again. First came the sound of screeching tires—and then a boom that made the cruiser's windows shake. Cars were skidding, swerving onto front yards in desperate attempts to avoid rear-end collisions. Cromag and Bennett avoided whacking the car in front of them by millimeters, but their luck didn't last.

As Cromag looked in the rearview, a Toyota Camry hurtled towards them, the terrified driver screaming. Cromag told Bennett, "Brace for a shock." The impact felt like a seismic event, and when it was over, they had a crumpled car resting on their trunk lid. *Dynamite—just what we need,* thought Cromag.

It was an accident all the TV stations would lead the news with that night. A flatbed truck owned by Hernandez Landscaping had centerpunched an open semi carrying three tons of lemons from California Citrus. Both trucks had overturned, spilling their loads all over one of the busiest intersections in the San Fernando Valley.

The best part? The landscaping truck had been laden with fifty-pound bags of chicken manure—and they had exploded all over the intersection, mixing with the juice of thousands of crushed lemons. Quite a cocktail.

The two trucks had slid over the asphalt, framing a perfect gridlock. No cars could move near or around the accident. The streets that fed the intersection were packed solid with trapped, crumpled cars. Jets of steam gushed from crushed radiators. Drivers were blasting their horns in exasperation, knowing it was useless to do so, but doing it anyway.

The drivers of the trucks were uninjured—miraculously—and had exited their vehicles. They were now confronting each other, with a growing crowd of spectators in attendance. Two young Hispanic guys, frothing at the mouth.

"Pince pendejo! Donde aprendiste manejar?" screamed one.

"*Cinga tu madre, puto!*" yelled the other.

Cromag and Bennett looked at each other, shaking their heads. They were already late responding to the domestic violence call. The swarming onlookers cheered, eager for the confrontation to escalate. The scene resembled a bullfight in Tijuana—and smelled far worse.

Cromag barked at Bennett, "Get in," and floored it in reverse. The Toyota that was propped on their trunk got bucked off and spun around like a top. The cruiser had bumpers like steel girders, and Cromag cleared the space he needed by butting and banging other cars out of his way. He made the fastest k-turn in history, the cruiser smoking its tires all the way.

He sought out the most resistance-free route he could find. He drove over front lawns, splintering picket fences and sending trash cans flying. They left a trail of cavernous ruts and huge divots of grass in their wake as they escaped from the chaos behind them. Other drivers had exited their cars and looked at each other in astonishment: *these are* cops *driving like this? And why are they heading* away *from the accident?*

Cromag looked in his rearview. The crowd had gotten loud and ugly. Riot control would need to be brought in, but that was for somebody else to worry about. Too much precious time had already been lost.

He hit the brakes and went into a controlled skid as they careened onto Desmond. It felt like they made the turn on two wheels. He glanced over at Lyle and could see his junior partner was a little unsettled. Here they were, doing seventy in a residential zone, going the wrong way down a one-way street. Cromag, the veteran, empathized, but hey: That's the way it is when you're a cop—*Sometimes you have to break some laws…to enforce others…*

They finally made it to De Garmo and hung a shrieking left. The address was in "The Projects," a huge, depressing glut of apartment buildings and narrow streets cluttered with trash and derelict cars. The Projects were the centerpiece of one of the most heavily-populated *barrios* of Los Angeles, and as such, were one of the most productive sources of domestic violence calls. Here you had thousands of low-income residents, mostly immigrants, most of them illegal, struggling to survive in their cramped, smelly shitholes. It was an explosive urban environment—with a very short fuse. There wasn't a week that went by they didn't get multiple calls like this. It went with the territory.

As they got nearer, the true cost of the delay caused by the accident became apparent. Things had escalated since the original dispatch call. The building was swarming with black-and-whites, the perimeter swaddled in yellow tape. There was a throng of curious onlookers, chattering feverishly in Spanish. It wasn't until he saw the Medical Examiner's van that Cromag realized they had arrived too late. What had started as a domestic squabble had become a homicide.

They showed their badges to the cop guarding the taped-off perimeter and went upstairs to a second-floor apartment. The hallway was dingy and dirty, with burned-out light bulbs in naked fixtures on the ceiling.

They went in slowly. There was a painting of the Virgin of Guadalupe hanging in the entryway. Baby clothes, diapers, and bottles were scattered all over the floor. The sink was choking with dirty dishes. An open package of tortillas was sitting on the counter. A pot of refried beans was simmering on the stove, with a frying pan full of fragrant *carne asada* sizzling next to it. The small table was set with plates and utensils. And the person who had been preparing the meal, a young *Latina* mother barely out of her teens, was lying in a pool of blood on the floor, with sixteen stab wounds in her torso and face.

The first-responder cops had cuffed the primary suspect: her boyfriend, who was found holding the knife in a stupor and looking down at the dead body of his *mammacita*. He had surrendered without incident and confessed on the spot, and was now awaiting transport to Division for interrogation and booking. Three children—a boy age five, a girl age four, and a baby less than six months old—were sitting on a shredded couch in the living room. There was a black-velvet painting on the wall, of a *bandito* brandishing six-guns, the kind of artwork popular among Hispanics. The children were silent, their eyes gaping in bewilderment. The baby was sucking on a *bobo,* Spanish slang for a pacifier. A policewoman was watching over them.

A feeling of futility engulfed Cromag and Bennett. *They were too late. This could have been prevented. If only they hadn't gotten caught in that fucking accident.* It was a sick feeling. Despite their best intentions, they'd been unable to prevent a tragedy. They felt helpless, themselves victims of a larger injustice that included this senseless murder. How could a day that started out so good turn bad for so many people, in so many ways?

To compound the sting, their presence as homicide investigators was more or less superfluous. It was a no-brainer crime scene. The cause of death was obvious; the murder weapon had been bagged, still wet with the victim's blood; they had a suspect in custody who had already confessed; and they had witnesses.

All that remained was for the CSI's to gather evidence to support what was already an open-and-shut case. As far as an investigation was concerned, they could pretty much mail this one in. They returned to the car, feeling defeated and useless, and headed back to Division. They remained silent and obeyed the speed laws the whole way.

CHAPTER 2

FAR ACROSS TOWN, IN STARK CONTRAST TO THE *BARRIO* IN Pacoima where detectives Connor Cromag and Lyle Bennett had been unable to prevent the City's fifty-eighth homicide of the year, the doors of the Excelsior Motor Car Company were opening for business. The prestige auto dealership had been a fixture in Beverly Hills since the days of silent movies, with a showroom that boasted an assortment of insanely expensive chariots equal in value to the gross domestic product of some third-world countries. Bentley's, Maybach's, Lamborghini's and Ferrari's—all gleaming, all incredibly costly—and all just waiting to be driven home by some fortunate member of the city's privileged few.

Corbin Kellerman, impeccably dressed in an Armani suit, had just sat at his desk near the showroom when a striking brunette entered and began walking across the floor. She was tall, shapely, and quite beautiful—a typical customer at Excelsior. She passed car after car, not even stopping to look inside, as most customers did. She was on a trajectory, as if she knew exactly what she was looking for.

Her behavior did not surprise Corbin. After years as Excelsior's top salesman, he had become well versed in the ways of the affluent. Celebrities were as common at this dealership as trailer trash might be at a Walmart, and women like this stunning brunette were garden-variety specimens. Dressed in Versace, accessorized with Gucci leather, she glided over the marble floor like a vapor.

Everything about this lady said high thread count. Corbin pegged her as either a star or the trophy wife of some uber-powerful studio exec. But Corbin's conjecture was irrelevant. Her identity would remain a mystery, unless she decided to reveal it. Women like this were inscrutable on purpose. The rich prided themselves on the maintenance of their anonymity; if they wanted to reveal their identities, they would let you know.

The click of her heels on the tile got nearer. It was time for Corbin to introduce himself. She had stopped in front of a fiendishly attractive Maserati Granturismo Convertible, and she appeared interested. *Time to help the young lady kick the tires…*

"Good morning. I'm Corbin Kellerman. Would you like to know more about any of our motorcars?"

She turned and regarded him half-seriously, almost bored, as if communication were drudgery. Another earmark of the rich, one that Corbin was all too familiar with. She pursed her lips just so, saying "Yes, I like *this* car."

"Aaah, yes…the Maserati Granturismo. One of the most highly-prized motorcars in the world." Corbin was not exaggerating. The Maserati convertible was among the current hot choices for those seeking instant visual evidence that they'd "arrived." In the epicenter of conspicuous consumption that was Los Angeles, an uncommonly over-accessorized motorcar fit in perfectly with the uncommonly-overhyped culture. For those who could snicker at its six-figure price tag, it was *the* car to drive, especially for a beautiful young woman. She had made an excellent choice.

"Would you like to take it for a test-drive?" Corbin asked. He did so as a courtesy to all prospective buyers, but in this case, he wondered if she was really ready to dance with four hundred and fifty-four horses, and fork over a hundred and fifty grand to do so. She countered right away—with a surprising reply.

"That won't be necessary. Is it available for me to take right now?"

"Yes, of course. It will take about five minutes to make it ready. "Uhm …" he always slowed down when he got to the part about payment. He knew from experience that the wealthy were touchy about money, as if bothering to mention the cost of an outrageously expensive item would be an insult to their affluence.

"… Were you interested in a lease arrangement?"

As everybody in the luxury car business knew, most such vehicles in Los Angeles were leased rather than purchased, so her response was totally unexpected.

"No, I'll pay cash."

CHAPTER 3

IT HAD BEEN A COOL OCTOBER NIGHT IN THE SAN FERNANDO Valley—good weather for sleeping. In his small house in Mission Hills, Detective Connor Cromag was snoozing soundly, right until his alarm went off.

His alarm played "Ventura Highway" by the group America. He liked waking up to it. It reminded him of his arrival in California decades ago. He had been young, full of the energy and dreams of youth. "Ventura Highway" had been the number one song on the radio. To him, the song had embodied the mystique of California, with its promise of a fresh start in life.

Now, years after having established a career, he still loved the song and associated it with a more innocent time. Its promise of a new day and good things often contrasted sharply with the reality of his life. That's why he liked to start each day with it. Kept his attitude proper.

He squelched the alarm and put his cellphone down, next to his badge and Glock. He kept those two items with him at all times. He even had a special dry nook where he parked them while showering. The gun and the badge substantiated each other—and together gave him the street cred he needed to be a homicide detective in Southern California.

It was still dark outside. It was at least twenty minutes before the sun would rub its eyes, stretch its arms, and get on with the business of warming and illuminating L.A. Getting up early was a habit Cromag had cultivated since his tenderfoot days at the Police Academy. His fellow recruits had given him the nickname "Crackadawn" for his habit of early rising. "Crackadawn Cromag" was always the first one in class, on the shooting range, at the training field.

He walked into the kitchen to address one of his morning priorities: coffee. If addiction to caffeine was, as some believed, a vice—then yes, Cromag was guilty of it. He couldn't start a day without it. He ground the beans and savored the aroma as the liquid dripped into the carafe. "The Elixir of Life," was what he and his brother Clayton called coffee. How true was that?

He finished the java and moved on to his next priority: getting to the gym. Exercise was part of his daily routine, essential to his lifestyle. Fortunately, he belonged to a gym with a location not too far away. He had joined many years ago and had been a member ever since.

He got into his car and headed for the freeway. Twenty-five years ago, when he had been a rookie, the freeway system of Los Angeles had been fast, efficient and a pleasure to use. Unlike other states, where drivers had to pay highway tolls, the freeways of California were indeed free, and were open and uncrowded.

All that had changed in the ensuing years. The growing volume of people and cars simply outpaced the capacities of the system. Now it was hopelessly inadequate, an ugly reminder of a failed dream that had become an urban nightmare.

The 101 Freeway was the primary artery connecting downtown Los Angeles with the suburbs of the San Fernando Valley. It was a study in frustration, and had helped Los Angeles earn the dubious distinction of having the most congested traffic in the nation. At any time—even pre-dawn—the 101 could be counted on to be bumper-to-bumper, a parking lot masquerading as a freeway.

Freeway congestion had become a part of every Angeleno's life—a "comes with the territory" fact that irritated anybody who depended on the system. On a list of the five things that were feared most by residents of Los Angeles, "Freeway Commuting" ranked very high—right after "Earthquakes" and "Wildfires."

Cromag got to the gym and had time for a quick workout before he headed into Division. He showered, dressed, and drove on Devonshire Street, always scouting and checking his surroundings with the eyes of the perennial cop.

After he crossed over Laurel Canyon Boulevard, he saw the familiar grim façade of Division staring at him through his windshield. The stark, imposing structure of Angeles Division Police Headquarters had been built in what had once been an idyllic residential corridor many years ago. It was a proud monument to justice and the rule of law, and the community around it had reflected those ideals.

But over time, the changing demographics of the city mutilated the once-peaceful suburban community around the police station. What had once been an ideal place to raise children was now an ideal place to score crack cocaine, or get a blowjob from a street whore.

This same scenario of urban blight had become rampant throughout much of the San Fernando Valley. The wide streets, beautiful parks, and never-ending orchards of citrus and olives that had drawn families to the Valley in the 1950s, changed over time, under the assault of a burgeoning population of illegal immigrants, the homeless, and gang members.

In this urban battle zone, Angeles Division Headquarters stood as the last bastion of law and order, an island of good in a raging sea of evil. This island was where Detective Connor Cromag worked, and it was home to his team of detectives and forensic investigators.

Cromag parked and entered the building. He nodded to the desk sergeant, then went upstairs to Homicide. This is where he spent most of his waking life. He'd never even considered any other alternative to being a cop. He had decided on a career in law enforcement when he was in his teens, and had pursued his dream relentlessly.

He had gotten a degree in Criminal Justice and then applied to the Los Angeles Police Department. He was accepted and did his basic at the Police Academy in Elysian Park. He became a patrolman in short order, never taking his eyes off the prize he wanted more than anything else in the world: to be a detective.

Many other metro police departments did not require their detective candidates to pay their dues as police officers first, but the LAPD did—a minimum of four years as a police officer. After four years as a beat cop, he applied for the detective program. When he was accepted, it was the happiest day of his life.

He trained at the FBI's National Academy, graduated with honors, and became a rookie detective. In smaller metro operations, detectives often investigated a variety of crimes, including homicides, but the city's department was large enough to warrant a division devoted exclusively to homicides.

Cromag soon went from general detective to homicide detective, and his career flourished. He had good communication skills, which he piggy-backed onto his perceptiveness and intuition, and the mix gave him a unique talent for determining whether people were being honest or not. He was a natural.

Cromag worked his way up the ranks, and four years ago had been appointed Lead Homicide Investigator, the supervisor of the department. He had a team of detectives working under him, and had hand-picked an elite squad of talented, dedicated professionals to assist him.

Lyle Bennett, age 34, was his second in command and had also graduated from the FBI Academy. He was sharp, smart and intuitive. He was a good man.

Rounding out Cromag's squad was Tom Dupree, a 37-year-old specialist in BPA (Bloodstain Pattern Analysis); George Simington, a forensic pathologist in his early forties who had transferred from the Atlanta, Georgia PD; and Robert Alcord, the "baby" of the team—a California born-and-raised CSI who had recently come on board and had just celebrated his twenty-eighth birthday.

Habitually, Cromag always arrived early and today was no different. He poured himself a coffee and sat at his desk. It was Lyle Bennett who arrived next, greeting Cromag as he did every morning. "Hey, Sarge, how ya' doin'?"

Cromag, who was out in the field more often than not, relied on Bennett to brief him on the latest developments. "Good so far, Bennett. What've we got?"

"The bad news is that our key person of interest in the Hermosillo slayings just lawyered-up, but the good news is that we don't have any new homicides."

"Wow—it's gonna be a peaceful day," Cromag said. A "peaceful day" in Cromag lingo meant a day without any new homicides.

Little did Cromag know that at the very moment he was uttering those words, events were transpiring that would spell the end of his peaceful days for a long, long time to come.

CHAPTER 4

THE MASERATI GLEAMED IN THE SUNRISE JUST STARTING TO peek over the San Gabriel Mountains. It had rained the night before, cleansing the fetid detritus of smog that usually blanketed the Valley. The morning air tingled with freshness—an expectancy of new beginnings. Droplets of water beaded up on its mirrored finish as it grabbed the curve of the freeway offramp.

The driver had input an address into the car's navigation system and it had performed flawlessly. She looked up at the sign on the building. "Exceleron Fitness," it said, and she mouthed the words slowly, syllable by syllable, repeating the name in the way someone does when they're learning a new language. She exited the car and walked towards the entrance.

At the counter, a young redhead dressed in tight leggings and an Exceleron Fitness t-shirt, got up from her chair and greeted her. "Welcome to Exceleron Fitness," she said. "How can I help you?"

The woman looked at the girl's nametag and spoke, reading it verbatim. "Hello, Rose Williams Membership Coordinator." She said it in an emotionless manner, with no eye contact, and no pause between words. Her delivery was so devoid of expression, that Rose thought the woman had gotten one too many botox treatments and had paralyzed her facial muscles. But suddenly the woman smiled, and it was a smile so beautiful and disarming that Rose felt awkward.

"I would like to become a member, Rose Williams," she said, reverting to her prior robotic aspect, her eyes staring right through her. Rose felt the same way she did when she got a solicitous phone call and wasn't sure if the caller was real or a robocall droid.

Rose took a quick visual inventory of her—in the silent, efficient way that women assess other women. Not like a man does—with his crude, top-to-bottom scan of eyes, face, breasts, ass and legs—but a woman's assessment: more concerned with what is *on* the body: makeup, jewelry, clothing, shoes, accessories.

Rose's review was thorough and perceptive. She noted the Versace threads, the Bottega Veneta handbag, the gold rings, the diamond tennis bracelet—all expertly coordinated, and all being carried by perfectly-manicured feet sporting Christian Louboutin pumps. Everything about this lady said "A-lister," no doubt about it. Rose was impressed, even slightly jealous, but she knew better than to display any catty behavior.

"Of course, …" Rose said. "Here's an application. Fill out the front and back completely. Here's a pen." She motioned to a group of chairs off to the side. "You can sit over there."

The woman filled out the form and returned. She handed Rose the application and a wad of cash. Rose looked down at the woman's name.

"Eve Nouveaux?" Did I say that right? Do you pronounce the last name "New-voh?"

"Yes," the woman said.

Rose created a new member file and handed the woman a membership card. "Well, congratulations for joining Exceleron Fitness, Eve. This is your membership card. It will give you access to any of our locations, nationwide. We have fifty locations here in California alone."

"Yes, I know," the woman said. She started to walk away, but Rose just had to say something that had been on her mind since she'd first seen her. "By the way, I like your shoes," she said.

The woman turned to her and looked directly into Rose's eyes, again with that vacant stare that Rose found disturbing. "Do you? Take them, they're yours." She took off her shoes and handed them to an astonished Rose. Then she reached into her handbag. "And here is the receipt. I just bought them. If they are the wrong size and you need to exchange them, you shouldn't have any problem."

You could have knocked Rose over with a whisper. Here, a total stranger had just gifted her with a pair of Christian Loubotin "Red Bottom" open toed pumps—eight-hundred-plus bucks a pair—and had not batted an eyelash. The magnitude of the gesture had no more effect on the emotionless donor than if she had given Rose a stick of chewing gum. For the third time now, Rose had witnessed an undecipherable and disturbingly weird facet of the woman's behavior, and it made her uneasy. She simply muttered "Thank you," and watched in gaping silence as Eve walked out the door.

Later, when questioned about the incident, Rose would describe the woman as "incredibly detached." Rose's assessment was correct, but the woman's detachment was not like that of the wealthy, who are insulated from life's setbacks and challenges, and become quasi-emotionless. Nor was it the detachment of the terminally ill, who perceive the inescapable approach of death and vacate their earthly aspect in response to it. No—this woman's air of detachment was the product of something else—something very different.

After Eve Nouveaux returned to her car, she opened the trunk and reached in to get a brand-new pair of Louboutin pumps—exactly like those she'd just given to "Rose Williams Membership Coordinator." She had purchased four pairs, all exactly the same, because she liked them. She got back in the car and reached into her Bottega Veneta handbag—one of three she had purchased the day before at Nordstrom in the Newport Beach Fashion Square Mall. Eve believed in being prepared, even if outfitting her operation ran into six digits.

She retrieved a smartphone from the bag and got to work. Her fingers moved over the app screen with a speed and precision that spoke of far more than just a high level of competence. At first glance, it would seem that any adolescent could have given the same demo. But a closer observation would have proven she was far more skilled than a typical tech-savvy teenager. She had a focused touch and rapidity that was almost machine-like—it rendered her rapidly pecking fingers a *blur*. It would have required a stop-motion camera to capture the individual keystrokes and swipes.

She downloaded a directory of all the Exceleron Fitness locations in California, then integrated that data with the map application on her smart-phone. She traced an itinerary that started in the Santa Clarita Valley, swung east through the Foothill Communities, then laced its way into the San Fernando Valley, winding up in metro Los Angeles. She did all this at blinding speed—so quickly and precisely it would have left most observers not only impressed, but awe-struck—and in some cases, even shocked and fearful.

She dug into her handbag and pulled out what looked like a charging cord. But it was different. It had a normal USB terminus on one end, but the other end featured a narrow cylindrical cone. She inserted the USB coupling into the smartphone and put the conical end deep into her own ear. But it wasn't music or a podcast she was seeking. She was going to transfer data.

She set the phone to transmit the gym location data and her mapped itinerary directly through the earpiece. To ordinary ears, it would have been digital gibberish, like the weird gargling of an ancient fax machine. But to her it was as soothing as soft music, evidenced by the euphoric manifestations on her face. She lay back and her eyes glazed over, with her eyeballs moving rapidly, as if she were in the deepest stages of REM sleep.

Within minutes she opened her eyes and became alert as a falcon. She activated the Maserati's nav system, and spoke an address command to it.

"There it is," she said, as the route to her next destination appeared in vibrant color. The Maserati's interface and graphics were exceptional. "Estimated arrival in ten minutes," said the droid voice. "Perfect," Eve said.

She hit the gas pedal and the Maserati growled in response. She headed onto the boulevard.

CHAPTER 5

. : ⠛:.: .⠂

ON A NIGHT LIKE SO MANY OTHERS, CONNOR CROMAG WAS asleep in his home in the northeast corner of the San Fernando Valley of California. It was the kind of deep, restorative sleep that is the reward of those who work hard, are honest, and have sincere hearts. His cat, Tiny Dancer—as she did every night—was curled into a purring ball of warmth between his feet.

Cromag slept, ignorant of the world and its concerns. Above him, in the indigo canopy of night sky, billions of pinpoints of light shimmered. On this night, across an inconceivable expanse of space, there was one twinkling star where events were taking place that would soon impact not only Connor Cromag's life, but the lives of every creature on Earth. Cromag could not possibly have known this, however, so he slumbered peacefully, a comfortable captive of his dreams.

This singular star of interest was located in what astronomers had named the Morbiddon Nebula, a supercluster that blanketed a corner of the universe an incomprehensible distance from Earth. It was a sphere of hot, flaming gases, similar to that of Earth's, and—like Earth's—had a complement of planetoids in orbit around it. On the largest planet of the system, the star was just coming into view on the horizon—large, bright and green—as the planet's rotation positioned it to receive its daily allocation of light and warmth.

The identical event on Earth, where it is known as "sunrise," or "dawn," would signal the start of a new day, and it meant the same thing to the inhabitants of this planet. What Earth-dwellers call "the Sun" was known here as a

"Sunstar." And, as it is on Earth, when the Sunstar arced across the sky, there was light, and it was time to be active; when the planet's rotation cast it into darkness, it was time to cease activity and rest.

The planet was smaller than Earth, and completed a full rotation on its axis in far less time. "Days" and "nights" were only eight Earth-hours in duration. And it was much closer to its Sunstar than Earth is to its own Sun. The surface temperature at mid-day made equatorial Earth seem like an Arctic glacier in comparison. The extreme heat made the growth of any plant life impossible, and the landscape was barren and marked only by rugged formations of rock.

On the arid surface of this planet, near its equator, there was a cluster of buildings, a small settlement that resembled the barracks of a military installation on Earth. At the farthest perimeter of the settlement, a cylindrical pod that resembled the fuselage of an airplane—and not much larger in size—was being exposed to the first rays of morning light from the green Sunstar.

Within this spartan "biopod," as it was referred to on this planet, a form began stirring. To this creature and the others like it, who dwelled in similar structures spread across the hostile expanse, the biopod was home. The creature rose and stood erect. It closely resembled a human, similar in shape and appearance. Easily over six Earth-feet in height, it possessed broad shoulders, a powerful back, strong legs, and a handsome face with lean, chiseled features. This creature could have walked among the inhabitants of Earth and none would have been the wiser—for at first glance, it was virtually indistinguishable from an adult human male. And yet it was not human—far from it. It donned a hooded robe, black as the short night that had just ended. Another day had begun, and there was much to do.

He had no name. None of the planet's inhabitants did. He and others on this world were known—not by names—but by their *function*. All beings were identified by what they did. Each creature was assigned a specific function at a very early stage in its lifespan. And each creature carried out its special function for the duration of its existence.

This would have been a strange concept, indeed, for "Terraforms" (inhabitants of Earth) to grasp. On a planet like Earth, with more than six billion inhabitants, names had evolved as a convenient and effective way to identify and differentiate. Terraforms were given names at their time of origin, to be used thereafter in interactions with one another. The roots of this practice could be traced to the earliest days of Earth's existence, when life forms began to proliferate.

The evolution of so many different life forms on Earth had been a response to the challenges of existence. Species adapted and diversified to survive the conditions of a cruel and harsh environment. Bears that hunted in Arctic snow evolved to have white fur that afforded them better camouflage when stalking their prey; those in warmer latitudes kept their brown coats. Each required a different name, so that a "polar" bear could be differentiated from a "grizzly" bear. Earth soon found itself populated with myriad life forms—and an ever-burgeoning glossary of names by which to identify them.

On this planet of nameless life forms, orbiting its green Sunstar, a similar process of evolution had taken place, but many, many millennia prior to that of Earth's. At a point in their evolution, advances in science and technology had empowered the inhabitants with the ability to control their environment. Droughts and storms became a thing of the past; the word for "hunger" dropped from their language; disease and illness became relics of history.

Concurrent with the mastery of their environment came a decreasing need for adaptation and species diversity. As the need for adaptation and diversity dwindled, so did the variety of extant life forms—and the need to name them all. Over time, the population, once a melting pot similar to Earth's, became a homogeneous and efficient collection of perhaps a dozen different types of beings, each with a specific function. There were now Thinkers, Leaders, Instructors, and Providers—to name a few—whose responsibility it was to think, lead, instruct, or provide food for the others.

The nameless creature in the dark robe had been trained from his very first moment of existence to carry out his function, just as his fellow creatures had. But his function was not to lead, or instruct, or think. His function was to pursue and destroy any entities considered a threat to the planet. He did so because he was a Hunter—and that is what Hunters did.

CHAPTER 6

.: ¨.! .¨

IN A SMALL STRIP MALL IN SUNLAND, CALIFORNIA, THE OWNERS of the True Tattoo Studio had opened their doors for business. William "Street Bill" Thompson and Rusty "Dynalow" Langhorne were outlaw bikers who had ridden for years with the Messengers of Doom motorcycle club, before pooling their resources to open the tattoo studio they had dreamed about all their lives.

They had acquired their nicknames by virtue of the bikes they rode. William Thompson rode a Harley "Street Bob" and so, with a poetic tweak, became "Street Bill." Rusty Langhorne rode a Harley Dynaglide Low Rider, and thus was christened "Dynalow," or "D-Low" for short.

The pair were walking advertisements for their enterprise. *We're talking heavy ink, bro.* These guys were *tatted*, man—from their scalps to the soles of their feet. Sleeves, leggings, gloves, neck collars, you name it. Street Bill and D-Low bragged that the only uninked spots on their bodies were their assholes—and nobody ever bothered to press them on it for visual proof.

Street Bill was the first to notice the smokin' hot lady who was headed their way. "Yo, D-Low—check this out," he said, motioning with his chin to the supermodel that was approaching. Yep, there was no doubt: she was walking towards *their* door. "Go figure..." murmured Street Bill to himself.

"Please come in here, please come in here," D-Low said in whispered tones, panting and whimpering like a puppy with a treat held inches from its snout. Within twenty seconds she was standing in front of their counter.

The boys glanced at each other and exhaled in unison. It wasn't every day a goddess walked in to their shop.

"Can I help you?" D-Low asked. He was sure she was lost and was probably going to ask for directions.

"Yes," she said. "I would like a tattoo."

Street Bill and D-Low glanced at each other in disbelief. *A supermodel? In our shop? And she wants a tattoo?*

D-Low was the first to recover his faculties. "Well, you came to the right place. That's what we do here," he said, trying not to trip over his tongue as he got the words out.

"What would you like?" Street Bill asked, as he waved his hand at the images adorning the walls.

She looked at the images rapidly, darting her head here and there as she focused her gaze, like a bird of prey scanning a field for mice.

Then, as suddenly as she had started her recon, she stopped and asked, "Do you have any others I can choose from?"

"Sure," Street Bill said. He handed her a fat notebook and motioned her to a chair near the counter. "This is an expanded assortment of what we can do, with some client photos towards the back. Take your time." She sat down in the chair and began perusing the binder.

"D-Low," Street Bill said, "I'm gonna run a few errands. I will leave this young lady in your capable hands." He got up and left the shop, winking his eye at D-Low as he exited.

She leafed through the loose-leaf binder quickly, and then stopped abruptly when she found an image that caught her eye.

"I want this one," she said.

"OK, no problem. Come back here to the work area and we'll get that done for you." He escorted her to the rear of the studio.

"Where'd you want me to put it?" D-Low asked.

"Here," she said, and in one fluid motion, she turned her back to him and lowered her skintight leggings over her hips and down to her knees. D-Low's breath caught in his throat. It was one of the finest asses he'd ever seen on a woman.

"I want it here," she said, as she mapped out the area, tracing her finger in an arc over her tantalizingly sculpted butt-cheeks. She licked her lips sensuously for good measure, to make sure that she had his attention.

D-Low was incredulous at first, as he realized he was getting sexually aroused! The lumber mill was opening for business in his trousers, no doubt about it. He was embarrassed, but then forgiving, as he realized the beauty of his subject would make any healthy man respond in like fashion.

He was daunted at the prospect of working on so magnificent an ass. Like some pristine canvas, or a flawless block of marble, it lay there before him, and he would be the artist that would transform it and forever change its appearance. Though he had inked a hundred rear-ends before, none had been as awe-inspiring as this one.

He daydreamed and started to wonder if Da Vinci or Michelangelo ever got wood before beginning a job. Then he snapped out of his reverie. *You're not in the Sistine Chapel, for Chrissake*, he thought to himself, *You're in a fucking tattoo shop in a strip mall in the armpit of Los Angeles.* The reality check brought him back to earth and the blood began retreating from his crotch.

"OK, just lay down on the table and I'll get started." As she lay face down on the table, he thought to himself, *one tramp stamp, coming up…*

He spent the better part of two hours inking the girl, and he did a good job. After twenty years in the business, he wished he had a nickel for every tramp stamp he had put on a lady. He wondered about the etymology of the term "tramp stamp." First, why the area above a woman's coccyx and butt-crack had become one of the most popular locations for women to get inked. And second, why was it nicknamed "tramp stamp," as if only women of questionable virtue got them? *Go figure,* he thought to himself.

When he was done, he took the money from her and showed her to the door. "Now, don't swim or sun-bathe for two weeks. You don't want that masterpiece to fade," he chuckled.

A minute after she left, Street Bill came back from his errand. "I just saw the supermodel leave. Nice sled, too—a Mozz—a black convertible." D-Low nodded his head, vacantly. He was still thinking about the unbelievable ass that he had just put a tattoo on.

"So how did it go?" Street Bill asked. He was sporting an impish smile, as if he were expecting to be told something juicy.

"Well," D-Low said, "aside from the fact that she had the most incredible caboose I've ever seen, it was pretty routine..." he grinned, waiting for the expected impact his lurid description would have on Street Bill. When he could see that Street Bill's eyes were steaming over with a prurient leer, he continued.

"I started getting hard the minute she dropped her drawers. It took all my control to keep from slipping her the salami right here in the shop."

"Really?" Street Bill mouthed the word silently, in a trance as his imagination revved up. He was salivating.

"I will say this, though—she had some of the softest, most beautiful skin I've ever worked on, I mean it was *perfect*—without a pimple, freckle, or blemish of any kind..."

Street Bill thrived on lechery; he couldn't get enough of this. "Go on..." he said, licking his lips.

"But the weirdest thing while I'm inking her was her reaction—which was no reaction at all! Usually, a gal gets a tramp stamp, since it's such a sensitive area, she's squirming and whining about the pain and discomfort. This gal didn't move a muscle, like I wasn't even touchin' her. Really weird."

"What'd she end up getting?"

"A black widow spider—the one with the bright red hourglass on its abdomen," D-Low said.

"A black widow, huh? Go figure..."

CHAPTER 7

. : "..: ."

FITNESS. BEING IN SHAPE. THERE WAS NO FINER FEELING. Cromag looked at himself in the mirror as he got ready to go to the gym. Many years ago, when just a twenty-something, he had made a commitment to fitness. A commitment he'd honored for more than twenty years now.

Like so many others who had been athletic in their youth, Cromag wasn't aware of any slippage in his level of fitness until he got a wake-up call. While on foot patrol through the city of San Fernando, he had confronted some graffiti artists tagging a building, and gave chase. After a couple of blocks, he became winded and weak and realized he'd lost the ability to sprint. He couldn't run if his life depended on it. The punks taunted him, laughing when they realized he couldn't keep up.

That was it. The moment he learned the hard truth about staying in shape: That physical fitness is "on the house" until you hit your late 20s, and after that you have to pay for it—with exertion, sweat, and strict control over what you stuff in your piehole.

So Cromag began a fitness routine in earnest. He joined a gym—and devoted himself to getting back in shape. Early on, he encountered a book called *The StrongPath*, and it changed his perspective. From it, he learned some important things about achieving any goal. He learned that "will power" was over-estimated in its importance to the pursuit. True, will power is essential at the beginning of a quest. But the key to long-range success lies in *making something a habit*, instead of relying on will power.

Once you made something a habit—whether a fitness program, dietary plan, or work procedure—it took will power out of the equation and made everything simpler. It was no longer your will power struggling with "should I do this today, or not?" Instead, it was a habit you had adopted—*something you did without thinking.* Duh.

This important transition freed your quest from the influence of will power (or, even more importantly, "won't" power!) and removed it from a decision-making loop altogether. Once something becomes a habit, you just "DO IT," case closed. It was then that Cromag finally understood how clever the execs at Nike had been to seize on the phrase "Do It" and anchor their marketing campaign to it.

Now Cromag was in his mid-forties, but you'd never know it by looking at him. Blessed with boyish good looks, a nice build, and a voluminous head of red hair, you had to look him over twice before taking a stab at his age. Perhaps most important, at a time when the midsections of most men head south—never to return—Cromag maintained a trim, muscular waist. Last thing he ever wanted was for somebody to mistake him for Poppin' Fresh, the Pillsbury Doughboy!

He got into his gym clothes and headed for the Mission Hills location of Exceleron Fitness. He had been a member for nearly twenty years, and this location was close to his home. It made the habit of staying fit that much easier.

He was a chronic gym rat. Hardly ever missed a workout. He used to joke that his mother had given him a dumbbell in the crib rather than a pacifier. He was committed, a true believer. His fitness program gave his life structure and purpose, and reduced his stress level as well.

The gym was really noisy when Cromag arrived. Typical Monday. *Weekend backsliders coming in to get the stink of indulgence off themselves.* The place always had twice as many people on Monday, compared to other days. The gym had a good mix of members, ethnically and age-wise.

There were the geriatric late-comers, desperate to regain a modicum of strength and mobility; the sinewy youngsters who came more to flirt and ogle rather than to work out; and the hyper-fit men and women who, like Cromag, were addicted to fitness and needed their fix on a regular basis. The whole gang was here this Monday.

Cromag had just completed a set of leg presses, and was dabbing at his face with a towel when there was a change in the ambience of the gym. It was subtle at first, but gained momentum as it spread.

One after another, men stopped exercising. Weight stacks stopped moving and clanking. The booms from the dropping of heavy plates halted. And the chatter that was the background noise of the gym tapered off. Everybody stopped talking because their attention had been diverted. The usual chaotic cacophony morphed to near silence, broken now by only one thing: the sound of jaws dropping.

There, breathing and moving among them in real life, at the very same nondescript gym they came to every day, was a *goddess!* No other way to describe her. Perfectly proportioned, beautiful, breathtaking. Tall, she was— what some might refer to as "statuesque"—and yet, her movements were anything but stiff. She passed from the entrance to the center of the gym like a miasma, gliding with a fluid sensuality that commanded all to focus on her perfect form in motion. Her breasts were round and large, but—as evidenced by the fact that they jiggled tauntingly with each step—they were *real*. So many women sported surgically-crafted chests, it was hard to tell the difference, but with her there could be no doubt.

Panning down her exquisite form, from the spectacular breasts to an impossibly narrow waist, the eyes of Cromag and the other men traced her curvatures, centimeter by centimeter, so as to slowly savor each tantalizing glimpse and let it swirl around their retinas. The exposed midriff, tanned and toned, was exceptional. Her wickedly-rounded hips framed as gorgeous a *derriere* as Cromag had ever seen on a woman.

It was an ass sculpted in such scintillating proportions, that those viewing it were awe-struck. The expanse of that magnificent bottom was covered by a leotard so tight and form-fitting it looked like it had been sprayed on. The creamy, silken flesh of her buttocks flowed out of the leotard and tapered into long, sinuous legs. So shapely, so strong, so firm.

Cromag was as captivated as the other men, and struggled in his mind to come up with a word he could use to describe this woman, should the need arise in a later retelling of the incident. *"She's fantastic, superlative, magnificent,"* he said, frowning at the insufficiency of those words to capture the precise essence of this female. *What is the word I'm looking for?* He demanded, and then in a flash he knew what that word was. The woman was *perfect. Yes, that's it!* She is completely and absolutely *perfect.* Cromag was stupefied, and so were the others. Did they have any other choice?

Suddenly, as quickly as she had appeared, she left. She looked around the gym as if making a final recon of the place, and then exited. The eye candy store had closed for business rather abruptly, and it took the patrons a few seconds to grasp it. The men shook their heads as if exiting a narcotic fog. Exclamations of "Whoa!" and "Wow!" echoed as they looked at each other, as if to say, *did you see what I just saw? Was that real?*

Cromag chuckled, realizing that all men are the same everywhere and always act so predictably when it comes to certain things. He was guilty as charged, just like the others. He loaded up the barbell and got down to business.

CHAPTER 8

ON THE PLANET WITH NO NAME, THE HUNTER HAD RISEN EARLY to make repairs to his biopod. A meteor shower during the night had sent shards of cosmic debris hurtling like missiles onto the planet, shattering some of his heat shields. He selected special reflective garb to protect him from the Sunstar's blistering heat. As he was laying out the garments, he felt a peculiar sensation at the base of his skull. He was being summoned!

The process was always the same: he would feel a vibration at the back of his neck; a warm sensation would engulf his skull; and then he would hear words in his mind. Telepathic thought-speech was how the inhabitants of the Hunter's planet communicated with each other.

The ability to transmit thoughts instead of speaking had evolved over much time. The first ones to become aware of the telepathic power had been the Leaders and Thinkers, not surprisingly. They had mastered the art and then taught the others.

As thought communication proliferated, the need for speech dwindled and finally disappeared. Eventually, most of their race lost the ability to speak at all; they were only capable of uttering shrill chirps and guttural grunts. Speech—and the ability to produce it—had become a vestige of the past.

There was only one group on the planet that still used spoken language: Hunters. They were the exceptions to the rule, for reasons that were linked to their function. Their pursuit of wrong-doers often led them to other worlds— where spoken speech was the only method of communication. For this reason, all Hunters were taught to speak, from the very moment their life-function was decided upon. Like earth schoolboys forced to study Latin, they spent hours acquiring and practicing speech. Ironically, though the use of spoken words was considered ancient and primitive by most, it was a high art among the Hunters, and well-respected by the Leaders and Thinkers. They knew it was a necessary skill in a universe largely-populated by savage creatures who still spoke words. It was a skill that would always need to be preserved and taught to a select few.

The Hunters learned not just the language of their ancestors, but that of other beings as well. Hunters were fluent in many exotic tongues, and when the need arose, were expected to acquire fluency in new ones in short order. They subjected themselves to intense immersion learning in order to do this. Hunters were known for their ability to absorb new knowledge rapidly.

Recently, the Hunter had been refreshing his command of other tongues. The learning sessions had been conducted strictly in spoken words. Because he had spent so many days using his voice, hearing it and the voice of his Instructor, the unexpected telepathic summons had startled him. He had not communicated with thought-speech for a while. And it had been even longer since he had been summoned.

To be summoned was always a thing of great importance. This morning the summons had come from the Leader Commander himself. The Hunter was being called to a special meeting—and it was to take place at the hub of all governing activity: The Core. The Core was an ominous monolith that pierced the sky from a cluster of sharp mountains at the planet's equator. It was the home of the Leaders, Thinkers, Instructors, and Guides—those who controlled things. From The Core, they administered the directives by which the planet sustained itself and conducted relationships with others in their sector of the Nebula.

The last time he had been summoned to The Core had been long ago. It was the time when the inhabitants of his planet had first become aware of the threat posed by a race known as The Morbiddon. The eponymous Morbiddon were the beings for which the Nebula had been named, and they were the dominant species in the sector. They had been there the longest, were the most advanced, and were considered the rulers of the Nebula.

For many, many orbits of the Sunstar, even before the Hunter's creation, the Morbiddon had been just and benevolent rulers. They had shared their science and technology freely with others. They were respected and revered by all.

Then, inexplicably, things changed. The once-generous and kind Morbiddon became surly and protective, refusing to share their knowledge. The respect and reverence with which they had once been regarded, were replaced by fear and loathing. Alienation begat more alienation, and soon there arose within the Morbiddon leadership a frightening movement that gained rapid momentum. It was based on raw and brutal imperialism. The Morbiddon now believed that their policy in dealing with other races should be one of subjugation, rather than cooperation.

Their technological superiority helped fuel their rabid sovereignty. They turned their intelligence and resources from the pursuit of harmony, to an unfettered lust for the resources of other planets. The desire to sustain and help others was replaced by a desire to conquer and oppress.

At that time, when the Morbiddon's intent had become apparent, a stage of high alert had been declared by the Leaders of the nameless planet, and every Hunter had been summoned to The Core. The elite cadre of Hunters could be likened to the soldiers of an Earthling army, or the police who enforced laws. They were highly trained in combat and the pursuit and eradication of those who threatened the planet's well-being. The purpose of the first gathering had been to make all citizens aware of the Morbiddon threat, and to mount a counter-offensive.

Of the many things that had been discussed that day, the most significant was a decree issued by the Leaders: The race which had been known as the Morbiddon, would from that point on, be known by the new function they had chosen for themselves. They would now be known as The Destroyers.

It had been many orbital cycles since that prophetic gathering, and in the interim, the Destroyers had left a gruesome trail of brutality as they cut a swath of destruction through the sector. They conquered one planet after another and made the inhabitants slaves. The conquered races had to swear fealty to their new Masters, and surrender their resources and freedom—or perish.

The Destroyers were merciless, and soon became the most dreaded scourge to blight the Nebula since the ancient epidemic of Monothalion Fever.

The outbreak of Monothalion Fever had decimated the planets and taken the lives of nearly eighty percent of the inhabitants of the sector.

Now, the Destroyers threatened to surpass even that quota of destruction. They were relentless, unstoppable, and despite the valiant efforts of the resistance, it appeared they would soon conquer the Hunter's planet and their domination of the Nebula would be complete.

And with absolute power, why should they stop with the Morbiddon Nebula? There was a universe full of other beings, other planets they could conquer. These were dire circumstances. These were the issues facing the inhabitants of the Hunter's planet. All these events had been the backdrop to the urgent summons commanding the Hunter to come to The Core at once.

CHAPTER 9

CROMAG HAD AGREED TO MEET HIS BROTHER CLAYTON AT THE gym on Tuesday morning. This was common practice for them. Clayton was dedicated to fitness like his brother Connor, and weight training was better with a partner. It also gave them a chance to stay abreast of each other's lives.

Cromag had already arrived and plated up a barbell for a quick warm-up. He was right in the middle of the set when someone called out to him.

"Hey, Connor!"

He recognized the voice instantly. There were only two people on the planet who addressed him by his first name: Police Captain De Carlo, who only used it to convey an insincere "chumminess" that did not really exist between them; and his brother Clayton. Since there was a snowball's chance in hell that De Carlo would ever go to a gym, it had to be his brother. To his co-workers and professional associates, he was "Detective Cromag" or "Sergeant Cromag" or simply "Cromag," but to his brother Clayton he would always be "Connor."

Cromag laid the barbell to rest and thought about the social conventions surrounding names, and his in particular. There was an interesting back-story to his surname. His reddish hair and blue eyes were a definite tell as to his Celtic ancestry, and people often pigeon-holed him as such at first. Then they would encounter his last name. "*Cromag?? That's not Irish or Scottish! What is it?*"

Truth was, his family name was actually *Corroumeiagh*, a daunting mouthful even for those who spoke his ancestors' tongue, let alone those who didn't know Gaelic from garlic. Connor's grandfather, Daniel, was eager to assimilate when he emigrated to the United States. So, he did what many of his compatriots had; he changed his surname: to *Cromag,* hoping to clear any potential hurdles that a difficult-to-pronounce name might represent. From that point on, in his newly-adopted country, he was "Daniel Cromag."

He settled in Allentown, Pennsylvania and had one son, whom he named Tobias. Tobias, who was Connor Cromag's father, had a restless spirit, and moved to California with his wife and young son to pursue work in the aircraft industry. Companies like Lockheed and Boeing were riding a wave of fat government contracts in the early 1950's, and they were hiring workers on the spot.

Tobias moved his family to Burbank, California and dug in. A second child, Clayton, soon followed, and they were a tight and happy family until Tobias Cromag was killed in a freak industrial accident. Connor was only twelve, his brother Clayton, five. The tragic death of his father marked a coming-of-age in Cromag's life. New responsibilities were thrust upon him. In addition to helping his widowed mother, he saw it as a primary duty to protect his little brother Clayton, to help him as much as he could, and mentor him in any way possible.

It was Connor who fended off the bullies, who taught Clay how to box, how to drive, how to use tools, and how to be a man, basically. They were as tight as two brothers could be, and they loved each other deeply.

They trained together as often as they could. Each brother, respectively, regarded their sessions at the gym as more than just bonding time—it bordered on sacred ritual. A mandatory part of this ritual was ribbing. As Clayton ambled up to join Connor, he had a grin on his face.

"Hey, big girl," Clayton said. "You need some help with that weight? Looks like it might be kind of heavy for you." Cromag countered with the most serious expression he could muster, from a face that was actually bursting to smile.

"Well, it's about time you got here, Clay. Did you finish playing with your dolls and decide to come to the gym with the men?"

They guffawed in unison. This was how a typical workout began for the brothers Cromag. Every session combined exercise with good-natured kidding and verbal snipes targeting the other's manhood. They were always jousting with each other this way—trading barbs and jibes in between hoisting iron. The two men smiled, and then embraced.

Clayton and Connor Cromag were unmistakably brothers—glance one told you that. Clay was a younger, slightly smaller version of Connor—well-built, with a handsome face that the ladies ate up with a spoon. He had a way with women, and he knew it. He was the top salesman at a Chevrolet dealership in Tarzana. Both brothers were dedicated to exercise and had been members of the gym for years. Connor loved his kid brother more than a rare steak—and would do anything for him.

With the ease and familiarity that comes only after many shared training sessions, they made their way around the gym quickly. They would "spot" each other on lifts, as training partners do, constantly peppering their dialogue with put-downs and jokes.

"Clay, you sure you don't want to use smaller dumbbells? Like the ones in the women's weight room? Wouldn't want you to get hurt…" Cromag joked.

Clayton responded. "Thanks for that tip, brother. I've heard you're quite an authority on muscles, especially this one right here …" he said, grabbing his crotch.

They brayed like jackasses and moved on to another station. This was how they conducted their workouts—and like all the others, this one seemed to be over too soon. They made their way to the locker room, showered and toweled off. They walked to the lobby and Clayton's attention immediately became fixed on a nubile blonde with substantial breasts and a well-rounded ass, who had just left a spinning class. He elbowed his brother as he whispered, "Wow—Connor—check that out. I've love to have her ride *me* for a while."

Cromag shook his head. The comment was *so* Clayton. "Is that all you think about?"

"Man does not live by bread alone—nor by bench presses and squats, brother. I'm just a red-blooded male."

"Yeah, right," said Cromag, and then he suddenly remembered the unbelievable woman he'd seen the day before. "Wow!" I almost forgot," he said. "You missed the most beautiful female you've ever feasted your eyes on. She was here yesterday morning. Came in, walked around, and then left. Smokin' hot!"

"Too bad," said Clay. "But if she's a member maybe I'll see her some other time. Plenty others to keep me busy in the meantime," he said, motioning with his chin to the top-heavy blonde who'd snagged his attention earlier. "You want to commit to our next workout? How about Thursday?"

"I'll have to check my schedule. I'll get back to you." Cromag said, leaving his brother to ogle another hottie who had just walked by.

CHAPTER 10

ERNESTO CABRILLO HAD BEEN LIVING UNDER THE RADAR IN L.A. for three years now. Like so many of his illegal alien *compadres*, he'd been lured to the United States not by its promise of opportunity and riches, but simply as a means to survival. It was a way to put food in the mouths of his impoverished family in Zacatecas, Mexico.

Guys like Ernesto were called "wetbacks," a derogatory reference to the act of illegally crossing the Rio Grande river that separated Mexico and the United States. But Ernesto was not a wetback in the literal sense of the word, for he had crossed over on land. He'd been smuggled in by a *"coyote"*—a man who shepherded human contraband into the United States.

Ernesto had crossed the Sonoran Desert into southern Arizona, and made his way to Los Angeles by bus. He had friends there who taught him how to survive and prosper as an illegal. Three years had passed since that time, a fact made all the more significant because he was burdened by an additional challenge: he was mute. He had been born without vocal cords and could only make grunting noises.

Though he was incapable of speech, he learned the ways of the *barrio* quickly. He joined the nation of illegals already entrenched in Southern California. Astonishingly, a young man like Ernesto could sneak into the country, get an I.D. and a job, and even marry and have children and eventually grow old and die—all without ever needing to become a citizen or learning how to speak English.

Today was the third anniversary of his arrival in the States. He owned a car and was driving to work—another perk of life in California. The state allowed undocumented aliens to obtain driver's licenses.

He'd gotten a job at the Sunland location of Exceleron Fitness, as part of the maintenance crew. He communicated by using a combination of sign language, body motions, and facial expressions. Despite living in constant fear of *"la migra"*—the Immigration authorities—he came to work every day, busted his ass cleaning urinals and sweeping floors, and did as he was told. He shared a one-bedroom apartment in Sun Valley with ten other illegals, and sent most of his income to his family in Mexico.

Today he had arrived early, before the gym opened, and was cleaning the carpet in the weight room. The gym wasn't dirty, and would never have a chance to become so. Not when he spent hours each day vacuuming, wiping down equipment, and dumping trash.

Although he was incapable of speech, his hearing was excellent. He heard someone come through the front door—a good two-hundred feet from where he was working. He was behind one of the vertical structural columns that went from the floor of the gym to its skylighted roof. The columns had broad sides almost four feet wide. He wasn't sneaky by nature, but his life as an illegal taught him to keep a low profile. He inched around a corner of the column to grab a peek.

There, loading up a barbell, was one of the most beautiful women he had ever seen. She was alone and didn't realize he was watching her. He watched her move, her motions fluid and determined, with long legs so toned and sinuous her musculature could be seen outlined beneath the sheer fabric of her leotard. Her *culo* was breathtaking—an expanse of buttock so full and perfectly sculpted he could not avert his gaze.

She bent down and displayed her cleavage, the pendulous breasts fairly bursting at the sheer cloth. He knew they were *pechugas verdaderas*—real breasts—because they jiggled tantalizingly as she moved. On top of everything, she had the hair and features of a Latina goddess. He was infatuated and indulging himself, getting an eyeful, until he saw something he would never be able to "unsee" for as long as he lived.

The woman had been loading the barbell with forty-five-pound Olympic plates, and accidentally dropped one on her foot from a height of three feet.

The weight and impact were enough to turn a person's metatarsals into cat litter—and evoke a commensurate reaction—but she did absolutely nothing! She didn't flinch, or scream out. Her expressionless face remained completely devoid of any grimace or agony. All this was unbelievable enough, but then she picked up the plate—and with a flick of her wrist—flipped it all the way across the room, as if it weighed no more than a cracker. The iron plate crashed into the wall, gouging out a huge chunk of plaster. She looked around to see if anybody had seen what she'd just done. Ernesto stifled his astonishment and ducked behind the column, missing the sweep of her gaze by micro-seconds.

Ernesto's heartbeat was galloping; he was sure it was audible across the room. He gasped, trying to breathe without making noise. Had she seen him? What would she do? Would she toss him across the room as she had the iron plate? He trembled. That was a forty-five-pound plate and she had tossed it effortlessly with one hand like it was a flour tortilla!

He remained hidden behind the column, afraid to move. Unbeknownst to him, the woman had left the weight room right after throwing the plate, but his heart continued to race with fear. Suddenly, a body appeared from behind the column; Ernesto nearly went into cardiac arrest. But it was just Robbie, a young white guy who worked with him.

"Ernesto! Good morning, you must have gotten here early." Robbie looked at Ernesto and could see he was a little bent out of shape. "You okay, buddy? *Todo bueno?*"

Ernesto shook his head side to side, put his hand on his stomach, and grimaced. "Oh," said Robbie. "You don't feel good, huh?" Ernesto nodded his head, grimacing even more. "Maybe you should go home. It's okay, I'll let the boss know you got sick and had to leave."

Ernesto nodded, and left like a rocket. He was still hyperventilating. He knew what he had seen could never be shared—with anybody. After all, he was an illegal, and he was mute. Who would he tell? What would he say? Who would believe him?

CHAPTER 11

IN THE WOMEN'S LOCKER ROOM AT THE GYM, THE SCINTILLAT-ing brunette who had just rocked Ernesto's world was donning her exercise wear. The skin-tight black leotard drew attention to her curves like a highway sign in a mountain pass. Her large nipples threatened to burst through the fabric, and her camel toe was so pronounced and prominent it was a geographical wonder in the land of male lust. She looked at herself in the mirror and approved. Perfect attire for what she was about to do: go hunting.

The gym had gotten crowded since she'd arrived. Inside the weight room, Manuel Osorio was finishing up a set of bench presses. Manny had been a high school football and wrestling star at Oakbrook Christian Academy, and though those days were now ten years behind him, he had made it a point to stay trim and strong. He pushed out the last rep and let the weight stack hit bottom with a thwack.

"Pretty impressive," he heard someone say. He looked up to find a gorgeous woman looking down at him and sporting a radiant smile—with teeth so white and perfect she might have walked off the set of a toothpaste commercial.

"Oh, this is nothing," he said, genuinely humble. "Just a warm-up set." He scoped her out, top-to-bottom, from that flaring smile, down to her breasts, her hips, ass, and her long, long legs. Each step of his visual descent offered a vista more breathtaking than the last. *And what was she wearing? —How could anything be that tight???*

"I wasn't referring to the amount of weight," she said, pursing her lips, then opening them and licking them. She swept her gaze down Manny's body, lingering at his crotch, making sure she conveyed her intention.

Manny was a little taken aback (*The most beautiful babe I've ever seen in here is impressed by me? BY ME??*) but regained his composure. *Okay*, he thought to himself; *I'll take the bait; I gotta see where this ends up.*

"Do those big, strong muscles run in your family?" she asked, like a love-struck teenage girl.

"Yes, they do," Manny said. "My father won the Amateur Mr. Southwest bodybuilding title back in 1960, and my grandfather was actually a circus strongman with Ringling Brothers."

"Hmmm," she purred, as if she'd just gotten a whiff of freshly-baked pie. "So, it's hereditary…that's a good thing." Then she shifted her stance abruptly, turning around so her butt was inches from his face.

"How about me?" she said, "Do you like what you see?" She cupped one hand on her ample bosom, flicking her forefinger over the taut nipple, and ran the other hand tantalizingly over her hip.

"I sure do…" he said, his eyes glazing over. His imagination was now sprinting.

"Would you like to see more?" she said in a half-whisper, running her tongue over her lips.

"Yes… I would…" he said. He was already taffy.

"Do you have a place nearby?" Before he could say "yes," she was already heading for the exit. "I'll follow you," she said.

Manny could barely drive his car, he was so excited. He kept checking his rearview to confirm that this ethereal creature was actually following him, that he wasn't dreaming. And what a car she had! This babe was not only beautiful, she was rich! *There's gotta be a catch,* he thought.

They reached his house in Shadow Hills with the speed of a jet. He had floored it all the way to get here as quickly as he could — *before I wake up*, he had joked to himself, as he felt G-forces on the sweeping curves of Sunland Boulevard.

She pulled up right behind him. They exited their cars and Manny appraised her chariot fully. *No wonder she was able to stay on my tail … A new Maserati—wow!* They entered his house. He took a deep breath.

She was facing him. No pretense. No distractions. "Wanna hear some music?" he asked. She nodded, bathing him in a come-on stare that made his knees buckle. "You want a glass of wine or anything?"

"What I want is *you*," she said, with a hungry look, like a leopardess about to pounce. They went into the bedroom and she undressed in front of him, revealing her perfection with no clothing in the way to hamper his undiluted enjoyment.

Manny Osorio now found himself standing inches away from the most sexually desirable female he'd ever seen. This was eye candy crafted by Heaven's most talented confectioners, and he had a sweet tooth that wouldn't quit. He kissed and licked her breasts, lightly savoring and biting her nipples. He ran his hungry hands over her ass-cheeks. She was enticing beyond description. At the juncture of her thighs, she had a well-manicured Brazilian, with a "landing strip"—just a sliver of pubic hair on her mons. Below, her pink labia were pouting, moist and glistening. His penis was throbbing with anticipation. She looked down at his erection and smiled.

"Turn the music up loud. I like it loud," she said. Manny cranked the stereo.

He lay on the bed and she went down on him, taking him into her hot, wet mouth. Her huge breasts jiggled, her nipples grazing his inner thighs as she sucked him. She continued to lick him to pounding tumescence.

"Hmmm," she said, her breaths coming in hot gasps, "I want you inside me …"

She straddled him and lowered herself onto his erection and took it deep within her. Manny groaned in ecstasy as she rose and fell on his penis, her buttocks slapping his thighs in erotic rhythm.

"Does it feel good?" she asked, moving her hips rhythmically.

"Yes, yes, don't stop…" he said.

Manny was powerless in the grip of such consummate pleasure. Little did he realize this was the last five seconds of pleasure he would ever know. In the brief interlude that followed, there was no sound to be heard but *Metallica* shredding away, as Manny silently lost his life.

CHAPTER 12

.: ":.: .'

THE DISPATCH BLARED FROM THE SCANNER AS CROMAG WAS leaving Sun Valley, heading east on La Tuna Canyon Road. "Code one-eight-seven"—a homicide. *So much for my run of peaceful days,* thought Cromag. The address was a residence in Shadow Hills.

When he arrived, Bennett's car was already there, parked under a spread of huge Eucalyptus that lined the front boundary of the property. He got out and walked up the long driveway.

Nice place, he thought. Meticulous landscaping swaddled around a six-thousand-square-foot house. Shadow Hills was one of the last remaining equestrian enclaves in Los Angeles. Pricey homes built into the hillsides. Lots of acreage, seven-figure price tags.

The scene was already webbed in yellow barrier tape. *I've seen enough barrier tape to encircle the earth three times over...* he thought, reflecting on twenty-five years as a homicide investigator. He walked up to the first responder, a young cop with a buzz-cut fade.

"What've we got?" Cromag asked him.

"One victim. The master bedroom. No witnesses," the cop said. "It's pretty gruesome, sir."

Aren't they all? thought Cromag. *When is murder anything other than gruesome?* He mentally steeled himself for what had become a familiar drill: a dead body, no witnesses, a critical quest to find evidence that would help solve a mystery. Certain things always remained constant at a murder scene.

Someone had murdered a person. Since there were usually no witnesses, all the police had to rely on was evidence. Evidence was the "silent witness" that helped solve crimes.

There was an old rule about criminal investigation that had been hammered into his cranium when he was a rookie: the perp either leaves something behind, or takes something with him. Therefore, every square inch of the scene has to be considered a source of evidence. It was critical to observe it, acquire it, and document it as thoroughly as possible. Anything less stringent than striving for perfection could provide a defense attorney with a bowl of cherries, and result in a walk on the part of the perp.

In short order, the members of Cromag's investigative squad arrived. He greeted them curtly and rounded them up on the front walkway before entering. They were all top-notch criminalists who had weathered many an investigation: His partner and second-in-command, Lyle Bennett; along with the CSI trio: Tom Dupree, George Simington, and Robert Alcord.

Cromag motioned for his team to follow him inside. On their way to the victim, Cromag took inventory of the surroundings. Italian marble floors. Imported crown moldings. Plush window treatments. All the furnishings were top drawer, and you wouldn't expect anything less in a home of this caliber: Roche Bobois furniture, Neiman Marcus accessories, the whole nine.

Wealth always added a separate dimension to any murder; a good percentage of homicide cases involved a murder/theft, and this was something that had to be considered. Maybe a burglar had been startled and had become a murderer to escape? It was Cromag's job to find out.

Before entering the master bedroom, he assigned each team member a portion of the scene to examine. Dupree got the walls; Simington was in charge of the furniture; Alcord got the floors. He and Bennett would examine the body and immediate surroundings. They would examine, and examine, and examine again, taking notes and photographing all. Then later, they would switch assignments and do the whole procedure all over again, so that every square inch of the crime scene ended up being examined twice. This was just investigative SOP—standard operating procedure.

"Okay," he said. Let's go."

Cromag was the first to enter the bedroom and froze in mid-step. He gasped audibly when he saw the victim. The amount of blood was astonishing—and he had been sexually mutilated. Cromag's career encompassed twenty-five years' worth of murders—and this was easily the most brutal killing he'd ever seen. Nothing else even approached it.

As each team member entered in succession, they too, gasped out loud. The scene was a ghastly portrait of horror, rendered by an artist so frighteningly psychopathic it left them mute. Bennett was the first to recover his speech. All he could say through his numbness was "Oh my God…"

The victim lay on his back, spread-eagled on the bed. He was wearing an orange Metallica tank-top and naked below the waist. Directly opposite him, a flashflood of blood had saturated the walls, starting at the ceiling and running down to the floor. It was still glistening, and so copious it had gathered in a ghoulish crimson pool. The walls were painted off-white, and nothing could have contrasted with them more than the vermillion red of human blood.

Cromag looked at the wall, then looked at the body. He repeated this a couple of times. It looked as if a fire hydrant had been opened—with a geyser of blood gushing forth. If one traced the trail from the wall, back across the carpet, and up onto the bed, the source of the geyser was obvious: it had erupted right at the juncture of the victim's thighs.

The blowhole of the gusher was a neatly cut opening—surgically precise—from which now dribbled what little blood remained in the vic's body. The gaping, oozing hole was right where his penis and testicles should have been, or once were. And they were nowhere to be found.

"Jeezis," Cromag said, "Have you ever seen anything like this in your life?" His team's reverent silence served as confirmation: no, they had not.

The team conducted their investigation. They checked for a weapon, a bloody towel, even the poor guy's severed privates, but found nothing. It slowly became apparent that at this particular crime scene, there would be no low-hanging fruit as far as evidence was concerned.

It was bizarre. There was no detritus from a typical life-and-death struggle—no torn clothing, no upended furniture or broken lamps. The scene was so eerily docile it almost seemed staged. There was only the victim—missing his genitals—and a tankerload of his blood, everywhere.

The scene defied conventional analysis. The victim lay there, like he had slept while being mutilated, and died, and didn't move a muscle. How could that be? Despite repeated scouring, none of the team members could come up with even a hint of trace. One by one, they came up to Cromag with empty hands and disheartened expressions, remorseful that they'd not been able to capture even an iota of evidence. Cromag tried to lessen their disappointment, saying "it happens," but in the back of his mind, he didn't believe it himself. He had never encountered a homicide so devoid of evidence. No prints, no hairs, no fibers of torn clothing, no nothing!

The only thing they came up with was found by Alcord, who had examined under the bed. He came up holding a University of Southern California hoodie, with the "USC" logo embroidered in large gold and burgundy letters. "Sarge," he said, "Check this out. It looks a little small for him," gesturing towards the victim. He looked at the tag inside. "It's a woman's sweatshirt."

"OK, Alcord, bag it and get it over to Forensics," Cromag said.

Bennett's cellphone rang. He answered. "Okay, I'll let him know," he said. He turned to Cromag. "The Medical Examiner's on his way, Sarge."

"OK—work with him and help him in any way you can. I'm going back to Division. Get a prelim report from the ME and we'll talk about it when we hook up later." Cromag left.

As Cromag drove along Foothill Boulevard, he fell into an all-too-familiar funk he often experienced after an initial visit to the scene of a homicide. Here he was, a veteran of twenty-five years, who'd seen more murders than most detectives, and it never got easier, emotionally. Sure, he'd toughened himself since his rookie days, when the brutality and gore sometimes made him nauseous, but he'd never been able to fully shield his heart from the pain and grief of a murder. He knew he'd always be emotionally invested to some degree. He saw it as the one fault he had as a detective, if any. He couldn't help it. He felt for the victim, for the friends and family, who would have no choice but to suffer and endure their grief, all caused by an evil they had never known could even exist. Internally, he grieved and suffered along with them.

He arrived at Division and went to his office. He attacked the pile of correspondence overflowing his inbox, part of the daily tide of never-ending paperwork. He was reviewing overtime assignments when someone tapped on his door. It was Bennett. "Come in," Cromag said.

Bennett's face was painted with defeat. He had just met with the Medical Examiner and had come to brief Cromag on the preliminary findings—and those findings were not good.

For starters, there was no DNA evidence, an unheard-of circumstance when it came to homicides. "I don't get it, Sarge," he said. "It's the damnedest thing. A team of our best CSI's swept that place *down to the molecules*—and they didn't find any fingerprints, trace evidence, or even a chromosomal speck of DNA other than the victim's. How can that be? He must have had other people in there at some time! How on earth could a crime scene be so *antiseptically* clean? How is that possible?"

Cromag remained silent, as baffled as Bennett was. He just shook his head.

"And there's the matter of the victim himself. ME says the body wasn't moved from somewhere else and "posed" there, but that the vic was alive and lying on the bed right up to the moment of death. And he was killed in that position, with no sign of struggle or resistance, not even one wrinkle on the pillowcase."

"Whoa," said Cromag. "You're telling me the guy just lays there and lets somebody slice his *scungilli* off—just like that—and bleeds out with no movement or struggle? That doesn't make any sense."

"Nothing about this case does, Sarge. The only other thing is that they found evidence of some matter under the victim's fingernails, and they couldn't peg it for anything familiar. It wasn't skin, or hair, or fabric. It's on the way to the lab." He started to leave, but then turned around.

"And one more thing, Sarge. The ME says he's gonna conduct the post tomorrow morning and he wants us there at ten a.m."

CHAPTER 13

. : ":.: ."

THE NEXT MORNING, AFTER THE SQUAD ROOM BRIEFING, Cromag and Bennett went to Angeles Mercy Hospital. Angeles Mercy was centrally located in the area that was Cromag's turf, and so it was an ideal location for something crucial to every homicide investigation: the morgue.

Typically, morgues were located on the bottom floors of hospitals. The morgue was the last stop before someone was buried or cremated. Cromag and his crew were regular visitors to this part of the world, but no matter how many times he went, he couldn't shake the feeling of uneasiness he felt each time he went for a post-mortem examination, or "post," as it was known.

The morgue at Angeles Mercy was deep in the hospital's bowels, and was accessed via service elevators. These elevators were cavernous, capable of holding multiple gurneys of stiffs. As Cromag and Bennett descended, Cromag thought of his many visits to the morgue—and especially his first one.

He'd just been awarded his shield and was investigating a stabbing—an ugly, gang-related murder. The gang connection might have put a negative bias in the mind of another investigator, but to Cromag, impartiality was the key to successful detective work. Despite a victim's affiliations, beliefs, or livelihood, that victim deserved a fair and unprejudiced investigation into the cause of his death. Procedurally, in Cromag's book, a gang-banger got treated the same as a Beverly Hills banker.

On his first visit, Cromag had met the forensic pathologist in charge: a big, hearty German guy by the name of Otto Gerlach. Otto was one of those guys who look scary but turn out to be as threatening as baby rabbits. He was warm, friendly, and eager to help any young homicide detective just starting out. They hit it off immediately, and from that point on, Otto became Cromag's mentor, schooling and coaching him in all things related to autopsies and post-mortem examinations.

During their first meeting, he had given Cromag a tour of the morgue, pointing out the stiffs laid out on the tables for different stages of processing. "Yah," he said, pointing to a body, "dis one was shot in a drive-by shooting," then moving on to a body sticking halfway out of the freezer, "Und dis one, was a heroin overdose. See the tracks on the arms? Dead give-away, huh?" he said, chuckling at his crude pun.

After the tour, Otto had asked Cromag to give him his honest reaction to the place. Cromag felt a little awkward, but got up his courage and said, "Well, to be honest, I find this place to be a little cold and sterile."

Gerlach guffawed, almost falling over backward with excitement. "Yah! Yah! Exactly! Dat is what it is supposed to be—cold to retard decomposition of the bodies, and sterile to avoid contamination! You got it!"

Cromag had laughed then, and he chuckled again now in remembering. Sadly, Otto was no longer in charge of the morgue. He had retired a few years ago, and then had been killed in an automobile accident while vacationing in the Adirondack Mountains of New York. Yes, Otto Gerlach was not the guy they'd be meeting when the elevator doors opened—that responsibility would fall to Dr. Abraham Steineck, the new hotshot ME. He was waiting for Cromag and Bennett when the elevator doors opened.

"Call me Abe," he said to Bennett, extending his hand for a shake. "Don't be afraid, I just washed my hands, and I don't touch the stiffs anyway—yuck!" He said, grimacing like a young girl confronted with a worm. "*You* I already know," he said, frowning at Cromag, as if to dismiss him.

Steineck was young, a recent graduate of medical school. He had landed the plum job of Medical Examiner at Angeles Mercy from a field of candidates. He was smart, sure—but he was an asshole. This was his first gig with a big-city crime unit, and in short order he had managed to alienate all the detectives he had contact with.

He was quite taken with himself, sporting an obnoxious air of superiority while speaking to any and all with an extremely condescending tone. He was more than a little cocky—a screaming-out-loud egotist, as a matter of fact—and showed none of the humility or deference you might expect from a rookie talking to a veteran. *I don't like you*, Cromag thought, two minutes into their first meeting—*and there's nothing you will ever be able to do to change that.*

What exacerbated Steineck's pompous posturing was the fact that he had a staff of three autopsy technicians to help him. Also known as morgue assistants, or "dieners," they did all the grunt work. They handled, moved, and cleaned corpses as needed for post-mortem exams. Steineck treated the dieners like chattel, even though in most cases he was only half their age, with half their experience. He didn't ever want to get his fingernails dirty—and he let his dieners know that he didn't have to, *because you are going to do it for me, peon!*

Cromag and Bennett followed Steineck to an exam room. The victim, Manny Osorio, was laid out on a slab. Next to the slab, on a stainless-steel cart, were the tools of the medical examiner's trade. Cromag recognized them from the tutorials he'd received from Otto: there was a Bone saw, used to cut through bone or skull; an "enterotome," the special scissors used to open the intestines; a Hagedorn needle, used to sew up the body after examination; a rib cutter, designed to cut through ribs; and a skull chisel and Stryker saw, used to cut through the skull to remove the brain. And of course, an endless assortment of scalpels and scissors.

Steineck posed himself next to the victim, as if he were a magician preparing to perform an illusion on stage. "Do you know what the cause of death was?" He tossed the question out to Cromag and Bennett with a sly grin on his face, acting every bit like a guy who already knew the answer and was asking them a trick question.

"Let me guess," said Cromag sarcastically. "He bled out."

The cocky grin widened on Steineck's face. *The smug little prick.*

"Well," he said, in a haughty tone, "While exsanguination was the cause of death, there are some inexplicable circumstances surrounding it. See these two incisions?" He pointed to cuts on each of the victim's upper thighs, close to his groin. "The femoral arteries were severed. This, in addition to the excision of his genitals, caused an extremely rapid loss of blood. But that isn't the baffling part."

Cromag and Bennett looked at each other quizzically. "What do you mean?" asked Cromag.

"The victim's body contained an unidentifiable compound similar in effect to curare—yet very different."

"Curare? As in the curare used by South American pygmies with blow-guns, to paralyze their prey?" asked Bennett.

"Well, not exactly. This compound paralyzed the victim immediately, but without stopping his heart. He lay motionless, but his heart kept beating, which accounts for the geyser of blood at the crime scene. The toxicologist is analyzing the substance right now, but so far, we're stumped. Never seen anything like it."

Steineck ordered one of his dieners to slide Osorio's body back into the freezer. Then he left without saying another word.

CHAPTER 14

THE GYM WAS SPARSELY-POPULATED, BUT IT WAS STILL EARLY. There were some isolated seniors huffing and puffing on cardio equipment, and a personal trainer was showing a newbie a stretching exercise on the mats in the corner.

In the weight room, two guys were grunting their way through sets of deadlifts. In the rear of the room, facing the back wall, was Cromag. He loaded an Olympic barbell with plates and hoisted it off the floor, "cleaning" it in preparation for an overhead press. He thought about his long commitment to weight training. *I wish I had a nickel for every pound I've lifted over the last twenty-five years…*

With a herculean effort, he pushed the barbell upwards, locking his elbows as he reached the pinnacle of the motion. He let it down and then repeated the movement. He was looking for one more rep when his concentration got shot to shit by someone who suddenly appeared behind him.

"Why don't you put some poundage on that bar?" a voice asked. "You'll never get big lifting girly weights, you know."

Cromag ignored the jibe, because he knew its source. He completed the last repetition and set the barbell back on the floor. It shook the ground like a stomping T-Rex. He turned to face his brother Clayton.

"Hey, bro," he said, and they embraced.

"All joking aside," said Clay. "That looks like a new personal best for you. Am I right?"

"Yeah," said Cromag. "Feeling strong today."

The rest of their workout went as expected, but Clayton could tell something was bothering his brother. He mentioned it. Cromag didn't like to talk shop with Clay, and when he did, he didn't share much.

"It's nothing, Clay," he said. "It's just work. Got a new case yesterday—a pretty violent homicide." Clayton didn't press him any further and they finished the session in silence. Cromag said he would be in touch about scheduling their next workout, and left for work.

On his way into Division, Cromag got a call from Bennett.

"Hey Sarge, remember that mystery substance they found under the vic's fingernails?"

"Yeah… what about it?"

"Well, it's got the lab geeks stumped. They're telling me it's not human skin, or animal tissue. And it's not plastic, or cloth or plant matter of any type."

"So, they know all the things it's *not,* but they don't know what it is? What're they gonna do?"

"They're kickin' it upstairs, Sarge—it's being flown to the FBI for further analysis."

CHAPTER 15

THE NEXT MORNING, CROMAG ATTENDED A TOWN HALL MEET-
ing hosted by the Mayor at City Hall. It was a carbon copy of the meeting from
the month before: updates on neighborhood crime, the latest statistics, a question-and-answer session to air gripes. Same old, same old. Cromag was heading back to division on the 5 Freeway, almost in a state of highway hypnosis,
when the shrill voice of dispatch bitch-slapped him to alertness.

"All units … we have a one-eight-seven at 5348 Mountain View Way in
La Crescenta…"

187. Murder. This call had Cromag's name on it. "This is Cromag, Unit
27—I'm on it."

He got into the fast lane and punched it. He jumped on the interchange
to the 210 Freeway at Lakeview Terrace, and it triggered a painful memory.
The community of Lakeview Terrace had been a sleepy, nondescript little
place until an event occurred that would forever cement it in the annals of
civil disobedience. In the parking lot of what had been a convenience store
at the time, a black guy named Rodney King had been stopped for question-
ing by the police. He had some priors for possession and public intoxication,
and the incident soon escalated. Other squad cars showed up, a crowd gathered, and the guy ended up getting the shit stomped out of him by a mob of
baton-wielding white cops.

Most of the spectators were black. Many of them recorded the whole
thing on their cellphones. It went viral, of course, unleashing a shit-storm

of epic magnitude. The cops were charged and the city became polarized—black versus white—as the urban populations held their breath awaiting the outcome of the trial. Uncannily, all the officers were acquitted—an outcome so shocking that even the Mayor of Los Angeles at the time held a press conference and asked publicly: "Did the jurors watch the same video footage we did?"

The black population of Los Angeles, fuming over the injustice, exploded in violence. In Compton, considered by many to be the flashpoint of the riots, looters and roving gangs almost burned the city down. Business owners in Koreatown hovered like snipers on the roofs of the buildings, armed with rifles to protect their shops. Gangs of roving bangers raided malls and retail outlets, smashing windows and looting. It was an ugly chapter in the history of Los Angeles and its Police Department.

As Cromag sped on through Shadow Hills and Sunland, he was glad the incident had predated his career. When he started ascending the stretch bordered by the green, forested foothills of Tujunga, he knew he was minutes from his destination.

He exited on Lowell Avenue and went up to Foothill Boulevard. The area hadn't changed much in the last twenty years. Still quiet, with lots of mom and pop shops and a small-town feel. He made a left on Pennsylvania Avenue and gunned it the rest of the way: up, up, into the ritzy communities of the foothills—homes with astonishing views and staggering price tags.

He turned on to Mountain View Way and slowed down. Yeah, this was the place—no doubt about it. Bennett's car was already there, parked next to a black-and-white. It was a Craftsman home built in the 1950s, part of a tract that had been built after World War Two. The perimeter was already cordoned off with yellow tape.

He went to the front door. There was no cop there, and the door was open. He followed the murmur of voices upstairs. He could hear men speaking in the first bedroom on the right. As he rounded the door frame, he froze.

Oh, no…not again…

There, on the bed, looking as peaceful as a napping child, was a well-built young guy—maybe in his late twenties—and there was a gaping, bloody hole at the juncture of his thighs. The walls looked like they'd been fire-hosed with blood, now dripping and puddling on the floor. The sheets and mattress were saturated with it. Cromag looked at Bennett, then at the bed, then back to Bennett. Lyle had never seen a look like that on the Sarge's face.

"Do we have an ID?" asked Cromag, almost whispering.

"His name is Clifford Shaw. He's twenty-seven. He was supposed to attend a family lunch and never showed up, never answered his phone. They got concerned and called 911."

Within minutes the rest of the CSI team arrived. One after another, they entered the room and nearly convulsed. This was now the second homicide in as many days, with the same *modus operandi*. Victim was a young, athletic male in his late twenties, seemingly "posed" or displayed on the bed with legs and arms outstretched. It might have been a portrait of a young man in calm repose, except for a couple of gruesome details: he was dead; missing his penis and scrotum; and his blood was everywhere.

As with the first homicide, a geyser of blood had gushed from his crotch and covered the nearby wall. And despite the defensive struggle that would have been expected with such an attack, the victim looked as calm as a sleeping newborn, but with his eyes wide open and no longer seeing. It was a duplicate of the first crime scene, as if it had been scripted.

The team conducted their search and evidence-gathering. Simington retrieved an article of clothing from underneath the pillow next to the victim's head. He held it up. It was a skimpy tank-top, with the "PINK" brand logo in large letters on the front. The brand was popular among women. Cromag had seen many a female at the gym clad in such sportswear.

"Now all we have to do is find the owner of this," Simington said half-heart-edly, knowing such a search would make finding the proverbial needle in a haystack a walk in the park.

Bennett had been rummaging through a nightstand on the side of the bed and pulled something from the drawer.

"Wow, Sarge—look at this." Bennett said, holding up a hypodermic syringe and needle in his latexed hand. "The guy must have been a junkie. Maybe this was a drug deal gone bad? Or a cartel hit? Those cartel boys have gotten pretty gruesome—what with all those decapitations…. Maybe this is the latest way they 'send a message,' you know?"

Cromag looked at the syringe momentarily but did not comment. He searched the nightstand on the other side of the bed. He withdrew his hand, holding a pharmaceutical vial. He examined it closely.

"That isn't dope he was shooting," said Cromag. "They're steroids." He held up the vial and displayed its label. "He wasn't a junkie. He was a bodybuilder."

CHAPTER 16

AFTER COMPLETING THEIR PRELIM, BENNETT LET SIMINGTON take his car and he rode back to Division with Cromag. No words were exchanged. It took them a while to recover from the numbness inflicted by the crime scene. Bennett finally broke the silence.

"Sarge, Steineck went back to the first homicide to re-conduct the evidence sweep. He supervised it himself, step-by-step."

Cromag was taken aback. The Medical Examiner went back to personally conduct a repeat investigation? Certainly not standard operating procedure.

"Why would he do that?" asked Cromag.

"Because the first sweep came back with nothing. He just couldn't believe the CSIs came up with zilch in terms of evidence. He was ranting and raving about 'incompetence' the whole time he was there. But when it was over, I found myself wishing for some bacon to give him—to go with the egg he had all over his face. His personally-conducted investigation ended up with the same results: zero."

Cromag suppressed a smirk and they reached Division without any further conversation. He let Bennett out and then headed home. The events of the last two days were beginning to weigh on him, in a way that no other case had ever done. He pondered the circumstances as he drove surface streets instead of the freeway. He needed time to think.

Two homicides in succession. Not only was each murder tainted by an aura of unimaginable evil, but they both bore the same distinctive "signature"—a young, athletic male brutally murdered and mutilated in an abhorrent way. And there was little or no evidence to go on. Baffling! And the fact that this was the second murder in as many days portended of something very disturbing to Cromag. These killings were the work of a nascent serial killer who was just getting started and not wasting any time between kills.

In Cromag's experience, one-off homicides often occurred suddenly, in the heat of the moment, and were usually fueled by passion. Murders by serials, on the other hand, were often planned, and typically cold and especially brutal. These two murders bore a chilling stamp—not of a jilted lover, or a gangbanger looking for payback—but of a true psychopath, one with an agenda known only to himself.

It was only two days since the first homicide, and no reports or information had been leaked about that case. So, there was no way this second killing would qualify as a "copycat" murder. It was too distinctive to be a coincidence. This was definitely the work of the same killer, and realizing it made Cromag shudder, as if Death itself had just tapped him on the shoulder, wanting him to notice something similar about both crimes.

CHAPTER 17

THE HUNTER HAD RECEIVED HIS TELEPATHIC SUMMONS AND knew that he must waste no time in responding to it. The repairs to his biopod's heat shields would have to wait. He put away his tools and headed in the direction of The Core, its structure towering like a gleaming spearpoint over the barren expanse around it. As he got closer, he saw other Hunters marching in procession toward the massive gates that surrounded it. As always, the entrance was flanked by a cotillion of Guards. Entry was permitted only by those who had been summoned. He filed in with the others, and the gates shut behind them.

They entered a transporter shaft and traveled far below the planet's surface. A hallway led to an immense arch that had been cut into the stone, and the Hunters passed through it until they stood before two foreboding doors that ran from the floor to a terminus in the ceiling far above them.

This was the strategic center of The Core. He had been here only twice before. He and the other Hunters were led into a great hall. Leaders, Thinkers and Guides were already assembled there, and the level of tension among the crowd was palpable. There wasn't a single one among them who didn't already know why they had been summoned: news about the looming threat of the Destroyers.

He felt the familiar throb in his skull that preceded thought-speech. All grew silent as the Leader Commander rose and walked to an elevated platform from which he could address the assemblage.

"As some of you may know, we have had a specially-trained team of Hunters conducting an intelligence-gathering operation on the Destroyers' home planet. During our planet's last seven revolutions, the Destroyers have not made any attacks or strategic maneuvers, and have scaled back their warlike incursions in the farthest regions of the quadrant. We now know why."

The Leader Commander paused for a moment, and the level of telepathic communication among the excited crowd reached a near-seismic level that made the Hunter's head feel as if it would shatter. The Leader Commander raised his hand, and all grew silent.

"It appears there may be a balance of justice in the Universe after all. When all seems threatened by the darkness of doom, a shining glimmer of hope often appears. The Destroyers—wholesale merchants of death, virtually unstoppable—now find themselves in a battle none of them could have foreseen, and it is a battle for their very existence."

The crowd was stunned into silence at first, from such totally unexpected news, and in addition, they had not expected the Leader Commander to convey his message in such philosophical tones, but it was fitting that he prefaced his announcement in such fashion. As the potential significance of what he had said became apparent, a feeling of hope and excitement swept through the cavernous chamber, and indeed the planet itself, like the shock-pulse from a nuclear reaction. Frenetic bursts of thought-speech and spoken words filled the hall. The Leader Commander raised his hand and waited for the frenzy to subside before continuing.

"Their enemy is an entity so seemingly insignificant they were not aware of its threat. Its assault could not even be detected at first—let alone defended against—and yet they have now learned their enemy is powerful beyond measure, and capable of decimation on a scale that surpasses even that of the Destroyers. This enemy has targeted the Destroyers—and the Destroyers alone—thus making it our ally. This news comes at a time when an ally has never been needed more."

The crowd frothed with excitement; many wept with joy. They looked as one towards the Leader Commander, who himself was overcome with emotion and struggled to maintain his composure so he could continue.

"This 'ally' is an organism not even visible to the naked eye. It is a microbe that attacks the Destroyers on a cellular level. The contagion it spreads not only produces a high mortality rate among their population, but it renders any survivors sterile, and unable to reproduce. Quite simply, if left unchallenged, this microbial scourge will cause their race to become extinct. Strangely enough, we and the other species in the sector are immune to the disease. It has singled out the Destroyers exclusively."

This news about the contagion—and how it had the potential to annihilate the Destroyers, was a message of hope so profound that many were left unable to communicate—either with spoken words or thought-speech. They embraced each other, smiling, tears of gratitude flowing freely among all. Just moments ago, all had seemed futile, their world doomed, but now there was a light that banished the darkness from each of them. The Leader Commander shared in the exultation, and then asked for silence once more so he could continue.

"This is indeed a time for celebration, but we cannot fall prey to any delusion that the threat is over and we can relax our vigilance. The Destroyers are cunning and powerful—as we all know—and they will respond to this new challenge with all the might they can muster. This has forced them to re-align their priorities. They have no choice but to shift their focus from conquering worlds to learning how they can conquer this microscopic foe—if that is even possible. They will commit their vast resources to a vital search for something—*anything*—that will help them stave off the threat of this disease.

"In the meantime, our team of clandestine operatives will continue to gather information and will pass it along as it becomes available. Return to your dwellings and be thankful for the intervention of this microscopic ally."

CHAPTER 18

.: ":.: .'

CROMAG HAD ARRIVED AT DIVISION SHORTLY AFTER SUNUP. Like many other detectives in the Department, he worked a standard rotation of nine-hour days, with weekends off. In reality, however, since he was the supervisor of Homicide, he was on call 24/7. *What a life.*

He devoted his morning to doing busy work—those repetitive administrative functions that demanded constant attention: completing time sheets, signing overtime authorizations, looking over search warrants, reviewing court orders. He looked up at the clock. In about ten minutes his team would start showing up.

Lyle Bennett was the first to arrive. No sooner had he set his coffee down than his phone rang. "Detective Bennett," he said, and as he listened, his expression morphed from pleasant to grim. "OK, got it," he said. "6520 Day Street in Tujunga. We're on our way."

Cromag and Bennett had worked together so long they communicated damn near telepathically. Cromag knew the call had been about a new homicide. He commanded the squad to meet at the crime scene. Then he and Bennett went to their car and roared out of the Division lot.

"Sarge, I hate to start the day off on a negative note, but remember that substance they found under the first vic's fingernails? The sample that they sent to the FBI Central Lab? Well, it's got them completely stumped."

"What? What do you mean?"

"Well, they called this morning to update us." He pulled a small notepad from his shirt pocket. "This is what they said: *'It appears to be some sort of advanced polymeric compound that is impervious to heat, cold—or conventional analysis. Quite frankly, we are baffled.'* End of story."

"That's it? The Federal Bureau of Investigation gives up? Are you kidding?" Cromag frowned and shook his head. This news was more than disturbing. The last thing their fruitless investigation needed was another inexplicable mystery. The circumstances of the case didn't add up, and now, the best crime lab in the country was clueless about the only evidence they had recovered. *What will happen next?*

They reached the intersection at Sunland and La Tuna Canyon. Cromag decided to stay on surface streets and made a quick right. They shot up La Tuna Canyon Road, avoiding the freeway. They blazed their way up to Foothill Boulevard; made a right on Haines Canyon Road, and then a right on Day Street in Upper Tujunga.

Halfway down the block they saw the cluster of black-and-whites, bubbles flashing. They parked behind the last patrol car. Barrier tape everywhere. And a crowd of curious onlookers to boot—a complication Cromag did not welcome. Three patrol cars had already responded and the cops were swarming.

"Who's the first responder?" Cromag barked, holding his shield up high so all could see.

"I am, sir," a young patrolman said. Cromag approached him. "Victim is a black male, 28, name of Rodney Culbertson. He's in the guest room at the back of the house. Appears to be the same M.O. as the recent homicides, sir."

Wonderful, thought Cromag, as he surveyed the surroundings. He saw a young black woman sitting on the front steps, sobbing uncontrollably while another woman attempted to console her. This prompted him to ask the young cop, "Any witnesses?"

"Not of the crime itself, sir. But that woman over there is his sister. She was supposed to have lunch with him today. When he didn't show up, she drove up here—and that's when she found him. She doesn't have anything more to offer right now—she's in a state of shock."

Within minutes, the rest of the CSI team rolled up and got out of their cars. "All right … let's get this over with," said Cromag, as he led the way into the house.

The victim was in a small room towards the rear of the house. He was face up on the bed, with arms and legs extended. *This is getting tiresome*, thought Cromag. Apart from the bedroom décor, the crime scene looked identical to the first two: a bloodbath featuring a victim with severed genitals. It was only four days since the first murder had been committed, and here was number three already, done up in identical fashion. And—even more discouraging— the other circumstance that was now identical between all three murders was the fact that there was zero evidence, not even the slightest trace.

Cromag looked under the bed, careful to avoid the blood-saturated rug. There was an article of clothing there, which he retrieved and held up. It was a sweatshirt bearing the logo of Exceleron Fitness, the same chain of gyms Cromag belonged to. Bennett looked at it, and then looked at Cromag.

"Exceleron Fitness? That's the gym you go to—isn't it, Sarge?"

"Yeah, it is," Cromag said, pausing for a moment. "Go ahead and bag this. I'm gonna talk to the sister."

He walked out to the front steps. The crowd had tripled in size, and by now the press had arrived. *Oh, Christ—just what I need now…* Reporters were firing questions at him; he waved them off with a stern "No comment!" and walked over to the victim's sister, who had calmed down a little.

"I'm Sergeant Cromag. Can I ask you some questions?"

She looked up at him, her eyes rimmed with tears, and nodded slightly.

"Did your brother live alone?"

"Yes."

"Is there anybody you can think of that would have done this to him?"

At this she broke down and wept. She stammered between sobs, "No… no… he was a phys ed teacher at La Crescenta Middle School. He was a great guy. All his students and co-workers loved him. I can't imagine anybody want- ing to do this to him."

"I noticed he had some Exceleron Fitness sweats. Was he a member there?"

"Yes, we both are. Why?"

"Nothing, just part of the investigation. Thank you." Cromag left her his card. He and Bennett drove back to Division. Bennett could not recall a time when he had seen his boss so sullen and quiet. On the way back Cromag said, "I want you to do some background research on the first two vics. I want to know if they were also members of the Exceleron Fitness health club chain."

CHAPTER 19

SERGEANT CROMAG HAD CALLED A SPECIAL MEETING AND THE squad room at Division was packed and vibrating with energy. You could've shut the lights off and the room would have luminesced in the dark.

Cromag entered the room and the buzzing stopped. The Sergeant was a serious guy to begin with, but today he came in snarling, his face reddened, his pulse elevated. If you had looked up the word "pissed" in the dictionary, there would have been a picture of Cromag.

He held up a newspaper—that morning's edition of *The Foothill Chronicle*—and raised it high for all to see. Splattered across the front page was a banner headline in ninety-six-point type:

'JEWEL THIEF' KILLER STRIKES AGAIN
3rd Victim Found in Tujunga

Cromag pointed to the headline. "Jewel Thief? Are you fucking *kidding* me? Whose deformed brainchild is this?"

"Not us, Sarge," Bennett said. "Pretty sure it was Barry Lennox. He's taking credit for it."

"Lennox? That jerkoff reporter?"

Bennett and others around him nodded their heads.

"Jeezis Fucking Christ!" Cromag looked like he was going to pop an artery in his neck. After years of dealing with a voracious press that sought every opportunity to sensationalize murder and sell more papers, he had very little tolerance for the media—especially for scumbags looking to make their bylines household words. Guys like Barry Lennox.

Barry Lennox, barely thirty years of age, had slithered his way up through the scumpits of bottom-feeding journalism very quickly. The guy had a sixth sense for sleaze, scandal, and murder—he could smell it in the wind. In the waters of big-city crime, he was like a rogue shark. He could detect a developing story from even the slightest chum-trail of rumor or hearsay. If it was gruesome, and capable of generating headlines, he would find it—and milk it for all it was worth.

In this case, Barry Lennox had arrived on the scene right after the 2nd homicide had hit the scanner. He had overheard the CSIs calling the murder "the second one" where the victim had been found brutally murdered and minus his privates.

It was a short and perverse creative leap for Lennox to mint a catchy nickname based on that information. The victims were not only brutally murdered, but the perp had severed their genitalia. Genitals are called "family jewels" in slang. Lennox, the consummate slime scribe, connected the dots and came up with "The Jewel Thief Killer."

He ran with it, it went viral, and now, the department and the city were stuck with it. Publicly, it was a disgrace. But privately, despite the nickname being in extremely bad taste, there wasn't a single guy on the force who didn't have to suppress a chuckle when he heard it for the first time. It was funny, in a macabre sort of way. And it sold newspapers—Jeezis did it sell papers!

Cromag poured himself a coffee, reclaimed his calm, and then turned to a presentation easel standing to the left of the podium. He removed a large sheet of paper covering the easel. There were three mugshot photos mounted on it: a woman and two men. Uneasy murmurs rumbled through the room. Many of the detectives and CSI's recognized the photos.

Cromag took out a laser pointer and tapped it on the palm of his hand as if it were a baton. He cleared his throat. "Welcome to Serial Killers 101."

"So, when does someone graduate from being a garden variety murderer to a serial killer?" he asked rhetorically, but did not give anyone a chance to respond. "Most experts are in agreement that a serial killer is someone who murders at least three people, with the murders taking place over an extended period, with an interval of time between them. In this case, our killer has 'broken the mold' and transcended the classical definition by murdering three victims in less than a week.

"The United States has more serial killers than any other country in the world. Some experts attribute this to a number of reasons which we will not go into here. Suffice it to say that the serial killer represents a true challenge to investigation. Why? Because there is no rational explanation as to why they commit their murders, moving the whole scenario to a different playing field than what most of you are used to.

"In typical homicides, motive is more or less simple to identify, and is usually attributable to greed, jealousy, or anger—and usually directed at one person. When that person is dead and out of the picture, the compelling force also disappears. That's why most homicides are 'one-offs'.

"I've studied serial killers, and learned a lot from research, but have never participated in an actual investigation, like this one. These are uncharted waters for me as well."

The detectives and CSI's pondered his statements with grim and quizzical expressions.

"The FBI has come up with three classifications for serial killers," Cromag continued, as he unveiled a second easel to the right of the podium. On it were three words: MEDICAL. DISORGANIZED. ORGANIZED.

"The first category is what are known as Medical serial killers. This type of killer is rare, but usually is a person who has entered the medical industry as a way to feed their perversion and carry out their kills. Could be a doctor, a nurse, an orderly. The setting of a hospital or care facility provides good cover, since people are dying on a regular basis. These types of serials are usually smart and know how to cover their tracks. If the death appears to have been the result of natural causes, there is no need to search for a perpetrator. That's why they're hard to catch.

"Example of a Medical serial killer: Genene Ann Jones," Cromag said, aiming the beam of his laser pointer between the eyes of the female who stared out from the photo. "She worked as a pediatric nurse in Texas and was known as 'The Angel of Death'. She killed an unknown number of children—an estimated forty-plus—by poisoning them. She would inject drugs that would create a medical crisis in the patient, and attempt to revive them, but they would die. She had her run in the 70's and 80's but was eventually captured and convicted, and is currently incarcerated."

Cromag pointed to the second key word on the easel. "Disorganized serial killer. Yeah, I know, nothing catchy about the name, but it does capture the key trait. These serials rarely stalk their victims or plan their kills. Most times, the victims are people who unluckily wound up in their path through no intention. Disorganized serials strike on a whim or when an opportunity arises. They make no effort to remove evidence or cover up their tracks. They often move frequently, even relocating to different states to avoid capture. These killers are typically not too bright. Under-educated, and very antisocial. Loners.

"Famous example? A local boy, I'm not proud to say: Richard Ramirez, the 'Midnight Stalker,' who terrorized California for about five years, from 1984 to 1989. He was convicted of thirteen murders and sent to prison, where he died after twenty-three years on death row."

As Cromag sighted his laser on the forehead of Ramirez' photo, the crowd nodded their heads in recognition of his infamy. Most of them had been just teenagers when Ramirez cut his swath of brutality and murder, but the high-profile case had dominated the media—it was everywhere and couldn't be ignored. It had made an indelible impression on anybody who was around at the time.

Cromag focused his pointer on the last category. "Organized serial killer. This perp is often the most difficult to identify and apprehend. Usually very intelligent and meticulously organized. They plan their kills well in advance. They pay attention to detail. This type of serial takes extreme precautions to 'sanitize' their crime scenes. Very little latent evidence.

"They commonly stalk their victims—sometimes for days—in preparation for the kill. They make contact with their victims, gain their confidence somehow, and then take them to another location to commit the murder. Afterwards, they usually go to extreme lengths to prevent discovery of the body—until it is convenient *for them*. I know it sounds perverse, but these types of serials often take 'pride' in their work. They follow the media in the aftermath, and get their jollies by outwitting the investigators. Poster boy for this type of killer? None other than Ted Bundy, a name I'm sure you're all familiar with." Cromag zapped the photo of Bundy with his laser, then clicked it off and faced the room.

"I believe we are dealing with an *extremely* well-organized serial killer here. Ted Bundy took great pains—and pride—in being able to leave virtually no evidence at murder after murder. Granted, the forensics technology of the 70's was nothing compared to what it is today, but that being said, the killer we are now dealing with makes Bundy look like a cub scout."

CHAPTER 20

CROMAG WAS DRIVING ON COLORADO BOULEVARD IN Pasadena when Bennett called.

"Remember you asked me to research whether or not the first two vics were members of Exceleron Fitness like the third one? Well, your hunch was right. All three victims were members."

"OK, now we may be getting somewhere," Cromag said. "I want you to contact Exceleron Fitness, find out which branches those victims were members of, and get on-site at each location. Get Simington or Alcord to help you. Once you're there, determine when was the last time each victim clocked in. Get whatever CCTV footage is available from their surveillance cameras. Then get it over to Digital Forensics and tell them it's a rush job. I've gotta see the Captain. I'll meet you at the lab this afternoon."

Bennett asked Alcord, the rookie, to help him. They divided up the three locations. He assigned the Valencia club to Alcord, and he took the other two. Separately, they went to each location and queried the computer log-in records to verify the identity of each victim. They determined the last time the victims had used the facilities. Then they got a copy of the surveillance footage from each day, at each club—and took it to the forensics lab to be analyzed.

While Bennett and Alcord were carrying out their assignments, Cromag headed to Division for his meeting with his superior, Captain De Carlo. He'd been summoned unceremoniously, and already knew what the topic of discussion would be: the three brutal murders for which they still had zero evidence and zero leads. The news had already leaked and gone public, throwing the city into a state of panic. The Mayor and Chief of Police were screaming at PD for results.

He approached the door to Captain De Carlo's office and tapped on the door. "Come in, Detective Cromag," the voice within said. The way he said it let Cromag know the Captain had been expecting him. *Oh boy, this should be fun…*

Captain Carmine De Carlo was fifty-eight years of age, with a slight paunch and thick head of salt-and-pepper hair. Lifetime cop. He'd been wooed for the Angeles Division Captain's job after a very successful, high-profile stint in one of the New York City boroughs. During his tenure in the Apple, he'd inherited a corrupt, sloppy department known for mediocre performance and had turned it around, posting some pretty impressive stats in the process: a fourteen-percent drop in homicides; a seventeen-percent drop in rapes; and a nearly twenty-percent decrease in burglaries and other petty crimes. Pretty impressive, Cromag had to admit.

De Carlo had achieved those stellar numbers by instituting a relentless and unforgiving work ethic—and setting an example for his men to follow. Unlike many high-ranking Officers who felt they'd done their grunt work early in their careers and now took pains not to get their shoes dirty, De Carlo hopped right into the trenches with his subordinates. He'd show up at crime scenes and personally supervise inspections; he'd spend afternoons at the morgue with medical examiners; and he took particular pleasure in personally supervising the interrogations of persons of interest. He had a formidable reputation for demanding and getting results. And now, by any standard, Cromag's squad was failing miserably in that department.

"Connah," he said, his vestigial New York accent as prominent as the broad nose on his face, "Please come in … have a seat." Despite having lived in California for five years now, he occasionally slipped back into Big Apple dialect, and more often than not, when he wanted to appear chummy with his subordinates. Cromag sat in the chair facing De Carlo's desk.

De Carlo now reverted to the dialect of a pissed Police Captain, which has no telltale link to any geographic region. "You know, Cromag, FBI statistics show that only sixty-seven percent of murders have been solved since

1980. That's a pretty dismal average, and it looks like your progress with this so-called Jewel Thief Killer isn't going to boost that any time soon."

De Carlo always clothed his jabs in sarcasm, and Cromag didn't appreciate it. But he remained professional, and used the Captain's cited statistic as a springboard for his response. "Yes, Captain, and FBI figures also show that the thirty-three percent of homicides that go unsolved can be attributed to either a lack of evidence, lack of witnesses, witnesses who refuse to cooperate, or lack of motive. In this case, choose any one, or all. There's no evidence, no witnesses, no motive that we can tell. Even the forensic geeks are stumped— they've never encountered even one, let alone *three* crime scenes—so totally devoid of any trace or DNA evidence. We've got our backs to the wall—and I'll be the first to admit it. I've been investigating murders for twenty-five years and have never encountered a mystery like this one."

"We gotta come up with some results heah, Connah," he said, his voice now emanating from Brooklyn again. Cromag's honesty and exasperation had softened him a little. "Do you have any leads whatsoevah?"

"Just this morning, we learned that all three victims were members of the same health club chain. As we speak, my detectives are rounding up surveillance video that may help us."

"Okay, detective. Keep me posted. You're dismissed."

Cromag headed to Forensics. He knew he'd just dodged a major bullet. He had bought himself a little time, but that didn't provide him with any relief. It made him even more tense, and more determined to learn the identity of the killer.

CHAPTER 21

CROMAG TOOK THE STAIRWAY UP TO THE THIRD FLOOR. THIS was the home of Forensics—a long, narrow hallway with well-lit rooms on both sides, housing microscopes, computers, and analytical equipment. Forensics technicians in lab coats darted in and out of the rooms, nodding to him as he passed by. At the end of the hall he reached his destination: DIGITAL FORENSICS.

The Digital Forensics lab was the pride of Division. It boasted the latest tech equipment, and was staffed by the most capable forensics experts in law enforcement. The higher-ups had lobbied hard to staff the operation with the best-qualified candidates available. They were young, crackerjack techs who could work magic with soundtracks, wiretaps, surveillance footage, and cell-phone grabs. There wasn't any type of audio or video recording they couldn't unlock, decipher, and enhance, to get the evidence they were after.

Cromag remembered the "prehistoric" era of video evidence, and how quickly it had all changed. Back in the day, the recorded footage detectives relied on was pathetic in quality—grainy, poorly lit image scrambles usually captured by a lone surveillance camera that had been in the right place at the right time. It was hit or miss, but as bad as the quality was, the evidence was often very effective in building cases. Over time, this became obvious, and it translated into a push to develop better equipment and analytical software.

The development of sophisticated software had dovetailed with a prolif-eration of the means to capture data. Nowadays, there wasn't a square inch of the city that wasn't being filmed 24/7: fast food restaurants, convenience stores, traffic intersections, malls, banks. Surveillance cameras were everywhere. In addition, there were dashboard cams, body cams, and aerial drones. Even Joe Citizen could capture usable evidence with his cellphone.

The key to maximizing the effectiveness of all this raw footage was the cadre of digital forensics experts—the "monitor geeks" that staffed the labs. Armed with an overwhelming array of technology, they could instantly find details that in the past would have required hours of painstaking perusal by human eyes.

The programs could crunch raw footage and distinguish men from women, and children from adults, based on size, walk speed, and other factors. It was an embarrassment of riches from an investigative standpoint. Conversely, in the interest of preserving anonymity, they could selectively blur a license plate, or the face of a witness, without compromising the integrity of the video.

As Cromag entered the room, he saw a female lab tech viewing footage on a monitor. He cleared his throat discreetly to get her attention. She turned around abruptly. Cromag was startled by how pretty she was. Blonde hair, sapphire-blue eyes, creamy skin, and a voluptuous figure. *You shouldn't be buried up here with all these dweebs ... you should be on the cover of a magazine,* Cromag thought.

She was likewise smitten by what she saw. Here was the Lead Homicide Detective, who could moonlight as a Calvin Klein model. He had chiseled features, great hair, blue eyes, and a pair of shoulders so broad she could've taken a nap on them. As if that weren't enough, this Detective Cromag had a smile that could liquefy a glacier in a couple of heartbeats.

In another time and place, she might have kissed him right on the spot. But this was the digital forensics lab! She had to maintain a professional distance. This was only their first meeting. *But hopefully not our last,* she thought. She looked at him and smiled.

It was the most beautiful smile Cromag had ever seen. *They've been hiding this woman up here on the third floor all this time? And I didn't know it? What kind of detective am I, anyway?* Cromag started to speak, but she beat him to it.

"Hello, Detective Cromag. I'm Linda Evans. I will be helping you today." She turned, inviting Cromag to follow her. "We've been expecting you.

Detective Bennett arrived just a while ago with the surveillance footage you want to analyze. We've got it loaded on our main bank of monitors. Please follow me."

Anywhere, thought Cromag. They walked down the middle aisle of the lab, flanked on both sides by researchers with their faces plastered to glowing monitors. They were screening footage in slow motion, fast-forwarding, winding and rewinding, zooming in and out, tweaking and editing. Cromag and Evans walked another fifty feet and were soon facing a wall of monitors mounted on the wall. Bennett was there, spellbound, looking at flashing electronics and swirling images. He heard them approach, and came out of his trance. They exchanged greetings and sat in chairs facing the monitors.

"Okay, Detective," Linda said to Cromag. "You're driving. What would you like to see first?"

"How about the footage from the Valencia location? That was the home base of our first victim."

Linda nodded silently and motioned to the left-most monitor in the bank. Bennett said, "OK, Manny Osorio arrived at the gym at 9:00am. Let's start with the feed from the camera at the entrance."

Linda manipulated some controls and the footage started rolling. They reviewed the images of members leaving and entering the gym. Suddenly—a burst of recognition: "Stop!" said Cromag. "Right there—rewind that—the guy with the Metallica tank-top. I think that's him."

Linda rewound and slowed the stream until it featured the image he'd recognized—a young male in an orange tank top featuring the band, Metallica. "There it is," Cromag said. "Can we zoom in?"

"Of course," said Linda. "We can do a loose zoom, like this…" As she spoke, the screen filled with a head-to-foot shot of the subject. "…Or we can get really tight, like this…" She tweaked the control and suddenly they could see the pores in his skin. "Back off a little," said Cromag. "I just want to get a close-up of the face."

Linda zoomed out slowly and locked the image so that Manny Osorio's head filled the monitor. Cromag and Bennett looked at each other and shared their mutual recognition. "That's him," said Cromag.

In similar fashion, they repeated the procedure with the footage streams captured by the cameras at the other two Exceleron Fitness locations. In both cases, they were able to isolate the sequences showing the arrival of the other two victims, and identify them in close-ups.

"That's amazing, Ms. Evans," said Cromag. "Now we need to see if we can spot these victims when they leave the club. That could be anywhere from ten minutes to two hours later, depending on how much time they spent exercising."

"Not a problem," said Evans. "We can code the specific parameters of each victim's appearance, clothing, height, weight and gait, and build an image profile specific to him. Then we can go through the footage from the rest of the day, and compare that profile to the images of every person who left the gym until we get a match. It's like a 'video fingerprint,' and if there's even a close similarity, we can drill down and examine it."

Cromag and Bennett nodded in agreement and asked Linda to proceed. They started with the Manny Osorio footage, streaming on the first monitor. Linda isolated the image of him entering the gym, and input specific commands on the keyboard. She hit the "enter" button and the screen blurred and became pixelated as it analyzed the data at staggering speed.

"It's making coffee now, we'll let it percolate for a while," she joked.

Within minutes, the screen froze and locked on a frame. Linda got tight on it. It was Osorio. He was leaving the gym approximately one hour after he'd arrived. But he was not leaving alone. "Whoa," said Cromag. "Okay, let's slow down a little; looks like we're getting to the good part. Can you enlarge the image of the person walking next to him?"

Linda did as best as she could, but within a second, they had walked through the door, and both Osorio and his companion had their backs to the camera. They remained that way, walking away from the camera until they were out of range. Linda was disappointed with the lack of a frontal view, and turned to the detectives, expecting to see disappointment on their faces as well.

Instead, Cromag and Bennett were gaping, having seen something in the footage that made their hearts fibrillate. The person walking next to Osorio was wearing a USC hoodie—similar, if not identical, to the hoodie retrieved at the first homicide. "Now," said Cromag, "Can you capture that same type of image fingerprint on this figure?"

"Of course," Linda said. She turned the computer loose and it went through its manic gyrations, flashing images in rapid succession until it stopped. Cromag said, "Let's see if we get a match between that profile and anybody in the video captures from the other two locations."

Linda turned her attention to the other monitors, which were streaming the footage from the La Crescenta and Glendale locations. She set the process in motion, and like a slot machine, each monitor spun images until it stopped and locked on one frame in particular.

There, displayed on the three monitors, were the three victims, exiting the gym with a companion. And the companion certainly didn't look like a man. Rounded hips, long hair, and prominent backside, with a gait uncharacteristic of a man.

In addition, the person walking with the second victim, Clifford Shaw, was wearing a tank-top emblazoned with a "PINK" logo. Cromag and Bennett recognized it. It looked identical to the one retrieved at the second homicide. There followed a moment of silence, but then a sensation of revelation that was shared by all three, as if to say, "*Are you thinking what I'm thinking?*"

"I'll be damned," said Bennett. "It's a woman."

Cromag and Evans concurred. Cromag said, "I had a suspicion, but the odds of my hunch being correct were pretty slim. The percentage of women serial killers is so low I didn't want to conjecture until we had pretty good evidence. I wasn't sure until now. This person is seen with each of the victims shortly before their deaths. That's no coincidence. In addition, she's wearing articles of clothing identical to those found at the first and second slayings. I think this may be our killer. And that means our killer is female."

CHAPTER 22

.: ".: ."

CROMAG AND BENNETT VAULTED BACK TO THE SQUAD ROOM.
He told Bennett to let the team know their number one suspect was female.
Then he went to Captain De Carlo's office and knocked on the door.

"Come in," De Carlo mumbled. Cromag entered. "Ah, Detective Cromag,
just the guy I wanted to see. You have an update for me?" He was wearing the
synthetic smile that he sported when he was stressed or pissed but didn't want
to appear that way.

"Yes, sir." Cromag said. "We've isolated the visuals of the victims exiting the gyms. Without exception, each victim was accompanied by someone. Further analysis confirms that this person is the same one with all three
victims. Finally, we feel our person of interest is not a guy. We're pretty sure
our suspect is female."

De Carlo had been drifting off during Cromag's summary, but the word
"female" snapped him back to attention.

"A woman? I'll be damned... what are the odds of that?" said De Carlo.
"But I might have guessed, as outrageous as it seems." He was silent for a
moment, then resumed suddenly. "Well, whatever rumors might have been
circulating that the killer was a gay man will probably be squelched now. I,
myself, was baffled about the gender of this monster, but I can't say that learning our killer is probably a woman provides me with any relief. Anything else?"

"Yes, sir," Cromag said, "And this is what pretty much confirms to me that
this is our gal: The woman's sweatshirt that was found at the first homicide

and the woman's tank top that was found at the second homicide showed up on the tapes—being worn by our suspect as she exited the gyms with victims one and two. I'm convinced it's her. Forensics is drilling down right now to see if they can come up with any more information."

De Carlo leaned back in his chair. He looked like he was almost about to break into a smile. This was as close to being "pleased" that Cromag had seen the Captain since the murders began. "Connah," he said, reverting to his condescending ploy of addressing Cromag by his first name, "This is exactly the type of bone I've been waiting for, to throw to the press. The mayor's been snapping at my butt-cheeks like a piranha. The public has been ravenous for something—*anything*—that might shed some light on the killer's identity. I think we're ready to call a press conference so we can share some of these crumbs with them. I will contact you with further details, but leave your calendar open tomorrow."

"Yes, sir," Cromag said, and shut the door behind him. No sooner had he reached the stairwell leading down to his office than his cell phone rang.

"Cromag," he said.

"Detective Cromag. Hi. It's Linda Evans in Forensics. I've had a chance to conduct some further analysis on the video feeds and there are some things I think you need to see. Can you come by?"

Cromag's tone softened like butter on a stove. "On my way," he said to Linda, almost slurping into the receiver. He stopped in the squad room and grabbed Bennett, who was munching on a doughnut. "Evans has something she wants us to see. And by the way, the Captain is calling a press conference for tomorrow. Fore-warned is fore-armed."

They marched out of the office and shot upstairs to forensics. Evans was waiting for them. "We have to stop meeting like this, Detective," she said. *I hope not anytime soon,* Cromag thought. *Wow, she's so beautiful, and she has a sense of humor,* he thought, trying desperately to resist the hypnotic effect of Linda's blue eyes.

"As long as we're welcome here, we'll keep coming, Ms. Evans," He said, responding with the same flirtatious demeanor she had greeted him with. None of this interplay was lost on Bennett, who smiled inwardly and took mental note of the blossoming intimacy between the Sarge and Linda Evans.

They sat down in front of the wall of monitors. When they were seated, Linda began her presentation.

"I have two things I want to show you. The first, is that I was able to do an image profile of the female suspect by analyzing characteristics of her posture, gait, and proportions, as seen from the footage of her exiting the gyms. From there, I created a hypothetical profile image in reverse."

"In reverse?" Bennett asked, his brows knit by confusion.

"Yes, in other words, so that we can see what this woman looks like *approaching* the camera, instead of walking away from it. I was hoping we might get a frontal view and zoom in on her face."

"And?" Cromag asked, hungry for more.

"Well, the results are not encouraging. I'll show you." She synced up the video streams as she had before, extracted the data, and used her virtual composite to do a match-analysis of all the footage of women entering the gym. Within minutes, all three monitors locked on potential matches. But it was disappointing. In each case, the woman was not only wearing huge sunglasses, but also either a hat or a hoodie that obscured her facial features. "See what I mean?" said Evans. "A dead end."

Cromag said, "Hmmm," but then added, "You mentioned you had something else."

"Yes," said Evans. "I don't know if it will help us, but look at this." She fast-forwarded all three monitors and synced up the sequences that showed the victims exiting with the mysterious female. She isolated the sequence on the first monitor, the Valencia location. She let the footage stream a little, following the victim across the parking lot to his car. When she had reached a certain point, she froze the screen in mid-frame.

"Do you see anything unusual?" she asked, like a grade school teacher quizzing her students. When she was met with silence on the part of the two detectives, she pointed out an area on the monitor. "See this ... what do you make of that?" She had pointed to a dark area on the perimeter of the shot, near some trees that lined the side of the gym.

Cromag almost stuck his nose to the screen to get a better view. Suddenly, revelation washed over his face. "There's somebody there, hidden behind the tree," he said.

"That's right," Evans said, beaming as if her star pupil had aced the quiz. "And in the footage from the La Crescenta club, focus on this area behind that white van." They looked closely, and both Bennett and Cromag saw a dark figure trying to maintain his stealth in the shadow of the van.

"And finally," Evans said, "We have the footage from the Glendale location." She pointed to a dark figure crouching behind one of the granite columns that framed the entrance to the gym. "I'll be damned," said Cromag. "Can you zoom in?"

"Your wish is my command, Detective," she said, and then did a simultaneous enlargement of all three screen images. There was a person there—a man—and he was dressed in a dark hoodie and wearing dark sunglasses. Evans did a comparison and the computer screen displayed a banner at the bottom that said "100% match." The guys in all three shots were one and the same.

Cromag smiled at Linda. "Good work," he said, but there was something else that had piqued his curiosity. "Can you get even tighter? There's something I'm noticing that I need to take a closer look at."

Evans zoomed even closer to the man's face, a little too rapidly at first, as it blurred into a mosaic of pixels. Then she backed off slowly, until the image sharpened on the monitor.

"Stop! Right there!" said Cromag. There on the monitor, was an image of the mysterious stranger, enlarged to a screen-filling close up. "There—see that? That green glow on his neck right below where his Adam's apple is? What *is* that? Looks like some kind of amulet or pendant." Linda zoomed in tight. There, in all three grabs, was the mysterious stranger with an amulet nestled between his collarbones. An amulet that was glowing emerald-green.

CHAPTER 23

THE HUNTER'S PLANET HAD COMPLETED SEVEN ROTATIONS since the pivotal meeting where all had learned of the epidemic threatening the Destroyers. As each day beneath the green Sunstar passed, the feeling of relief among the populace grew until it was almost palpable. The entire planet and its inhabitants seemed to relax. All except the Hunter.

His training had taught him to maintain constant vigilance and expect adversity. Threats were always lurking. The Destroyers were a perfect example. Even the wisest among them had not foreseen the attack they were now battling against! Nothing was guaranteed. The future and the secrets it held would continue to be a mystery as unfathomable as space itself. All one could do was to be prepared. He lay back, trying to comprehend it all, when he felt a throb at the base of his skull. He was being summoned to The Core again.

When he arrived there, he was alone. There were no other Hunters. And no Thinkers or Guides. Instead, the Leader Commander, the supreme entity who ruled the planet, met him alone, and they descended far below the surface to a private chamber.

"Hunter," the Leader Commander said, "an important decision has been reached. We have evaluated the skills and capabilities of all the Hunters and you have been selected."

"Selected for what, Leader Commander?"

"You have been chosen to carry out a special mission. Please listen carefully. There are very few on our world who know what I am about to share with you."

The Hunter became as still as the stone in the chamber walls. He looked into the eyes of the Leader Commander to convey his understanding. The Leader Commander nodded and continued.

"The Destroyers have identified a substance that can help them fight the microbial infection. The substance gives them immunity to the disease."

The Hunter was disturbed by this news, but he did not show his disappointment, or any other emotion, for that matter. It was something that Hunters just didn't do. His face betrayed nothing and remained inscrutable.

"That is unfortunate," the Hunter said. "Does my mission have something to do with this new development?"

"Indeed, it does," said the Leader Commander. "It will be your mission to prevent the Destroyers from obtaining this substance."

"I am honored," said the Hunter. "When do we depart? And why are there no other Hunters here to learn about the mission?"

"Because," the Leader Commander said, "you are to carry out this mission alone."

The Hunter was shocked, but again, he did not reveal his discomfiture. He maintained his composure and spoke in an even voice.

"Surely they will send an army to retrieve the substance," the Hunter said. "What effectiveness can I possibly have by going against them alone?"

The Leader Commander was silent, weighing very carefully the words he would choose next.

"Our covert operatives have only the barest threads of information, so I cannot provide specifics, but the Destroyers have developed a new technological advancement that will enable them to retrieve the substance in a cunning way. The method does not rely on combat involving armies of warriors, but instead, on an evil subterfuge carried out by just one entity—an agent designed to conduct the operation alone, with no other support.

"This operative will be sent alone to the world where the anti-microbial substance is found. You will learn in a moment where this world is located. Your seek-and-destroy operation will be carried out in complete secrecy. There will be no armies, no teams—just one agent against another. We are going to send our bravest and most capable Hunter—that is you—to engage and defeat their operative."

At this point, the Leader Commander's thought transmission seemed to bore into the Hunter's skull, as if to further emphasize the importance of what he was saying.

"Know this, Hunter. The very future of all beings in this sector lies in the successful completion of your mission. If you should fail, and their operative returns with the immunological substance, the Destroyers will survive and resume their quest to dominate every life form in their path."

"Yes, Leader Commander. I understand."

Though he had responded in an affirmative manner, the Hunter was flailed by doubts. He alone was being entrusted with a mission upon which the future of the universe depended? How could he possibly succeed? How could he defeat this cunning enemy? And where was he being sent?

Almost on cue, the Leader Commander was prepared to address the questions the Hunter had just asked himself.

"Come, Hunter," he said. He led him to a large, flat disc hovering above the floor in the center of the chamber. Its surface was translucent and shiny. The Leader Commander closed his eyes for a moment, as if in deep thought. Suddenly, an image appeared above the disc. It was a holographic representation of the Morbiddon Nebula, with its Sunstars and planetoids, complete and accurate in every detail.

"We are *here*, Hunter," he said, as a bright pointer appeared on the surface of the sphere representing their planet. "We are far below the surface, of course, but this is the starting point of your mission.

"You are going to journey far across the cosmic web, to a planet where the Destroyers' operative is being sent to obtain the substance. Our knowledge of the operation is incomplete, so we must conjecture as to the details, but we do know their operative is being prepared as we speak, and so you must prepare in like fashion.

"Your ultimate destination is inconceivably far from our home world," he said, as a new image expanded above the disc. It was a magnificent formation in space, composed of countless densely-packed Sunstars. "This is known as a 'supercluster,' and from this point forward, we will refer to it as the 'Andromeda

Galaxy.' That is the name by which it is known on the planet where you will carry out your mission.

"And this," he said, as he whisked across the universe and enlarged the image of another Sunstar, "is referred to as 'Proxima Centauri.' It is the next nearest Sunstar to the system the target planetoid is part of."

He continued to scroll across the universe at high speed, pointing out certain things to broaden the Hunter's understanding. Planets and Sunstar systems passed before him in a blur as his trajectory was displayed. All the Hunter could comprehend was that the distances were immeasurably vast, and that he was being sent to a planet on the very edge of space.

"This beautiful stellar formation is called 'Lanakea,' which means 'immeasurable Heaven' in one of the planet's languages." The image of *Lanakea* became larger and larger. The formation was actually a supercluster of many other galaxies. The Leader Commander magnified the view of one of the clusters.

"And *this*," said the Leader Commander, "is the planet you are being sent to. "It is one of many planets that orbit *this* Sunstar." He pointed to it, and as the image grew larger, the Hunter could see that the Sunstar was not green, like that of his own planet. It was yellow.

A glowing highlight appeared around one of the planets in orbit. The Leader Commander said, "Of all the planetoids orbiting this Sunstar, the only one known to contain humanoid life is *this* one." The light around the planet brightened and throbbed. "The planet you are being sent to is called 'Earth,' and those who live on it are known as human beings."

CHAPTER 24

CROMAG WAS DEEP IN SLUMBER, AND DREAMING ABOUT HIS childhood. He and his brother were playing in the forest and Cromag saw a large bird land in a nearby tree. When he turned to point the bird out to his brother, there was no one there. He looked around, but his brother was nowhere to be found.

The idyllic ambience of the dream became overshadowed with fear. "Clayton! Clayton!" he yelled, running through the forest, searching frantically and encountering only stark silence. He realized he had lost his young brother and feelings of remorse and grief engulfed him.

He was weeping in the dream, the pain so crushing he felt he would suffocate. *He had lost his brother. It was his responsibility to take care of his little brother, and he had failed.* His grief seemed interminable; he was awash in a torrent of tears, and then he heard music playing. It was the song *Ventura Highway* by the group "America"—faint at first, and then increasingly louder, until he woke up and realized it was his alarm tone. He exhaled with the incomparable relief one experiences when the worst nightmare imaginable suddenly ends with the realization, "*Wow…it was just a dream…*"

He got up slowly, still feeling groggy. *Oh my God, that was intense,* he thought. As nightmares often do, this one had made a profound stamp on Cromag's psyche—and left a lingering dread that would be with him the rest of the day.

He went to the kitchen, fired up some coffee, and threw a handful of bacon into the pan. The familiar aromas restored his sense of calm. He needed to be calm, because today he was going to be part of an event he always dreaded: a press conference. Press conferences were bad enough, but one like today's, staged against a backdrop of multiple unsolved homicides, pushed the stress level off the charts.

At any press conference, the most powerful defense against a blood-thirsty press and panic-stricken public was *information. Clues. Evidence.* But in this case, Cromag and his team had none to offer. *It's going to be a rough day*, he thought.

He devoured his bacon and eggs and washed them down with two cups of strong coffee. He got dressed and got on to the freeway. The press conference would have the comfort level of a medieval Inquisition, and he knew it. Only it wasn't taking place in a remote dungeon of some castle, but at City Hall.

Driving from the San Fernando Valley to the Civic Center downtown at the peak of rush-hour could easily qualify as one of the Labors of Hercules. *Fuckers couldn't schedule it for mid-afternoon, could they? Had to be first thing in the morning, the assholes...*

He slowly merged into the swamp of stagnant cars and proceeded to inch along. *What irony,* he thought—he was a high-echelon cop in one of the most dynamic police departments in the world, and yet he was utterly powerless against the urban phenomenon known as metro rush-hour traffic.

Traffic was so snarled and gridlocked, he could have had an escort of squad cars with sirens wailing, and it wouldn't have made an iota of difference. The freeway was a parking lot—wall-to-wall cars, cars, cars. He felt trapped, a feeling that would only be exacerbated once he got locked into a room with screaming reporters. He would have nowhere to go—and no news to report.

He finally made it downtown. He could see the monolithic tower of City Hall awaiting him, already judging him, holding him accountable for the paltry progress they'd made in the Jewel Thief murders.

The building was supposed to convey the strength and power of the city—or so said the mission statement of the architects who had designed it. It was actually modeled after a famous mausoleum. It had been completed in 1928, and up until 1964, had been the tallest building in the city. *Thirty-two floors of power, influence peddling, and corruption*, Cromag thought, as it loomed larger.

Jeezis, an image of the building was even on the badge that every cop in the city wore! And in keeping with So Cal's history of being the nexus of the motion picture industry, City Hall boasted a screen credit resume any actor in Hollywood would have killed for. The building had been used as a filming location or backdrop in countless productions, from the iconic TV shows "Dragnet," "Adam-12," and "Perry Mason." to big-budget flicks like "L.A. Confidential" and "Gangster Squad."

The building had even gotten its feet wet in sci-fi, making appearances in "The Adventures of Superman" and the 1953 classic "War of the Worlds." In that movie, the building was destroyed by alien invaders. As Cromag entered the quadrangle that bordered the Civic Center, he was wishing it had been destroyed in real life, sparing him the ordeal he was about to endure.

Cromag turned off Temple St. and drove to the rear entrance of the parking structure. Chaos was already fulminating at the front of the building. The steps leading up to the entrance were covered with cops, onlookers, reporters, and tourists, all swarming like vermin. Even the homeless had drifted over from Skid Row on Fifth Street to see what all the fuss was about. Every major network had a news van parked out front. They were ready to broadcast the spectacle to the waiting world.

Cromag parked and took the elevator to the Mayor's office on the third floor. He displayed his shield and bypassed the pat-down and screening by the metal detectors. He was packing his Glock, too, so a little extra attention was paid to him as he identified himself.

Security was as heavy as he'd ever seen it—testimony to the level of paranoia that accompanied the rampage of a ruthless serial killer. There were cops everywhere. Elite SWAT commandos were stationed around the perimeter and on the nearby roofs, brandishing automatic weapons. Choppers outfitted with machine guns hovered overhead. The Police Department was definitely representing here—in full force—and their presence was intended to intimidate as well as protect.

Cromag was escorted to the Mayor's office through a sea of bodies. He was greeted by Darryl Horvath, Mayor of Los Angeles, and Police Chief Carson Jorgensen. Behind them he saw Captain De Carlo, who acknowledged Cromag's arrival only with a worried look and a slight nod.

Mayor Horvath cleared his throat abruptly and said "Gentlemen. Are we ready?" His question was more rhetorical than anything else, for he was already making for the door that led to the press conference room. Cromag thought, *is a condemned man ever "ready" to be pilloried?*

They entered and the buzz stopped for an instant as the crowd realized the conference was about to begin, but then resumed unabated. Within seconds, the throbbing vibration of countless whispering voices reached a crescendo in the room, now filled beyond capacity.

The official flags of the City and the State of California were displayed on the wall. Microphones from every news agency sprouted from the podium like fungi after a spring rain. The Mayor advanced and the crowd silenced. A translator for the hearing-impaired took her position to the right of the podium.

All focused their attention on the Mayor, like a school of piranha after a bloody lamb shank gets tossed into a river. The press was drooling—and it was audible.

"Mayor Horvath! Is it true that the Jewel Thief doesn't leave any DNA evidence at the crime scenes?" someone shouted.

"Why don't the police have any leads, Mayor?" another shrieked.

Horvath raised his hand to silence them. "There will be a question-and-answer period at the end," he said. "Please hold your questions until then. Right now, I would like to turn the mike over to Sergeant Connor Cromag, who is in charge of the investigation." He looked over at Cromag and nodded to him. Cromag walked up to the podium and spoke in a voice steady enough to surprise himself.

"As you all know, this serial killer has now claimed three victims that we know of, the most recent murder having occurred in Tujunga two days ago. There have been no witnesses to any of the homicides, and very little evidence has been discovered that might aid the investigation.

"All of the victims so far have been young, athletic males in their late twenties. There doesn't appear to be any racial or ethnic slant to the killings. One of the victims was Hispanic, one was African-American, and the third victim was White. But they all had one thing in common: they were members of a health club chain known as Exceleron Fitness."

Murmurs of recognition spread like a rash. Doubtless, some of those in attendance were members of Exceleron Fitness themselves.

"Each of the victims was killed without any sign of struggle. Based on surveillance video that we have of each victim just prior to their deaths, they either knew the killer or were comfortable in allowing the killer into their homes. We are continuing to analyze evidence and will keep you all up to date."

The crowd erupted in angry shouts, like they'd been ripped off at a carnival sideshow that promised something spectacular and delivered something far less.

"That's it? That's all you can say?" one of the reporters barked, with others around him nodding in agreement.

"Yeah! How come there isn't any more information?" screamed another.

Cromag sensed the onset of anarchy and looked to the Mayor. Horvath raised his hand to still the seething crowd and went back to the podium. "I want to assure everyone here, and all the citizens of this city, that *nothing* is being spared in our search for this diabolical killer. Manpower and resources have been tripled to aid the investigative team. We *will* find him and bring him to justice! Now…we'll take questions, briefly."

As he yielded the microphone back to Cromag, pandemonium exploded, as the reporters stampeded for attention.

"Sergeant! Is it true that the killer amputates the genitals of the victims?" The question silenced the crowd faster than a loud explosion.

"Yes."

The victim mutilation was the most gruesome aspect of the murders, and it made the pack snarl with bloodlust. The noise reached a point where Cromag could barely hear himself think. He held up his hand to restore peace. When the roar subsided, a female reporter from the *Herald* spoke up.

"Sergeant Cromag, is it also true that so far, your CSI's have not been able to retrieve any evidence more than a few personal belongings and articles of clothing?"

"That's not quite true. Though the crime scenes are remarkably clean, we have retrieved some evidence that has been helpful. I will say this, however: the killer is very thorough and meticulous in covering any tracks."

A reporter from *SoCal Today* snatched the next question. "Sergeant, given the fact that the victims have all been young men, is it logical to assume that the killer may be a homosexual male?"

Cromag thought for a moment. "Ordinarily, that would be difficult to answer, since there are many psychological factors to be considered when attempting to profile a killer. But in this case…" he paused, "…We have reason to believe that the killer is female."

"*Female?*"

"*What?!*"

"*Are you serious?*"

"*No way!*"

The crowd went ballistic over this crumb. Cromag had responded to their hunger for a fresh, exploitable wrinkle with his juiciest bit of intel. Given the extremely low percentage of female serial killers throughout history, it was news they weren't expecting and it hit them like a torpedo. The noise level got so amped up, it made all the prior minutes of the conference seem like they'd taken place in a soundproof chamber.

"There will be no further questions, thank you." Cromag yelled, as he turned his back on the frothing mass of angry faces and left the room.

CHAPTER 25

COLTON DRUMMOND, AGE TWENTY-SIX, WAS WORKING ON HIS
Master's Degree in Business Administration at the University of California,
Los Angeles. The UCLA campus was located in Westwood, one of the more
upscale suburbs in the city. Westwood was a college town, a throbbing hub of
nightlife and extra-curricular activities.

"Colt" Drummond had been a high school football star and was awarded
an athletic scholarship to UCLA. He had good genetics—both his father and
grandfather had been top-tier jocks and had both attended UCLA as well.
He was strong and good-looking, and had never suffered for trophy-class
female companionship.

If ever there were a place to seek the company of supermodel-caliber
babes, it was Westwood. California had always had a monopoly on hotties,
and Westwood was the center of business. Beautiful coeds swarmed the
campus and packed the streets and shops in the tony little retail center known
as Westwood Village.

The phenomenon of California being a magnet for beauty was often
attributed to the motion picture industry. In the early twentieth century, when
the movie business was in full swing, the lure of Hollywood and its promise
of stardom became legendary.

It was once said that the prettiest girl in every high school in America went
to Hollywood seeking a career in motion pictures. Granted, stardom eluded
most, but many did not return to Podunk in discouragement. Instead, they

stayed in California and ended up working as secretaries or marrying automobile salesmen, maybe even having a daughter or two.

Over time, the female gene pool of So Cal became top-heavy in the attributes that made men helpless fools. Los Angeles—and by extension, its premiere seat of higher learning, UCLA—ended up having more beautiful women per square inch than any other city on the planet, except maybe Paris, France.

Colt Drummond, California born-and-raised, had grown up with pretty young girls at every turn. He had always had above-average girlfriends since his days in grade school, but when he became a student at the university the pickings took an exponential leap. Beautiful girls were everywhere. They lined up at the Starbucks, they browsed the shelves at the bookstore, they crowded the boutiques that lined Wilshire Boulevard, and many attended aerobics classes and exercised at the Westwood location of Exceleron Fitness.

Colt was a fixture at the gym, and took frequent advantage of opportunities to bed hot babes. But given the diminishing returns that accompany a prolonged indulgence in any pleasure, he'd gotten much more selective over time. After five years as a student, Colt was nearly jaded, and it took an extraordinary beauty to get his attention.

Just such a beauty appeared in front of him this morning, as he was replacing a barbell on its rack. She was a tall brunette, with a shape forged by the master wraiths of lust. With her piercing green eyes, long hair and deadly curves, she was simply stunning. Colt hadn't seen a woman of this grade in a long time, especially not in the gym; and *definitely* not two feet away from him and getting closer.

"Hi," she said, "Would you spot me on my bench press?"

"Of course," said Colt, who'd already morphed into 220 pounds of male putty.

She lay down on the bench and positioned herself. She lifted the barbell off the rack with very little effort, which impressed Colt. "Wow, that's a very respectable weight—pretty good."

"That's not all I'm good at," she said.

Colt had been to the rodeo enough times to know a come-on. He also knew from experience that extraordinary women often troll gyms for sport-sex, so he went along, more than willingly.

"Well, maybe we should see what else you can do," Colt countered, with an equal amount of barely-concealed seductive intent. "My name is Colt."

"My name is Eve. I'll follow you."

And it was that simple. Some of the greatest experiences in Colt's life had been those that were not planned, or complex, or burdened down in detail— they just happened. He and Eve left the gym side-by-side. They got into their cars and she followed him.

He looked in the rearview to make sure she was right behind him. Hers wasn't a car you'd lose sight of on a crowded freeway, either—a brand-new black Maserati convertible. They pulled up together outside Colt's campus apartment.

Colt offered her a drink. She responded by taking off her tank-top, revealing the most magnificent breasts he'd ever seen.

"How about if I drink some of your nectar instead," she whispered in his ear, before dropping to her knees. In seconds she had pulled down his gym shorts and was sucking him feverishly.

"Whoa, honey ... let's go the bedroom," said Colt, breathless. He was sporting an erection like a spear. They went in and he grabbed his cellphone before laying down on the bed. "Hey," he said, "do you mind if I take some selfies, just for a souvenir?"

"No, of course—go right ahead."

CHAPTER 26

.: ":." .°

IT WAS EARLY AFTERNOON WHEN CROMAG AND BENNETT GOT the call from dispatch: a "probable" homicide near the UCLA campus in Westwood. Cromag bristled at the use of the word "probable" by the dispatcher, but this was just department policy. Nobody wanted to identify or classify a serious crime until the experts—such as Cromag's team—labeled it as such. The policy was a little too politically correct, to Cromag's thinking. If it looks like murder and smells like murder, take a deep breath and let's cut the bull!

On their way to the scene, Bennett got a call on his cell. It was Patrolman Kenneth Morrison, a friend of Bennett's, who always provided an in-depth alert whenever he was a first responder to a homicide.

"Yeah, Ken—we're on our way," said Bennett. "The traffic's pretty thick. What? Again? Oh Jeezis … OK, we'll be there as soon as we can."

Bennett looked over at Cromag, who had already figured it out, based on Bennett's reaction. The Jewel Thief had just scored another one.

They headed towards Westwood, but God only knew when they'd get there. Los Angeles had garnered the award for "worst traffic in the country"—for three years running now—so it was a crapshoot trying to determine an ETA.

The crime scene was in one of the most crowded parts of the city. A nationwide survey of traffic accidents had identified the intersection of Westwood Ave. and Wilshire Boulevard as having the most traffic accidents in the entire country. And that's where they were headed.

They exited the San Diego Freeway at Wilshire. Within seconds they were in the thick of it. They snailed along and turned on Gayley, headed for the Valle Verde apartments, just a condom's toss from campus.

They wouldn't have needed a nav program to help them. A full four blocks away, all the signs of crime-related angst had blossomed and were flourishing. News station vans; patrol cars; roadblocks; spectators and reporters; there were even two news choppers buzzing overhead. In short, it was a zoo—but what other reaction could you expect to what was now the fourth homicide in five days? Everyone was jumpy, scared, and seeking answers. But none were forthcoming.

As they inched closer, Cromag remembered how the level of concern had increased with each successive slaying. The first homicide barely made it on to the radar. They had to wait twenty minutes for the DA to issue a search warrant to go inside. The second slaying caused everyone to perk up. The city was on amplified alert, and the air had the scent of a harsh new reality that was beginning to fester. The DA issued the warrant with lightning speed, and the media showed up in an eye-blink, along with an army of spectators swarming like maggots on a corpse.

By the time the third homicide had occurred, everyone responded with hair-trigger efficiency. The DA himself hand-delivered the warrant; the Medical Examiner showed up in person to evaluate forensics; and the cadre of bloodthirsty reporters appeared instantly, like a magic trick.

What would be the next step? Would the Police Chief himself show up? *Not too far from the realm of possibility*, thought Cromag, as he got closer and saw some of the city's key players already suited up and going through pre-game drills. Cromag realized that the presence of so much upper-level juice was—not coincidentally—linked to the public's heightened paranoia about a killer who was now making national headlines—and doing so with a shocking rate of frequency. Plus, in the wake of yesterday's nationally-televised press conference, all the swells had to at least give the appearance that they were performing beyond spec. A potentially career-making (or breaking) photo op or interview was lurking around every corner. The directive of the day was "CYA": Cover your ass!

Connor and Bennett parked, and plunged right into the shit-storm. People everywhere. Yellow tape. Flashing lights. Walkie-talkies squawking like angry birds. They approached the cop outside the door to the apartment.

"What've we got?" asked Cromag.

"A male grad student, name of Colton Drummond, age twenty-six. He was found alone, no witnesses. He missed a scrimmage yesterday and one of his teammates got concerned." Cromag and Bennett sighed in unison and prepared for the carnage they knew was awaiting them.

As they entered the bedroom, Cromag once again had the eerie sensation of having been transported through time to a medieval torture chamber, conceived by the most diabolical mind imaginable.

As per the script they'd now become familiar with and could re-enact blindfolded, the victim lay on the bed spread-eagled, in a blissful state of repose. Blood everywhere. And of course, conspicuous by their absence: the victim's genitals.

Cromag and Bennett donned latex gloves to do some light investigation. They weren't trying to steal any of the CSI team's thunder; they were just curious. And anyway, based on the track record thus far, it was a better-than-good bet that the team would not find any evidence at this crime scene anyway.

Bennett slid his hand under the bedsheets, and pulled something out. "Check this out, Sarge—the first time we've had any evidence like this." He held up a cellphone drenched in blood. "Bag it and get it over to Linda," Cromag said.

The team of CSIs arrived and began their sweep, but an air of futility pervaded the crime scene. They went through the motions half-heartedly, knowing that the Jewel Thief's trademark when it came to evidence was no evidence at all. Still, they conducted their search. Aside from the cellphone, the entire team came up with zilch. No surprise. They looked at each other, baffled and beaten into muted bewilderment.

CHAPTER 27

▪ : ▪▪:▪ ▪▪

ON THE PLANET WITH NO NAME, THE HUNTER PONDERED MANY things about his impending journey. He had heard of this "Earth" on occasion, most often when the subject of humanoid life had been discussed. He knew the inhabitants of Earth resembled those of his home world in physical appearance, but in little else.

For one thing, they were primitive, with limited capabilities, and their societies were still dominated by greed and war-mongering. In addition, they had not yet even mastered the basics of intergalactic travel. And worst of all, they all spoke with speech! What a challenge he faced trying to conduct his mission on such a savage world. But failure was not an option. He would succeed. He *must* succeed.

He had been given a written tutorial on Earth culture by the Instructors. He was reviewing it, familiarizing himself with the strange species that populated the planet. He had been taking a short respite when the Leader Commander summoned him.

This time they went to an area of The Core far from the secluded chamber of his prior briefing. They went down an unfamiliar corridor. A massive door restricted entry to all those but Leaders, who were the only ones who could open it, via thought-commands. The Leader Commander looked intently at the doorway, and it swung open slowly. They entered and the Leader Commander addressed him.

"Hunter, in preparation for your mission, you must become fluent in a specific language of human speech. Many languages are spoken on Earth, but you must learn one specific tongue. The language you must learn is the most widely-spoken one on their world. It is called 'English.' You have a very limited time in which to master it, so your learning protocol must begin at once.

"In addition," the Leader Commander continued, "the planet Earth is divided into many different regions, each populated by a different lineage of human beings. Each region has maintained its sovereignty and preserved its government, language, and customs over many generations.

"You will familiarize yourself with the people and practices of the region where you will engage the Destroyers' operative. As soon as we have gathered more intelligence, we will inform you. In the meantime, you will report to the Master Instructor to commence training."

The Hunter returned to his biopod and contemplated the responsibilities he was charged with. He had undertaken countless missions in the past, hunting enemies on other planets. Each time, he had undergone rigorous training—whatever had been necessary to prepare for his mission. He had been successful every time, but this fact did not spare him the concern he always felt prior to embarking on a new operation. And this operation caused him more concern than all the others he had undertaken in the past.

CHAPTER 28

CROMAG AND BENNETT WERE REVIEWING THE DETAILS ABOUT the Westwood murder when his intercom buzzed. The call was from Forensics. His heart began sprinting in anticipation.

"Hi, Connor, er-uh, I'm… I'm sorry, I mean Detective Cromag."

It was Linda Evans. Cromag smiled. He could just visualize her blushing crimson because of her unintended lapse into informality. It tickled him. "That's okay, *LINDA,*" he said, for mock emphasis. "You can call me Connor anytime." The thought that he and this beautiful woman were now on a first-name basis made his heart go giddy up!

"I've had a chance to isolate the data on the victim's cellphone. It's pretty interesting. Would you like to come here and review it?"

"I thought you'd never ask," said Cromag. "We're on our way." Cromag wished he were a fakir who could steady his fluttering heartbeat on the way over to Linda. She opened the door and lit his way in with a thousand-megawatt smile. Nothing had to be said; their eyes did all the talking. None of their romantic interchange was lost on Bennett, either. He figured it was his cue to reel in these two lovebirds. He cleared his throat.

"Ahem! How are you today, Ms. Evans?" Bennett said, and waited for her to float back down to earth along with the Sarge.

"I'm good, Detective Bennett. Thank you for asking," Linda said. "Please … have a seat next to Co- I mean, next to Sergeant Cromag, and we'll begin. Bennett could have sworn he saw Cromag blush and suppress a grin.

"Looks like the victim wanted a souvenir of his tryst," Linda said. "This cellphone has got audio *and* visual on it. We'll start with the visual data."

She had synched the phone to a huge monitor, and scrolled through some selfies the guy had taken while he was lying in bed. As is often the case with selfies, the end product fell way short of what was envisioned when the shot was taken. There were lots of blurry takes, some shots just showing what appeared to be someone's back, and one or two with Drummond's grinning face partially visible at the edge of frame.

The photos were pretty feeble, from an evidence standpoint. The two detectives had been hoping for a full-face portrait of his companion, but that was not to be. Chalk up one more on the list of disappointments associated with this investigation. They were about to get up from their chairs when Linda stopped on one of the photos.

It was the last shot that had been taken. The camera had been held higher aloft, from a perspective looking down on the bed. Colt Drummond could be seen flashing his grin, peeping out from behind something that was blocking the frame. And that "something" had a bit of blurry detail that intrigued Cromag.

"Can you enhance it, Linda?"

"Yes. I can do a VR2," she said. "That's a 'virtually-rendered reconstruction,' and what it means is that we take the image, frag it down to its essential elements, and cut and paste the pixels to come up with a rendering of what the entire scene would have looked like. It's like putting together a puzzle. We can then produce a sharpened version of whatever was blurred in the original image."

She zoomed in and began tweaking, cutting and pasting pixels, moving patches of imagery around the screen. As the enhanced image came into view, Cromag and Bennett were astonished. The fleshy pink amorphous shadow was now transforming before their eyes—clear and sharp. The curvature of hips, the roundness of female buttocks, the ecstatic face of Drummond in the background. There was no doubt: it was the backside of a woman—she was straddling the victim and having sexual intercourse with him.

As Evans continued to manipulate and fine-tune the image, they became aware of another image on the woman's back, just above her coccyx. Linda was on it like a stooping falcon. She zoomed and enhanced until the image was sharp.

"I'll be damned," said Bennett. "It's a tattoo—a black widow spider."

Cromag spoke. "You said there was audio as well?"

"Yes," said Linda. She backed up to the point just before the woman had mounted Drummond. She cued the audio up. The sounds of rock music gushed through the speakers. The victim had been playing his stereo—quite loudly as a matter-of-fact—and it dominated the ambient sound in the room, threatening to drown out all else.

"I'll filter out the rock concert and we'll see what's left," Linda said. She enhanced a thread of muffled vocal pattern. It was a voice, but it wasn't Drummond's; his mouth was shut as he fixed his gaze on the voluptuous female sitting on his erection. It sounded like the breathless, excited murmurs of a teenage girl getting fingered in the backseat of a car.

Linda isolated the mysterious little snippet and enhanced it. It was a woman's voice, and she was saying,

"Arousal."

"Tumescence."

"Engage."

The visual became hopelessly blurred and the recording now transitioned to what could best be likened to a porno film soundtrack. Moaning, "ooohs" and "aaahs," and heavy breathing: the last sounds Colt Drummond would ever make.

CHAPTER 29

CROMAG COULDN'T GET LINDA OFF HIS MIND. HERE HE WAS, neck deep in one of the most baffling homicide investigations in history, and all he could think about was how she had inadvertently toppled the barrier of workplace formality by addressing him as "Connor," instead of "Detective Cromag." It excited him to think about it, and his excitement snowballed.

When the team left the squad room for lunch, he made his move. *Only one way to get rid of a temptation: yield to it,* he thought, recalling a famous quote by Oscar Wilde, and his fingers were already pushing the buttons that would link him to Linda.

"Hello, this is Evans." *Oh God, her voice…give me the strength…*

"H-hello, Linda. This is Detec… I mean, this is Connor."

"Oh *hi,* Connor…" her voice tantalizingly warm and sweet, like heated honey.

"Linda, I was wondering…"

"Wondering *what,* Connor?" She added a teasing lilt to her voice, making it even more difficult for him. And she took delight in it—she wasn't going to make this easy on him.

Oh Jesus, I may as well just get it over with…

He blurted it out. "I was wondering if we could get together outside of this place. You know, maybe get a drink or something?" *There! I did it…* he finally exhaled.

Linda's heart went up three atmospheric layers. At last! She had been sowing the seeds of this encounter every time he had been down in her lab, and she thought maybe she had lost her mojo. But her intuition had been right—he felt the same way as she did! And the "or something" part of Connor's invitation intrigued her most of all…

"I'd love to. How about tonight?"

Am I dreaming? Did she actually say tonight?

"Yeah, sure. How about five o'clock? I can come and get you."

"Okay, I'll be waiting…"

Connor put the receiver down. The oldies hit by the Spinners filled his brain like an earworm. *"Could It Be I'm Falling in Love?"* He was floating, and would need a sturdy anchor to moor him to his desk for the few remaining hours before his date with Linda.

Time snailed along, but somehow, he got through it. Connor and Linda went out that night—and every night thereafter for the rest of the week. Cromag was hopelessly smitten. It had been so long—too long. These were uncharted waters for "Steamship Cromag," but he pushed ahead at full speed. All he could see was her beautiful face, framed by long blonde hair, her sparkling blue eyes like beacons, leading him to a safe harbor he'd been seeking for years. He was drunk with the sensation: warm, inviting, and more soothing than he could have imagined.

He went back in memory, and retraced the years that had brought him to this place of bleak bachelorhood. He had had girlfriends—more than a couple, in fact—and one or two had even shared his home for a while. But none of his involvements had evolved into the type of relationship that can change a man's life. The demands of being a cop's partner-in-life were too much for most women, and as his success rate in achieving a long-lasting relationship tanked, so did his hopes of ever being able to do so. Over time, he submerged himself in his work and ignored that part of his soul that was aching for a companion.

Until Linda! She had awakened a dormant part of his manhood—one he had sequestered like a novitiate and buried far away, underneath a mountain of professional obligations. Linda was *different*. It wasn't only that she was drop-dead gorgeous—but that she was uncorrupted by her beauty, unlike so many other attractive women.

When he was with her, life's concerns evaporated in the warmth of her affection. Linda was as sweet as a kitten; but incredibly, she balanced that sweetness with a no-nonsense grasp of her career and her life. She knew what a life devoted to law enforcement meant, and she seemed ready to go the next mile with him. He couldn't believe it was happening for him—finally.

On Friday night, they went to a little barbecue joint on Sepulveda Boulevard that had been one of Cromag's favorites for years. They stuffed themselves on ribs and brisket, as Cromag mentally checked off another positive on the "Linda attribute list:" *She's got a hearty appetite and enjoys a good meal. Pilgrim, your search is ended...*

They had sweet potato pie for dessert, a specialty of the house, and when they couldn't possibly consume another forkful, Cromag said, "Well, it's getting late; better get you home..."

"Why don't we go to your place instead...?" she asked, a flame burning behind those blue eyes; Cromag a helpless moth.

He brought her back to his house and his cat, Tiny Dancer, immediately walked up to Linda and sniffed her before rubbing against Linda's leg, a sign of affection.

Omigod, Tiny even likes her! This woman is perfect!

They took off their coats and were in each other's arms immediately, embracing and kissing each other hungrily.

"Oh, Connor... I've wanted you for so long... I've never wanted anyone so much..."

"Oh, Linda... Linda..." He could barely get the words out because he didn't want to deprive his lips of even one moment of the exquisite pleasure of kissing her, of tasting her. He picked her up like a newlywed and took her into his bedroom. They tore each other's clothes off.

The sensation of being completely naked in contact with her flesh inflamed him. It was like a powerful, mystical drug. His hands roamed over her curves, her hips, her ass. His mouth sought out her nipples, and he bathed her breasts in hot kisses. His hands found the hot wetness between her thighs and she melted in the crucible of passion.

"Oh, Connor," she moaned. "I want you inside me..."

Connor lay her on the bed and entered her, pushing himself deep into the hot, intimate embrace of her body.

"Oh, Linda… I love you…"

"Oh, Connor … I love you, too…"

They moved in heated rhythm, ravenous for each other, kissing and writhing on the sheets. She met his thrusts passionately and their tempo increased until they both erupted in climax, drenched in perspiration, barely able to catch their breath.

The afterglow was like a narcotic, a soothing delirium spent looking into each other's eyes. They spent that night together, making love until dawn.

CHAPTER 30

IT WAS A TYPICAL SATURDAY MORNING, AND IN KEEPING WITH tradition, a sizeable chunk of the city's population decided to brave the crowded freeways and head for the water. One of the destinations of choice on the coast was a few miles of famous beachfront that started in Santa Monica and ribboned south to Venice, California.

Winding through this stretch of sand was a special path that connected the Santa Monica amusement pier with Venice Beach. It was always packed with skaters, cyclists, and joggers. This area of California was where the So Cal mystique had been forged, a setting that inspired the Beach Boys to chronicle its charms in hit songs. Here was a world of permanent summer, endless surfing, and sexual promise, where there were "two girls for every guy." The whole nation bought into it.

Venice started out as a hippie enclave that attained notoriety for its "clothing optional" beach. Here, nudists and free-thinkers attracted throngs of wide-eyed tourists who copped a visual feel as they walked along "the strand." The strand, the West Coast version of an East Coast beachside boardwalk, was populated by street performers, hucksters, and vendors. It was lined with pop-up businesses that sold arts and crafts, sunglasses and souvenirs. Venice was a melting pot that attracted tourists, hippies, and the homeless.

Over decades, the times had changed, but not the basic vibe. Even now, after Venice had become gentrified, with real estate prices poking the ionosphere, the vagabond heritage of Venice hung around like a stain that couldn't be washed out. In keeping with the chill mindset that was the legacy of the flower children and the dopers, everybody accepted it and adjusted. Urban swells learned how to rub shoulders with street vermin, and life went on.

One of the landmarks of Venice that became famous was Muscle Beach. This outdoor gym-on-the-sand drew athletes who came to catch rays and show off their physiques. Southern California was the mecca of bodybuilders, and some of the biggest names in the sport started hanging out there. Soon, what started out as a crude little patio with a few barbells evolved into the premiere place to pump iron.

Muscle Beach was a mandatory hangout for muscle heads, along with gawking tourists, hot girls in bikinis, and all the nuts who claw at the fringes of spectacle. Nobody was quite sure who first came up with the name "Muscle Beach." It might've been a gym rat, a real estate developer, or a city council-man. Whoever claimed authorship, it didn't matter. The tag stuck—and the small oasis became an iconic symbol of the lifestyle in Southern California.

Nothing much had changed even now, despite the fact that Muscle Beach was already a septuagenarian in the world of SoCal legend. As the sun arced in the sky, the crowds would build and surround the small fenced area where sweat and sinew reigned supreme. Pro bodybuilders and aspiring hopefuls grabbed iron and grunted side-by-side. The spectators got an eyeful.

Brad "Biceps" Chandler was one of the faithful. He went to "the Muscle" every day—rain or shine—and he had established a following among the gawkers and bikini-clad groupies who clung to the fence, pushing their taut nipples through the chain link, hoping to make eye contact with their bronzed heroes.

On this Saturday, Brad showed up as usual and entered the paddock with the other bulls straining over their physiques. He maintained an air of aloof non-involvement. It was a demeanor he had worked on. It allowed him to scan the crowd intently, yet appear casual and disinterested while doing so. As his eyes swept the perimeter, they froze in mid-pan and locked on an outstand-ing specimen of womanhood. She towered above the teenyboppers and stood out like a lioness in a meadow full of rabbits. She was beautiful, muscled and magnificent—and she was looking directly at him.

Under the ruse of going over to spot a training buddy on a heavy lift, he approached her. The closer he got, the bigger her smile got. This babe was the hottest thing on the beach, hands down.

"Hi," he said. "What's your name?"

"Eve. What's yours?"

"Brad."

"Well, Brad, where did you ever get those huge arms?" Brad knew she was patronizing him, but it was all part of a game that he loved playing.

"From living right and being a red-blooded male," he said.

She smiled, and he hopped over the short fence so they could pursue their conversation more discreetly. "Come with me," he said. "Got something I want to show you."

"Okay." She couldn't have been more agreeable if he had suggested giving her a diamond bracelet. She put her arm through his and they left Muscle Beach and went to the parking lot. His white Chevy van was sitting right where he had parked it that morning. They went in the back.

It would be the last time he would ever enter his van.

Hours later, the maintenance crew that swept the parking lot at closing noticed Brad's van still sitting there. Prior to calling a tow service, they got out to get a closer look.

"If this van's rockin', don't be knockin'," one of the guys said, quoting the vernacular rhyme about the popularity of vans for sexual encounters.

"Yeah," the other one said. "I can remember my VW Microbus back in the day ... laid more pipe in that ride than in my bed at home. It sure came in handy for quickies."

They chuckled, but then something caught their attention and stifled the humor: a stream of liquid dripping from the rear of the van had pooled on the paving below. Red liquid.

"Whoa," said one of them. "I think we need to hold off on the tow and call 911 instead."

Within minutes the first responders came. The parking lot morphed from a deserted expanse of asphalt to a crowded crime scene. Squad cars howling in packs. Calls emanating from Venice Beach were usually high profile, and elicited response from both the Santa Monica and Los Angeles police departments, at the very least. And since a serial killer was currently at large, Playa Del Rey and Mar Vista joined the party.

The infestation of squad cars led to the to the inevitable glut of those who are drawn to wailing police sirens like leeches to blood. Right on cue, the network news vans and hovering helicopters showed up. All of a sudden, what had been an empty lot was the nexus of a rapidly-swelling media event.

This was the scene that confronted Cromag and Bennett as they parked on the perimeter and fought their way to the van through the swarming crowd of shock junkies. It was amazing how people got hooked on the adrenalin high that brutal crime provides.

They walked up to the cop guarding the van. There was a portable canopy set up around the rear doors, to conceal the gruesome spectacle within. Cromag ducked his head in for three seconds.

You gotta be kidding me.

Had this been someone's bedroom, there would have been no doubt. But it wasn't someone's bedroom; it was a public parking lot next to a beach. *Was it really the Jewel Thief?*

He and Bennett pondered the implications. Not the Jewel Thief's typical MO, that's for sure. When had she decided to start targeting victims at public venues? Apart from this strange circumstance, all other aspects of the killer's signature were definitely there: an athletic young male, spread across the floor, legs open, with his cock and balls nowhere to be found. And yes, blood: it was there by the gallon, all over the van's interior and dripping out the back door, transforming the vehicle into a bizarre abattoir-on-wheels.

Bennett went to talk to the cops on scene for additional details, and came back to brief Cromag.

"They were able to ID the vic by his wallet. It was just sitting there on the front seat. Money still intact. His name is Bradley Chandler, age 27," said Lyle. "Local bodybuilder, won a couple amateur titles, lives in Mar Vista. Comes here just about every day, according to the locals. I guess he couldn't wait to get to his apartment."

"Any witnesses?" asked Cromag.

"Not a one. Ain't that the bitch of it all? Must've been a thousand people here on a Saturday afternoon, and nobody saw anything or knows anything."

CHAPTER 31

. : ¨:.. .¨

"YOU MEAN TO TELL ME, THAT IN BROAD DAYLIGHT, IN ONE OF the most heavily-populated public venues in California, some guy gets his junk hacked off *in his van* and bleeds to death, and nobody hears it and there's no witnesses? C'mon, detective—whaddafuck??"

Cromag was standing at attention in Captain De Carlo's office. He dared not move a muscle while De Carlo was venting like this. This newest addition to the Jewel Thief's resume had blown the City's tolerance level to smithereens, and the PD was absorbing the shrapnel. The Captain's face was almost crimson; his pulsing carotid threatening to burst through his neck. Cromag stood there and weathered it.

"Are we sure it's our gal and not some copycat? Since when does she do her thing out in public, for Chrissake?"

"Captain, all the triggers for her were there, regardless of location. I mean, c'mon: Muscle Beach." Cromag said it as if the fact could not have been any plainer.

"Okay," De Carlo said, drifting into sarcasm, something he did without thinking when he was angry. "Okay, I see. She was there for a nice day at the beach and decided to get some penis and testicles for lunch, is that it?"

Cromag did not respond right away, and instead mused further, *how could she resist? A beach full of bodybuilders ... she must have thought she was in a candy store ...* He snapped back to attention and addressed the Captain's question about the possibility of a copycat.

"Captain, the one indisputable fact about this scene—and what makes it doubtful that it was anybody else *but* our suspect, is the fact that there was no evidence. You would think, in such close quarters, where you can't even push a broom, let alone sterilize a crime scene, there would be a hair, some epithelial cells, *something* to give us a lead. But there was nothing, just like the four previous killings. That fact alone makes me believe it's the same killer."

"Christ," the Captain said, exasperated. "So now the killer is branching out to athletic events and the like? Are we going to have to start watching other public venues frequented by young males? Given this, will she start practicing her sex organ surgery at Laker games, or at Dodger Stadium?" The veins in De Carlo's neck were throbbing in tempo with every syllable.

He is reaching new heights of sarcasm, thought Cromag, who remained silent until the maelstrom blew over and the office became calm once again. De Carlo wiped his brow with a handkerchief.

"That will be all, detective." De Carlo said, as he turned his back to Cromag, signaling that the ream-session was over. Cromag shut the door behind him, certain that he'd not heard the last from higher-ups regarding the Jewel Thief.

CHAPTER 32

IT DIDN'T TAKE LONG FOR THE RIPPLE EFFECT OF THE MUSCLE Beach slaying to reach the top floors of City Hall. The killing catapulted the Jewel Thief case to an extraordinarily-amped level of prominence in the consciousness of the city.

Mayor Horvath called a special meeting with Police Chief Jorgensen, Captain De Carlo, and Detective Cromag. The Mayor was fuming.

"I want you to watch this," he hissed, as he clicked on the remote that operated a television in his office. "It's a special report on *60 Minutes* on what they are calling 'The Jewel Thief Phenomenon.' I cannot, for the life of me, understand why the public has the kind of morbid fascination with gore that fuels this type of social media hunger, but it's out of control. Just sit back and watch."

The episode was a special report on the infamous serial killer who was now topic number one in the minds of the people. The show explored the social dynamics behind the case's meteoric rise to national prominence.

"Who is the Jewel Thief?" had now become a social media catch-phrase and internet meme. Graffiti artists had tagged the freeway overpasses of Los Angeles with screaming, multi-colored renderings of the question. T-shirts emblazoned with it were selling like hotcakes online and at swap meets.

Spectators at sporting events displayed posters with such taunts as "Is That Gal Next to You the Jewel Thief?" knowing that cameras panning the crowd would broadcast it to a national audience. The topic was everywhere, and news cameras couldn't keep their lenses off the spectacle.

The *Dictionary of Contemporary Slang* even recognized the term "Jewel Thief" as a synonym for an emasculating female, as in *"I could tell she was a Jewel Thief right away, so domineering. That was my first and last date with that bitch."*

The show offered up the theory that the epicenter of the cataclysm now rocking social media had been the slaying at Muscle Beach. Apparently, a bystander had recorded someone carrying a poster with "Who is The Jewel Thief?" painted in huge neon letters. It got posted on Facebook and the rest was history.

Whether or not the theory was true didn't matter anymore. The juggernaut had been set in motion and was hurtling forward at frightening speed, fueled by the explosive atmosphere that surrounds spectacular acts of brutality and violence.

Mayor Horvath shut off the television and asked, almost pleading: "What am I supposed to do? What are *we* supposed to do?" Nobody had an answer to that question. After an awkward silence, they were dismissed, and filed out of the Mayor's office.

The situation did seem hopeless. It's often been said that "the darkest hour lies just before the dawn." Little did Cromag suspect, as he drove back to Division, that he was about to see a glimmer of daylight—a break in the case—but one whose price would be the death of yet another victim.

CHAPTER 33

. : ".:. ."

ON THE NAMELESS PLANET, THE HUNTER'S SCHEDULED DEPAR-
ture for Earth was approaching rapidly. Since his last briefing, he had learned
how to speak the Earth language "English." In addition to learning its basic
grammar and pronunciation, he had studied a specific dialect of English—
the one spoken in the region where he would conduct his strategic operation.
Along with lessons in speech, he had been taught about the customs and
culture of the target region.

During his period of learning, he had taken up residence at The Core, to
facilitate his tutoring by the Master Instructor himself. The Master Instructor
was the sternest of taskmasters, who spoke few words and did not tolerate
weakness or inattention on the part of his pupils. Their first meeting had
been memorable.

"So," the Master Instructor had said, "You are the chosen one. The guard-
ian of our future, on whose shoulders the hope for our continued existence
rests." He was evaluating him, testing him, perhaps even taunting him, to
gauge what weakness—if any—might reveal itself and jeopardize so vital a
mission. All the while, the Hunter had remained as steadfast as the very rock
from which The Core was hewn.

"Yes, Instructor. I am committed to my function and will do whatever is
necessary to succeed."

The Master Instructor continued, "You will be sequestered alone and will
be allowed no company or recreation during this period. Your training will be

conducted at a level far exceeding any you have experienced in the past. And you will have no rest until your training has been completed. These measures are necessary because our time is limited. You will need to depart for Earth in twenty planetary revolutions." The Hunter felt that the Master Instructor was emphasizing the rigor his training would require, in order to reveal any latent weakness.

"Yes, Master Instructor," he said, looking him directly in the eyes.

Then, mysteriously, as if the Hunter had demonstrated some hidden attribute during this brief introductory exchange, the Master Instructor smiled, and stopped speaking momentarily. When he resumed, he had altered his tone, to one that was almost conciliatory, as if to acknowledge that his preliminary evaluation of the Hunter had been satisfactory. He spoke of the Hunter's past achievements.

"I know that you have been a Hunter for many orbital cycles, and have fulfilled your function admirably." He looked at him, as if waiting for some sign in his response. The Hunter said nothing, and the Master Instructor went on.

"I see furthermore that you are quite proficient in languages. You have learned to communicate in many tongues with speed and efficiency. That is a good thing."

The Hunter remained guarded. He would not show pride or any other emotion that might belie his unconditional commitment to his training.

"Yes, Master Instructor."

The Master Instructor then changed his tone again abruptly, signaling that their introductory meeting was over. "Very well," he said. "Your training will commence with the next rising of the Sunstar. Go to your quarters now."

And so, their first meeting had ended. As promised, his training had started on the following dawn, and as promised, had been rigorous beyond imagination. But he had not failed. He had learned all that he was required to.

And here he was now, his training completed, on the threshold of an adventure so fraught with implication he trembled at the thought of it. He had been summoned by the Master Instructor for a final meeting prior to his departure.

He went to the main academic hall of The Core and approached the Master Instructor. He nodded his head in salutation and was standing reverently before him, perhaps for the last time he would ever do so, and was unprepared for what happened next. The Master Instructor, an imposing figure with a presence as immutable and foreboding as the monolith itself, actually extended his arms and embraced him. He smiled and looked into his eyes.

"You've done well, Hunter. The Leadership made a wise choice in selecting you for this task. I know you will return victorious." If ever the Hunter had felt unable to contain his emotion, this was such a time, so overwhelmed was he by the Master Instructor's praise. But he remained strong, inscrutable.

"The Leader Commander would like to see us both," the Master Instructor said. "Come with me."

They left the academic hall and went to the large chamber where the Leader Commander had conducted the virtual tour of the universe during their previous meeting. He was waiting for them.

"I want to show you both something.," the Leader Commander said. "To review thus far, not long ago we learned where the Destroyers were sending their agent for the retrieval operation. Based on that knowledge, the Master Instructor crafted a proper curriculum for you. According to his report, you have performed admirably. Let us now focus on the target region." The Leader Commander focused his stare at the shimmering disk. An image of planet Earth appeared in orbit around its yellow Sunstar. He nodded at the image, and the planet tripled in size, magnifying their view.

"You know from your training that Earth is composed of land masses and water. The human beings live on the land masses, but are capable of traveling over the expanses of water, which are called 'oceans.'"

The Hunter opened his mouth and his eyes widened. He had heard about Earth's expanses of water in his schooling, but had no idea they were so large. The "oceans" of Earth amazed him. His home world suffered a severe scarcity of water that made it precious beyond measure, and yet here was a planet where the amount of water exceeded that of land. Astounding!

"This land mass is an example of what the Terraforms, or 'Earthlings,' call a 'continent.' This particular one is called the 'North American Continent.' Notice how it is flanked on both sides by oceans."

As the Hunter surveyed the North American Continent, a certain area of it became infused with green light. It was in the lower portion of the continent, and bordered an ocean. He looked up at the Leader Commander.

"This is where you will confront the enemy. It is part of a region known as 'The United States.' A 'state' is a smaller area controlled by its own governing body. There are a number of states in this land mass. The one you will journey to is called 'California.'" A red beam now shone down, illuminating the area he was referring to.

"The lower part of the California state is where you will engage your combatant. It is a large settlement—some twenty million earthlings live there. It is called 'Los Angeles.'"

CHAPTER 34

.: "..! .°

CROMAG AND BENNETT GOT THE CALL BUT THIS TIME IT WAS different. It was a homicide, all right—and at first glance it bore the Jewel Thief's signature—but certain elements were off. There was a dead guy spread-eagled on a bed, but he had not been mutilated in the usual fashion. His pride and joy were still intact.

There were small cuts at the base of the penis and top of the scrotum, but his genitalia had not been removed. This alone was enough of a shock, but the real bombshell came in the form of a living, breathing witness who had seen the killer and could help in providing identification.

Cromag and Bennett approached the witness, who was sitting on a couch in the living room. He was still trembling, hyperventilating with rapid, short breaths. His name was Benjamin Fuller. He was the roommate of the victim, David Shulman.

Fuller was draped in a blanket. "Mr. Fuller? I'm Detective Cromag ... and this is Detective Bennett. Can you tell us exactly what happened?"

"I ... I...c-came in and heard some noises ... they... they... were coming from Dave's room," he said, choking back tears, struggling to speak.

"What did you do when you heard the noises?" Bennett asked.

"I ... I tippy-toed up to the door, because ... because as I got closer it sounded like Dave wasn't alone. I could hear two voices."

"Two voices?" Bennett asked.

"Yeah … it… it was Dave and a woman. Sounded like they were having sex. You know—moaning and sounds of pleasure."

"And then what?"

"I got closer to the door and peeked in…" he started to shake even more noticeably, recalling the scene.

"What did you see?" asked Cromag, pressing in.

"I'll never forget it…" He froze, the recollection so horrifying it trapped the words in his throat. "…Dave was lying in bed, and the woman, she had long black hair, she was straddling him…"

"Straddling him?"

"Yeah, they were fucking alright, no mistake. She was on top—and Dave was digging it. I remember that she had a pretty big tattoo, right above her ass-crack."

"A tattoo?" Bennett asked.

"Yeah, it was a black widow spider … you know, big, black—with a red hourglass on its abdomen."

Cromag and Bennett glanced at each other in mutual recall of the video image from the fourth victim's cellphone.

"And then what happened?" Bennett asked.

Benjamin became transfixed in horror. "Then … then… all of a sudden, Dave's expression froze. He stopped moving … his eyes were wide open and so was his mouth, but he was completely expressionless, like someone had turned a switch off and sucked the life out of him … I… I've never seen anything like it—it was horrible."

"What did you do then?"

"I screamed at the top of my lungs. I told the bitch to get off him and I threw the door wide open. I yelled again and lunged at her. I was going to grab her and yank her off Dave."

"And?"

Before I could reach her, she got off Dave and shot straight up in the air, like she'd been fired from a cannon. Weirdest thing I've ever seen. I mean, how could anybody jump straight up like that? She almost hit her head on the ceiling. She went straight up and then spun around and landed on the bed, facing me. I looked down at her crotch and she was bleeding a little, like she was having her period or something.

Cromag and Bennett knew that the blood on her vulva would have been the victim's, from the incisions on his penis and scrotum. But had she cut him with a knife and then resumed intercourse? At what point would she have severed them completely? It was a mystery, but it didn't matter: she had undoubtedly used the same nerve poison to paralyze this guy as she had on all the others. She had probably been on the verge of mutilating him when the roommate barged in.

"What happened after she faced you and you saw the blood on her?"

"This is the scariest part… She stood up; she was at least six feet tall. I know that, because that's how tall I am and she was looking me in the eye. Never seen eyes so green… And then she grabbed my throat …"

"Yes?" said Bennett.

"And she picked me straight off the ground with just her one fucking arm, like I weighed no more than a pillow! She was choking me and I couldn't do a thing about it, she was so strong. I was helpless. Then all of a sudden, she just stopped and dropped me—and jumped right out the window—totally naked. She didn't even take her clothes … we're three floors up here, you know? … what kind of person can do that??" He was trembling in earnest, his face the color of "scared shitless."

"Did you try to pursue her?" asked Cromag.

"No… I blacked out right after she jumped. When I came to, David was lying there, dead. That's when I called 911."

"Okay, thank you," said Cromag. "Well, it sounds like you got a good look at her face."

"Oh yeah, I'll never forget it. She was gorgeous, I could never forget a face like that."

Cromag and Bennett had Benjamin Fuller transported to a safe house used to sequester witnesses in high-profile prosecutions, where there was a possibility of witness intimidation, or worse. The suspect had seen Benjamin, and was still at large. Cromag was not taking any chances with his only eye witness. Benjamin was given a sedative, with a police guard stationed outside the house and one in the room adjoining his.

They bagged the killer's jumpsuit and underwear and rushed it to forensics, but as feared, the clothing she had left behind yielded zero in terms of evidence. It was completely devoid of hair, or even skin cells. This, coupled with the roommate's account of the killer's physical prowess, pushed Cromag to a new, uncomfortable plateau of awareness. He was now more concerned about this killer than he had ever been with any other case he could remember. For the first time, he wondered *What the fuck are we dealing with here?* And for the first time in his career, he felt fear.

Benjamin woke up the next day, rested. The cop on duty said, "Sergeant Cromag wants me to take you to the station to meet with a sketch artist." They got into his patrol car and headed for Division.

The forensic artist at Division was one of the best, and his work had helped the department solve many crimes. Whether it was a composite sketch based on witness description, or a facial reconstruction from skeletal remains, he was often instrumental in providing the missing visual link to identification that would help crack a case.

The forensic artist spent a couple of hours with Benjamin, first getting a thorough description, and then consulting a facial identification catalog. The facial ID catalog contained a glossary of images organized by facial features, such as eyes, noses, chins, lips. Benjamin selected images that closely resembled some of the killer's facial features, and the artist did the rest, fine-tuning his sketch until he had a good likeness of the killer.

He held the sketch up for Benjamin. "Whaddya think?"

"Wow! That's her!" said Benjamin.

"A pretty good-looking woman," said the artist.

"Oh yeah," said Benjamin. "She was really beautiful."

Cromag and Bennett came and retrieved the sketch. They told Benjamin to wait in an interview room until they returned. Now it was time to take the next step: see what magic Linda Evans might be able to work with the drawing.

CHAPTER 35

BENNETT MADE ARRANGEMENTS TO GET THE MEMBERSHIP database for all the Exceleron Fitness locations in California. The database contained the personal information—as well as a head shot—of every member. Cromag told Linda what their plan was: compare member photos with the forensic sketch and hopefully, come up with a match. She said she could meet them in the lab that afternoon.

Cromag arrived early for their appointment, and since they were alone, he leaned in to kiss her. Linda was surprised at his boldness. "Connor … I don't know if we should … *should we*?"

Her ambiguity about whether a kiss was okay or not said everything he needed to know. He embraced her and soon they were lip-locked like two teenagers. "Oh, Connor … we better stop…" They heard footsteps in the hall outside the door and tried to regain composure as quickly as possible.

The footsteps belonged to Lyle Bennett, who knocked before coming in. As he entered, he sensed that some sort of impropriety had just transpired, so he grinned. "Hello, Detective Bennett," Linda said, trying to suppress the grin that had popped up on her own face. Cromag cleared his throat and attempted to appear serious.

"Okay, we ready to go?" said Cromag, with gruffness as genuine as plastic leather.

"Yes," said Linda. She scanned in the sketch, synced up the gym member database for cross-matching, and then entered the filters that would further define the search: Gender, female; Age: early twenties; Hair Color: brunette; Eyes: green. The computer screen displayed a blizzard of code as it crunched the search parameters.

"Exceleron Fitness has nearly 100,000 members in California alone, 30,000 of which are female. This could take some time," Linda said. "Why don't you guys grab a coffee and come back in about twenty minutes."

Cromag and Bennett shuffled out and headed for the commissary. Bennett took the opportunity to rib his boss a little, and do some poking around.

"So, Sarge … uhm, Ms. Evans has been a great help to us so far, hasn't she? She sure is a nice gal, you know …?" He was fishing to verify his suspicion that Cromag and Linda were an item, but Cromag didn't budge.

"Yes, she has been," said Cromag, trying to color his response with gravity. But Bennett could see that, despite his dry answer, Cromag was fighting off a smile. *That's what I thought. Question answered,* he said to himself, grinning from ear to ear.

They finished their coffee and went back upstairs to the lab. Linda was finishing up. "Bingo," she said. "I came up with three potential matches. She lined up all three head shots on the computer screen for comparison with the sketch. Sure enough, any one of them could be their suspect. One of them, in particular, caught Cromag's eye. He could swear he'd seen her before… but where? He turned to Linda.

"Can you print me out a copy of these photos? I want to get back to our witness and conduct a virtual line-up." Linda printed copies of the photos and the detectives shot back up to the interview room where Benjamin was.

"Do you know what a police line-up is, Benjamin?"

"Yes."

"Well, then you know the drill," said Cromag. "But we're going to do it a little differently. Instead of parading suspects in front of you, we're going to do it right here in this room with photographs. I'm going to show you photos of three suspects. I want you to tell me if any of them look familiar." He laid the photos down on the table in front of Benjamin.

His reaction was immediate. Recognizing the woman who had murdered his roommate was a painful shock. He started to shake and broke out in a sweat.

"What is it?" said Cromag. "Do you recognize her?"

"Yeah… yeah… th-this one—right here." He pointed to the photo on the right end of the line-up.

"You're sure?" asked Bennett.

"Y-yes … positive. N-no doubt."

"Okay, Benjamin. Thank you, we'll get a squad car to take you home." Bennett escorted Benjamin to the front desk and soon returned.

Cromag looked at the name on the photo. "Her name is Eve Nouveaux. This is our gal."

Bennett and Cromag went into turbo mode. This was the break they'd been waiting for, and it was time to run with it. Six victims had already been slaughtered, with more to follow, probably. They had no time to lose. Cromag handed Bennett the photo of Eve Nouveaux.

"Get this photo out to all the channels: All PD and Sheriff's departments in California; the FBI; and yeah, even Interpol. We gotta nail this psycho. I'll notify the Mayor and the Captain that we have a positive witness ID. Get whatever information Exceleron Fitness has on her: address, credit card info, where she works, whatever they've got. Then do a complete work-up on this Eve Nouveaux—background check, Department of Motor Vehicles, schooling, work history, where she shops, *where she gets her fucking nails done!* I want to know *everything* there is to know about her. Got it?"

"Yes, sir—understood." Bennett headed for the squad room. He would gather the other team members and divide the follow-up assignments among them.

Before Cromag went upstairs to give an updated report to Captain De Carlo, he called Linda. "This is Evans," she said.

"Linda, it's Connor. Our witness provided positive ID on one of the photos. Her name is Eve Nouveaux. Yeah, it's the break we've been waiting for. I feel like I can exhale, if just for a little while. It's a cause for celebration. How about dinner tonight?"

"I'd love to, Connor," she said.

CHAPTER 36

CROMAG WAITED A BIT BEFORE GOING UPSTAIRS TO THE Captain's office. De Carlo saw him approaching, and also noticed an encouraging look on Cromag's face—one that he hadn't seen there for quite a while. He motioned him in.

"What is it, Detective?"

"Sir, we've got a breakthrough in the Jewel Thief case."

De Carlo perked up like a bear smelling bacon. "Oh, *really?* Go ahead, I'm listening…"

"We've got an eyewitness. He helped produce a composite sketch. We matched the sketch against the gym's membership files and came up with a photo. He made a positive ID". Cromag showed him the photo. "Her name is Eve Nouveaux. We've sent out an APB and alerted all agencies. We're following up on building her profile."

De Carlo studied the picture. "She's a bit of a looker, isn't she?"

"Yeah," Cromag agreed. "Too bad she's a homicidal maniac."

"Well, this could be our break. I'm going to call a Press Conference for tomorrow. Good work, Detective."

Cromag hadn't even closed the door before the Captain was dialing City Hall. De Carlo was smiling: for the first time since the investigation began, he had good news for the Mayor and the Chief of Police.

The Press Conference took place at 10:00 am the next day. The Mayor had chummed the waters by announcing "a promising breakthrough" in the Jewel Thief case, and the media bore down on City Hall like sharks in a frenzy.

Everyone was there, waiting for what they hoped would be something different this time: Cops, city government swells, expert commentators, reporters, news vans, choppers—and a weary public—starving for any news that might relieve the bone-crushing tension they'd felt for weeks.

Cromag entered the Mayor's office and greeted Captain De Carlo, Police Chief Jorgensen, and Mayor Horvath. "Shall we?" said the Mayor, motioning to the door. *It's showtime,* thought Cromag, as he entered the conference room. A projection screen had been set up behind the podium as a visual aid. Mayor Horvath was visibly upbeat. He approached the podium and waited for the roar to dwindle, a smile on his face.

"Well, I am pleased to say that we have some good news—for a change—regarding the so-called 'Jewel Thief' murders. An eye witness has made a positive ID. If you'll look at the screen behind me…."

The photo of Eve Nouveaux blossomed on the screen, larger than life. The audience gasped. It wasn't just that she was pretty—*supermodel beautiful,* in fact—but how could this woman have murdered and mutilated six young men? The effect on the crowd was instant and profound. Disbelief spread like a contagion to every face. Some looked like they were going to faint. A few even looked like they were going to puke. A canister of tear gas wouldn't have produced the reaction the photo had. The noise subsided a bit, but then the reporters became rabid.

"Mayor! Mayor! Can we have copies of the photo to show the public?"

"Who is she?"

"Is she in custody?"

"Does she have a prior record?"

"Where is she from?"

"Is she a California native?"

"Did she act alone?"

The Mayor held up a hand and waited for the temblor to pass. He looked at Cromag and nodded his head, indicating that he was transferring the meeting to him. Before taking the podium, Cromag spoke to one of the staff members, who then proceeded to distribute papers to the audience.

"We are passing out photos of the suspect for your use in disseminating this information. We confirmed the ID with our eye witness just hours ago, so we have no other information on this woman, but are working diligently to build her profile. According to our records, her name is Eve Nouveaux."

"Detective!" a reporter shouted. "Are you sure this woman acted alone? It seems unlikely she could physically overpower six strong young men, and then murder them and…" he hesitated, not sure how to tastefully refer to the act that earned her the Jewel Thief moniker. "And … you know—mutilate them the way she did."

Cromag caught the Captain staring at him and knew what the look was for. He had to cover the department's butt. "I want to emphasize that this woman is still just a suspect at this point," Cromag said, "And until further investigation, shall remain innocent until charged." The comment was met with groans of disapproval.

Cromag hesitated. He did not want to share with the crowd the fact that she had used some kind of paralytic nerve agent unknown to science to incapacitate the victims prior to removing their genitals. But he had to give them something.

"Regarding whether or not she acted alone," he said, "There is evidence to suggest she may have drugged her victims somehow to make them less resistant to her attack." More tremors shook the crowd. They still weren't satisfied. They didn't want to shut the door on the possibility of an accomplice, given the circumstances.

"So…" a reporter spoke up, "If you're not sure whether she had an accomplice or not, are there any other persons of interest in the case?"

'Persons of interest,' Cromag scoffed to himself. *That terminology first popped up on some cop show years ago, and now everyone is using it.* Cromag and the Captain had differed on whether or not to show the photo of the mysterious stranger who'd been hovering around the gyms. De Carlo had insisted he make it part of the presentation. He had agreed to, reluctantly.

"As a matter of fact, there is another *person of interest*," he said, embellishing the phrase with just a hint of sarcastic emphasis. "Not much to go on in terms of appearance or witness description. This is a person who has been sighted at the gym locations where the victims were videotaped leaving with the suspect."

"Can you give us a description?

"Yes—somewhat. Please look at the screen behind me."

The screen grabs from the surveillance cameras were projected on to the screen, and were met with snickers, scoffs, and muffled laughs from the audience. Cromag was not surprised. *I told the Captain this would happen. What did we expect? It's just a photo of some guy wearing a dark hoodie, with dark sunglasses, you can't even see his face—and he's got a costume jewelry amulet around his neck. Looks like a character from a fucking comic book...*

One of the reporters cleared his throat to get Cromag's attention. Cromag recognized him as Barry Lennox, the smart-ass who had coined the name "Jewel Thief" way back when, and had been instrumental in turning the case into a spectacle.

"So, Detective ... exactly who is this person of interest—*Doctor Strange*?" He looked around, smirked, and the entire crowd burst into laughter.

"Admittedly, as I said, we're kind of slim on particulars regarding this POI, it's not much to go on, but it's better than nothing. I will mention that the amulet around this person's neck emits a green glow."

"Oooh," said Lennox, refueling, "Better watch out or he'll make you disappear with his magic necklace." He looked around and the crowd guffawed. Thankfully, another reporter spoke up and the crowd settled down.

"Now that this 'Eve Nouveaux' has been identified and her photo circulated, how soon do you expect capture?"

Captain De Carlo stepped up and interceded on Cromag's behalf. "We're working as diligently as possible. All resources have been re-directed to the manhunt...or should I say, 'woman hunt.' We will let you know. No further questions."

The press conference disbanded quickly. Cromag saw Bennett approaching him. "Wow, I'm glad that's over," Cromag said. "I escaped with my skin, at least."

"Sarge," Bennett said, in a tone that Cromag had now learned to recognize and had come to expect whenever Lyle provided him with updates on the case. "We did an exhaustive background check on this Eve Nouveaux..."

"And?" *Here it comes: bad news,* thought Cromag.

"The address she gave Exceleron Fitness when she signed up is some bridal shop in Sunland. Her employment reference and job contact info are bogus as well—no such company, no such address."

"How about a credit card?" asked Cromag. "How did she pay for the gym membership?"

"No records whatsoever—she paid cash."

"How about IAFIS and the other databases?"

"We ran her through all of them including the national crime databases."

"Yeah…?" Cromag was hoping against hope at this point.

"Eve Nouveaux doesn't exist. Never has. No record anywhere."

Why am I not surprised? thought Cromag. "Thanks, Bennett," Cromag said, resigning himself to further mystery.

CHAPTER 37

ON THE ANONYMOUS PLANET, THE HUNTER LOOKED UP AT THE night sky, as he had done so many times in the past. In the morning, he would be leaving his home world to make the journey to Earth. He would be embarking on the most dangerous—and most critical—mission he had ever undertaken. As the hours crawled by, he gazed up at the firmament through the portal in his biopod. It was ablaze with the light of myriad Sunstars. Would he ever enjoy this view again?

He tried not to think about the importance of his mission, about the sheer number of beings that would be impacted by its success—or failure. The fate of so many worlds—ones he had never even been to—rested on the outcome of this operation. And he alone was responsible for it. He felt the apprehension he had felt before other missions, only magnified ten-fold. Never had the fate of so many rested in the hands of one Hunter.

When the first slivers of green light pierced the portal, he knew it was time to leave. He had gathered his gear hours earlier. He loaded it into a small transpod, as the brilliant Sunstar slowly ascended in the sky. He looked back at his dwelling before climbing in. Would this be the last time he would ever see his home world? Who could say?

He arrived at The Core and all the other Hunters were gathered there to send him off. One by one, they embraced him and spoke to him, some using thought-speech, others conversing with spoken words. Any one of them could have been envious of his position, but they were not. Their concern and support were unanimous and genuine, for each one knew the chosen Hunter would be undertaking a mission of the highest importance and risk—and doing it *alone*. After he had exchanged well wishes with the last of them, he turned to the Leader Commander. He was ready.

He followed the Leader Commander through the interlock that led to the departure portal. The Leader Commander slowed his pace and turned down a hallway. *Where is he taking me?* thought the Hunter. The Leader Commander sensed his concern.

"Hunter, before you depart, there is something I must show you."

He followed the Leader Commander to a darkened laboratory. It became illuminated as they entered, and he saw an area cordoned off with a curtain. The Leader Commander drew the curtain back. There, on a table, was a body.

"Hunter, do you know what this is?"

"No, Leader, but it appears to be humanoid. Is it a life-form I should be familiar with? Is it a human being?" He was excited that perhaps this was an example of the life forms he would soon be in contact with. He had become familiar with the characteristics of humanoids, especially Terraform human-oids. The defining traits of earthling physiognomy were easily recognized, and actually quite similar to his. The form he was examining was definitely humanoid, but he could not be sure of its origin.

"It is not a human being, Hunter. It is not even a life-form. It is a biomi-metic, modeled after the human beings you will encounter on Earth."

The Hunter was familiar with biomimetic science. He had learned its history, and how nearly every race of beings in the Universe had developed biomimetics—creations that "mimicked" life, in form and function. Even the Thinkers of Earth had succeeded in developing crude biomimetic units which they called "robots," "cyborgs," or "androids."

Not coincidentally, the Morbiddon had been the originators of biomi-metic technology. Over time, before they became the Destroyers, they had catapulted the science of biomimetics to an entirely new level, and had even shared it with the other worlds in the sector.

But their benevolence vaporized in the fires of conquest that burned in the hearts of the Destroyers. The technology of biomimetics cultivated by the peaceful Morbiddon, became perverted as a tool of war wielded by the Destroyers.

They had realized the strategic potential of using covert operatives that mimicked the species they wished to conquer. Agents that possessed far superior strength, had no feelings, needed no sustenance, and would do whatever they were commanded. No one really knew what deadly developments were taking place in the biomimetic laboratories of the Destroyers, but the Hunter suspected that the mysterious figure before him had something to do with it.

"Hunter, the Destroyers have succeeded in developing what we believe is the most advanced biomimetic unit ever created. Our covert operatives have stolen a prototype model. This is what you see before you."

The Hunter examined the biomimetic more closely. It did indeed resemble an earthling in every detail.

"The Destroyers call it a 'Biosynth,' because it is a 'synthetic' human—identical in appearance and function. It is virtually indistinguishable from an earthling, and would require the closest of scrutiny to determine that it is not human." The Hunter grew silent as he contemplated the sinister implications of such a refinement.

"Your adversary on Earth will be a Biosynth of this advanced design, Hunter. We do not know its full capabilities, but we do know it has been specifically created to retrieve the life-giving substance the Destroyers need to survive. We expect this Biosynth to be nothing less than the most devastating weapon the Destroyers have ever created, a combatant that will stop at nothing to achieve its mission."

If the Hunter had been worried about his mission prior to this meeting, it paled in comparison to the concern he now felt. They walked to a transport shaft that took them up to the departure portal where he would embark on his odyssey to Earth. As they neared the transpod, the Leader Commander looked at him for a moment and then asked, "Do you have any questions?"

"Yes. How much time do I have?"

"That is a very important point, Hunter. There is a time constraint. The Destroyers are dying at a rate far beyond what they had projected, and it is essential that they complete their gathering mission as soon as possible. You will leave for Earth now. While in transit, we will provide you with the latest intelligence right up until the moment of your arrival. Once you arrive, you will have twenty-one rotational cycles of their planet in which to accomplish your mission. Remember that Earth is larger than our planet, and a rotational cycle on Earth is of longer duration than it is here, but nonetheless, your time is extremely short.

"We understand the magnitude of the task that awaits you, and on a strange world, no less. We had told you not to engage any earthlings while in pursuit of the Biosynth, but it is far more important that you succeed, even if it means that some Earthlings discover your identity. If you feel you may fail without some form of assistance, and it becomes necessary to reveal the nature of your mission to somebody on Earth, do so. The fate of countless worlds rests upon you."

As the Hunter climbed into the transpod, the Leader Commander spoke to him once more, perhaps the last thing he would ever hear from him.

"I remind you again, Hunter: From the day you arrive, the Destroyer's Biosynth *must leave on its return journey no later than twenty-one rotational cycles of Earth around its Sunstar.* If the Biosynth is prevented from returning by that time, the Destroyers will succumb to the microbial plague and perish, and will no longer pose a threat to the universe."

"Understood, Leader Commander. I will not fail."

He closed the door of the transpod, secured himself in his seat facing the controls, and engaged the engines. The roar made the craft shake. He rose from the surface, the powerful thrusters propelling his transpod ever faster from the gravitational clutch of his planet. He climbed higher and higher, until his home world was but a speck, and the vast expanse of space lay before him.

CHAPTER 38

ON THE SAME MORNING THAT CONNOR CROMAG BEGAN WORKing on matching the forensic sketch, Clayton Cromag had gone to Exceleron Fitness in Glendale. The Glendale club was his home court. He parked his custom Corvette convertible and turned around to admire it. It was all part of the package. He was young and successful. The hot car was a confirmation of what he had achieved and a measure of the recognition he merited.

To round out "the package," Clayton paid particular attention to his appearance. He wore tight-fitting T-shirts that showed off his muscles and rumbled around town in an eye-catching chariot. It sent a message targeted at a specific facet of the population: young, sexually adventurous females.

Cultivating sexual encounters had been his specialty since his late teens. He had experimented with different locales in his quest for one that would ensure a steady crop of hot sex. He had tried bars, work, social clubs, and online dating, but found the payoff to be paltry for the time spent. He even went to sensitivity seminars and joined book clubs. In the final analysis, the "hit or miss" nature of trolling for sex in those waters had yielded disappointing results.

It wasn't until he joined a gym—quite innocently, and with no ulterior motive—that he stumbled upon the most fertile fuck-farm ever. Here was a rich and sustainable valley of plenty that was constantly watered with streams of hot young females. The overworked cliché about "low hanging fruit" was more than apropos for this environment, for opportunity was everywhere, ripe for the picking, dropping on the ground around him. From the first day he had gotten into the world of fitness, he had started harvesting a bumper crop of pussy. With no end in sight.

The pursuit of women was a game to him, and in keeping with that spirit, he assigned pet names to the choicest females that populated his workout turf. He dubbed these hyper-attractive female specimens "Amazons." These were women who, in the game of genetic poker, had been dealt royal flushes in terms of physical attributes.

First, there was the "Uber-Amazon," a large-eyed Teutonic beauty gifted with perfect symmetry and flawless musculature. Large breasts, slender waist, wicked hips and ass. She wore tank-tops and extremely tight leotards that displayed her cut-and-curved body to perfection. She was fit and she knew it. She was aloof, inscrutable, and mouth-watering.

Next, there was a trio of young Hispanic girls whom he dubbed "Las Amazonas," out of respect for their *Latina* heritage. They were all petite—the tallest was barely five-foot-four on her tippy-toes—but each was a marvel of incredibly curvy, lust-inspiring beauty. They had large breasts that were firm, perky-nippled, and bursting from their tank-tops. Their toned glutes strained tauntingly at the fabric of their gym wear, and to watch them perform lunges or squats was a hypnotic experience. Their tight leotards displayed their labia like bas-relief Renaissance sculpture. Each had a plump, succulent camel toe that commanded the stares of every male in the gym. Two of them featured the brunette hair and dark eyes that were Hispanic trademarks. The third was an anomaly for a *Latina*: she had blonde hair and cerulean blue eyes. They spoke Spanish when conversing with each other, but were quite fluent in English if the need arose.

Then there was another *Latina* that Clayton dubbed "La Amazonetta," a petite, perfectly-proportioned little Venus who was also quite strong. She could squat her bodyweight without getting a single hair out of place—and bang out a set of reps that would leave most guys out of breath. This lower-body strength no doubt was the source of her spectacular glutes. So captivating was her caboose that males in the gym would stumble over each other to obtain a better visual of her walking away. It was an absolutely astonishing ass. She was brunette—of course—and had a beautiful face with brilliant white teeth which she flashed to great advantage at all the admiring males.

Rounding out Clay's coterie of exquisite Amazons was the "Slavic Amazon," a tall and sinewy interpretation of perfection with an Eastern European pedigree. She always wore tight tank-tops to showcase her sinewy, tanned deltoids and traps, contracting them slowly and sensuously when she knocked out a set of dumbbell raises. Clayton pegged her for either ex-military, or law enforcement, or maybe both. She had a beautifully-featured, serious look about her, with piercing hazel eyes that could probably get even the most hardened criminal to cave during interrogation.

Such was the stable of gorgeous specimens that Clayton enjoyed at the gym, but lest anybody got the wrong idea, his enjoyment stopped at looking. Yes, contrary to what might be expected, his Amazons were off-limits to him. When he learned that they were serious about fitness and came to his gym on a regular basis, the targets on their backs disappeared.

This was simply a matter of keeping his playground sustainable. Clay was into one-night stands, and when a woman he had bedded realized this, anger often resulted. Better to have the angry woman be an occasional visitor or one-timer than a regular. Nothing would screw up his coital enterprise more than pissing off a regular. A jilted hottie could spread poison about him to all the other women, making him as desirable as a chemical spill—and killing any future hopes. That's why he adopted a policy of "look but don't touch" when it came to the regulars.

But even with a strict policy of "hands off the regulars," it left a more-than-generous portion of desirables to be pursued. There were visitors on guest passes; sporadic exercisers; gals turning over a new leaf after the holidays; women who had just been jilted and were into "revenge fitness;" and so on.

There was also a virtual nation of babes who frequented gyms for the same reason he did: they were into sport-fucking, plain and simple. Gyms were playgrounds for these "one and done" warriors who were mining for hot sex. And the sweet icing on the cocksman's cake was this: There were so many different Exceleron Fitness gyms that Clayton could be an eternally-roving pussy-hound, constantly sniffing out new quickies at club after club after club. Such was the beauty of a fitness chain with dozens of satellite locations.

Clayton had lost count of his conquests. Sometimes it seemed like an indistinguishable blur of women. But every once in a while, when he started to feel jaded and began to skirt the boundaries of boredom, something new would happen along, to provide a refreshing stimulus that would renew and excite him all over again.

That is exactly what happened this morning. He had arrived in a funk, not really looking to score. He was working a pulldown machine when his internal radar blipped: *an attractive woman was coming into view on the perimeter.*

She caught his attention instantly, for she was exceptional. *Wow, I don't think I've seen you here before, sweetheart.* Clay mobilized. He approached her, planning to use the very words that had popped into his mind a second ago.

"Hi, are you new to the gym? I don't think I've seen you here before."

"Yes, I am," she said.

On a scale of one-to-ten, this woman was a twelve, no lie. *Easy, boy … play this one right, no need to scare her off right away.*

"Are you new to California as well?"

"Yes, as a matter of fact—I'm vacationing and just wanted to use the facilities today."

Bingo! Right answer. Clay could already feel an increased blood flow in his southern sector. It was time to steer the interaction by seeding the conversation with some not-so-subtle sexual innuendo.

"I'm a personal trainer," he lied, "And I can see that you're no beginner, you're so trim and toned. I've got some special routines I could show you … to take your fitness to a new level. I'm sure you'd enjoy them."

She pondered for a moment. "I would like that, thank you."

He proceeded to show her some movements with free weights, making sure he kept his body extremely close, touching her as much as possible under the guise of demonstrating proper form.

"Umm … you smell nice," she purred.

Jeezis, I've never seen eyes so green. He was mesmerized, but still focused. Then it was her turn. She picked up the ball and ran with it.

"What else can you do, to take me to another level…?" she asked.

Her lips are so inviting…

"Well, I do have some advanced movements—like the pro's use—but I can't really show them to you here, if you know what I mean." Her expression told him that she knew *exactly* what he meant.

"I would love to see them. Is there somewhere nearby where you can show me?"

"Oh, you bet. Let me get my stuff from my locker and I'll be right back." He went in to the locker room to retrieve his street clothes. He took that opportunity to text Connor, purposely keeping his message cryptic, so as to whet his appetite:

YO! I HIT THE JACKPOT AT THE GYM… DETAILS LATER

He returned to see her waiting for him at the front counter. They walked out.

"Oh, by the way—my name is Clayton."

"I'm Eve. A pleasure to meet you."

CHAPTER 39

CROMAG WOKE UP AND WENT TO THE KITCHEN TO FEED HIS cat. He suddenly remembered a loose end from the day before: the cryptic text message he'd gotten from Clay. He reached for his cellphone, eager for an update.

A look of disappointment swept his over his sleepy face. *That's strange.... I would have thought Clay would have texted me by now, bragging about his latest score...* No text. And his brother hadn't called or left a voice mail, either.

Clay had never missed an opportunity to tell Connor—in detail—about his sexual adventures. Cromag was concerned. He called the central desk at Division and asked to be patched through to the nearest patrol car in the vicinity of his brother's house.

"Yes, Sergeant, this is Officer Gordon," the cop said. "What can I do for you?"

"I need you to check on my brother. Address is 14514 La Tuna Canyon Road. He has a black Corvette convertible. If you see his car parked there at the house, don't disturb him, just call me back."

"Will do, Sergeant."

Cromag had instructed the officer to show up discreetly. He didn't want to scare the shit out of his brother, after all. *He might have a cutie in the sack with him.* He chuckled; that would be just like Clay. And that would be the only justifiable reason to go *incommunicado* for so long.

Cromag made some coffee and read the newspaper. The latest update on the Jewel Thief case was on page one, above the fold. COPS IDENTIFY KILLER. SHE'S FEMALE! Screamed the headline. The newspapers kept the investigation right in the public's face with prominent coverage like this. It had almost become a daily feature.

His phone rang. Expecting it to be Clayton, he smiled and was prepared to hammer him verbally, but then he saw it was a call put through dispatch. It was patrolman Gordon.

"Sergeant Cromag … I'm sorry to have tell you this, but something has happened at your brother's house. We need you to get here right away."

Cromag's throat tightened, a harbinger of impending dread that had become a kneejerk reaction after two decades in homicide. He felt bile start to rise in his esophagus. His breath grew short. He threw some clothing on, grabbed his badge and his Glock. In his haste, he forgot to lock the house, but that didn't matter right now. The only thing that mattered right now was finding out what Officer Gordon had meant by "something has happened…"

He had a portable bubble in his personal ride. It came in handy at times when you needed to transform an ordinary vehicle into a police car. He pulled it from under the seat, set it on the roof, and fired it up. He pointed his car in the direction of his brother's house, and launched into traffic like a heat-seeking missile.

He was fishtailing, weaving in and out of cars. La Tuna Canyon Road was not a major thoroughfare, but still had enough traffic to make the ride dicey, especially at ninety miles an hour. Were it not for the flashing bubble, his unmarked car would have prompted onlookers to call 911. The bright pulses of red and blue light kept tempo with his own heartbeat, as his anxiety increased. He threaded his way through thick clusters of commuters, and even crossed over into the stream of oncoming traffic to maintain his juggernaut pace.

All the while, driving like a stuntman, the major part of his attention was still locked on his kid brother. *Clay…Clay…please be okay…Oh God, please have him be okay…* He fought off tears, telling himself that everything would be okay. Maybe it was just a break-in, or an attempted assault. But then fear overcame his attempt to maintain rational calm, and he began to worry, to really worry.

He was getting close. He had kept his two-way on during the entire crazy ride, and the scanner had announced a call for all cars to converge on the address. *Uh-oh … that's not good. Oh, please God, let him be okay …*

He wasn't far away now. He nearly creamed a Cadillac SUV that had changed lanes abruptly in front of him. He stood on the brake pedal and averted the collision by inches. Instead of pulling the jackass over and cutting him a new asshole, as he would have done normally, he floored the accelerator and spun around in front of the Escalade, his tires smoking and squealing as he raced the last half-mile to Clay's house.

He brought the car to an abrupt halt in the middle of the street. Didn't bother to park it—or even shut the ignition off. He was running at top speed, his lungs gulping in air, his heart rate red-lining as he got close. He instinctively pulled his shield and flashed it at the cop on duty as he crashed through the yellow tape.

Oh, God … please have him be all right, please God … Cromag was not a religious man, but he was a spiritual one; and though he couldn't remember the last time he had gone to church, he knew when it was time to humble himself and pray.

He saw Bennett on the front porch and they made eye contact. In that instant, he knew his worst fears had come to fruition. Bennett's face was a portrait of shock. Cromag slowed down to avoid knocking him over. He looked into Bennett's eyes beseechingly. His heart was beginning to know what his mind did not want to accept.

"Sarge, don't go in there … you don't want to see it. Please, stay out here with me…" Bennett said, his face etched in pain. As Cromag's partner he was family, and Clayton was like a brother to him as well.

Bennett knew from experience that it was useless to try and restrain the Sarge; he might have better luck with a charging rhino. Their eyes met, their hearts spoke silently, and he let him pass, unobstructed. Cromag entered Clay's bedroom. From that moment, his life would never be the same.

There was Clay, sweet young Clay, on the bed. He looked as calm as a summer Sunday. Cromag allowed his eyes to roam down. The bitch had mutilated him mercilessly, as she had her other victims. He felt his breath get knocked out of him, as if a heavyweight had landed a shot to his solar plexus.

He almost fainted, but he took a deep breath and got a grip. He turned his back on the carnage and Bennett was waiting there.

Cromag was numb, unable to speak, but his face communicated all. It was an expression Cromag himself had seen so many times on the face of a spouse, or a next-of-kin, when he had told them, "your husband has been murdered," or "we found the body of your daughter in the river."

It was an expression which was indescribable, because it was so many emotions struggling to be felt at once: anger, denial, disbelief, grief, pain. Each one was fighting to gain dominance; to be felt, expressed on the face and released, but the chaotic flood of so many emotions at once made that impossible.

The knot of feelings made the face pained and contorted, yet with the bewildered innocence of a child. There was nothing like it—to see that expression on a person's face—and now it was Cromag's turn to wear it.

Cromag sunk to his knees by the side of the bed and screamed "No! No! No!" His body convulsed in spasms of grief. Bennett crouched beside him, with his hand on his back. All the cops and CSIs left the room, to let him have his private reckoning with death. There was no sound, but for the stricken sobs of a shattered man, helpless on the floor.

CHAPTER 40

IN THE AFTERMATH OF HIS BROTHER'S DEATH, CONNOR CROMAG underwent a startling transformation. He didn't start to crumble incrementally, as some do when they mourn; he quite simply fell apart completely. He morphed from the dynamic and resilient homicide investigator he had once been, to a pathetic, destitute figure helpless in the strangle-hold of grief.

He was given a week's bereavement leave, and retreated internally—to the darkest labyrinth of suffering imaginable. He didn't shave, or shower, or eat or exercise. He didn't even shit for three days. He didn't go outside or leave his apartment to check his mail. He didn't call Linda or return her calls, either. He didn't answer the phone at all. After years of being a leader, a poster boy for professional discipline, a man to be admired and respected, he slid into an abyss and became the antithesis of all those things.

When his parents had died many years ago, he had been a teenager, and did not grasp the significance of loss in the way he did now. His grief, now tempered with a more mature understanding of life, was much more profound, and knew no bounds. For the first time in his life, he learned the truth about the human soul and what causes it to experience its deepest levels of feeling.

It was not success, or attaining some pinnacle of achievement, or even love, that made the heart reverberate with self-awareness. Joy and happiness merely scratched the surface of the heart's potential for feeling. No, it was in *grief* and *mourning* that people experienced the truest depths of emotion the soul is capable of. The heart offers no more compelling proof of its existence than when it is broken.

He seemed destined to experience this revelation over and over in the days following Clayton's death. He would awaken after a brief, fitful attempt at sleep, screaming and sobbing, calling his brother's name—only to realize that there would be no response; he was gone forever.

He felt responsible for Clay's death. Hadn't he known there was a killer prowling Exceleron Fitness? Couldn't he have bent the rules and confided in his brother about it? Couldn't he have warned him? And then there was Clayton's text to Cromag right before he was murdered, alluding to a pick-up he had made. Why hadn't he understood the implications of what his brother was doing? His life was in danger! How could he have been so stupid, so blind not to see what was going to happen, and try and prevent it?

The recriminations of his guilt slashed away at him. His spirit bled internally, flooding his soul with the bitter bile of grief. For the first time ever, he felt as if his life wasn't worth living. He felt like giving up. He considered eating his Glock as a way to end his torment. He was circling the drain.

But then, on the brink of the precipice, something changed. Ever slowly at first, it gathered increasing momentum. He thought of the other victims of the Jewel Thief and their loved ones, grieving just as he was. His pain and suffering were not unique; he shared suffering with all those others. Whereas, in the past he'd been able to maintain a professional distance from the agony of loss, he was now up to his neck in it. This time, it was *his* brother, *his* flesh and blood, that the killer had ripped from *him.*

You crossed the line when you killed my brother. You drew family blood— and now you're going to pay for it. In the hours that followed, he forged a renewed resolve for justice. He would rise above his personal agony and do what he had to do. His need for grieving and healing was pushed aside, usurped by a molten anger that now fueled a new need: vengeance. He had but one directive now. One thing, and one thing alone, would dominate his life from this point on, no matter the cost. He would hunt this woman, and *kill her*—in as brutal a fashion as she had killed his brother.

CHAPTER 41

. : ": .: ."

IN THE WAKE OF HIS DECISION TO SUSPEND MOURNING AND concentrate on bringing the Jewel Thief Killer to justice, Cromag found himself struggling to bury his grief and go on with business-as-usual. One moment he would be on the verge of tears, and the next, be imagining a violent scenario where he would confront Eve Nouveaux and brutally kill her with his bare hands. He knew his fantasies of vindictive rage were not the healthiest way to transcend his suffering, but he could not help it—and dreaming of his ultimate vengeance gave him the determination he needed to break the shackles of mourning and get some measure of closure.

He gradually rejoined the human race. He went online and retrieved his emails. He went to the market, bought some groceries, and made a meal for himself. He called Linda and apologized for having gone radio silent, and was moved to tears when she sweetly told him she understood, she loved him deeply, and to take as much time as he needed—she would be waiting for him. What a woman!

He knew he was well on the road to normality when he had a familiar urge: to have a drink at his favorite little gin-mill. He got dressed, got in the car, and made a short hop over to Sepulveda Boulevard.

The Hilltop Bar & Grill was a dive bar, kind of weak in the "grill" department—as such places invariably are—but it was quiet, dark, and the booze was cheap. And it was just a half-mile from Cromag's house. He had always

CHAPTER 42

. : "..: ."

THE AIR LEFT CROMAG'S LUNGS. EVERYTHING WENT STILL AND silent. He at first thought it was a joke in very bad taste, but who would make light of his tragedy? And who was this guy to even know that his brother had been murdered?

I am the only one who can help you catch your brother's killer. The words the stranger had just uttered in a near-whisper now replayed in his mind at a roar. Cromag was awash in emotions he had tried to bury, tumbling like a surfer in the grip of a crushing wave.

I am the only one who can help you catch your brother's killer. Of all the words in the English language, this total stranger from god-fuck nowhere, had just spoken the ones that had the power to shake Cromag's world like no other.

I am the only one who can help you catch your brother's killer. Cromag wanted to cold-cock him right there—to shut this idiot's mouth before it could spew one more sacrilegious syllable about his beloved brother. Not only had he trespassed on sacred ground by bringing up his brother's death, *but he's whacked out enough to claim he alone can help me capture Clay's killer? Is he fucking serious? Let me just punch out this fuckwad and put an end to his charade.*

Cromag's hands coiled and tightened into fists. He was ready to deck the ass-wipe, but a more rational part of himself intervened and restrained him. Despite the rage in his heart that would have fueled an assault on this stranger, something held him back. There was something in the stranger's awkward style of communication, the way he was dressed, and most importantly, *something in his eyes* that gave Cromag pause.

Cromag had an internal "bullshit detector," an intuitive gift of discernment he had developed after years of dealing with criminals who were masters of deceit. He was fluent in all the dialects of untruth, and could smell a lie a hundred yards away. Oddly, nothing about this guy tripped his detector. There was just something about him that was different, and he couldn't finger it. The mystery captivated Cromag, demanded that he continue to listen. And—more than anything—if this nutjob really knew how to collar Eve, Cromag wanted to know!

Cromag got up from the booth, scanning the guy slowly and deliberately, starting at his feet, and continuing up to his midsection. The guy was pretty good size, dressed in black. As his eyes made their way up his chest, they froze in mid-sweep as they locked on something right above the neckline of his t-shirt. Connor became motionless—like a pointer spotting a pheasant. Was he really seeing what he thought he was?

Hanging around the man's neck was a chain, and suspended at its center, right at the juncture of his collarbones, was an amulet. An emerald-green amulet. And it was glowing.

Cromag reacted like he'd just been tagged by an uppercut. He staggered back, dazed, and regarded the stranger with a new mixture of caution and curiosity, because he now realized this guy was more than he had appeared to be at first.

Cromag recalled the surveillance videos he had screened with Bennett and Linda. He remembered the mysterious figure with the green amulet lurking in the shadows at Exceleron Fitness—at all three locations where Eve Nouveaux had trolled for her victims.

He remembered the dark hoodie, the furtive movements, and especially, the amulet, glowing green. Now that he was mere inches from it, he was captivated even more. Was his mind playing tricks on him? In his agitated state, was he more susceptible to crossing the boundary between reality and the supernatural? What exactly was going on here? The fact that he'd been power-washing his gut with whiskey, didn't help with a rational evaluation, either. He felt like he was on the verge of losing it.

"Hey, man," he said, his voice tinged with apprehension, "Just who the fuck *are* you, anyway?"

The stranger's face got grim. He looked into Cromag's eyes.

"Where I come from, they call me Hunter."

CHAPTER 43

CROMAG TOOK SOME TIME TO ABSORB WHAT THE STRANGER had just said—about two seconds worth. His tone was a little angry. "Okay, '*Hunter*' ... back to my first question: Who the fuck *are* you?"

"Connor Cromag, I will explain who I am and why I have come to you. I will explain all, but you must keep an open mind. What I am going to tell you will be met with substantial resistance by your rational mind. But you must listen to every word. Much depends upon it."

The seriousness with which the stranger spoke bought him some time with Cromag. *Okay, I'll humor this freak for a little bit longer and see what happens.* "All right, but first—question number two: What is that thing hanging around your neck?"

Hunter fingered the amulet. "It serves many functions, but its primary function is one of identification—in much the same manner as your badge," he said, pointing to Cromag's detective shield on the table. "It identifies me as one whose responsibilities are similar to yours: I hunt those who are harmful to others and eliminate them."

Connor scoffed out loud. "You mean to tell me you're some kind of *cop*?"

"In a manner of speaking, yes."

Connor guffawed so loudly the bartender looked over momentarily, then looked back. "Yeah, right. Okay, where on Earth do cops wear IDs that look like a Halloween costume?"

Hunter paused. "Well, nowhere on *Earth*, Connor Cromag."

Hunter's emphasis of the word "Earth," did not escape Cromag. Years of interrogating people had made him a master at interpreting spoken communication, subtle or otherwise. Cromag decided he would play along.

"Okay, wise ass—I get it. ... Now you're gonna tell me you're a cop from outer space?" He shook his head slowly, side to side, angry with himself for having given this dickbrain so much attention.

"Yes, Connor Cromag. I know it is difficult to believe. But you *must* believe me. I cannot over-emphasize the importance of your belief in what I am going to tell you."

Cromag again fought the impulse to be sarcastic, but lost the fight. "You mean if I don't believe you it will ruin your day, huh?"

"Far worse than that, Connor Cromag. Your future—and that of everyone on this planet—depends on it."

Oh, why didn't you say so to begin with? Who am I to jeopardize the future of Earth? Of course, I'll believe you, thought Cromag.

"Okay. Stop right there, nutso ... tell me *why* I should believe you. Crimes like this always result in a proliferation of whacko's, copycats and wanna-be skels who just want attention. I'm a detective, and I need facts—*evidence*—to support any story, especially one as looney as yours."

Hunter sighed. "Very well, then—as you wish. Let us review the case and the evidence you have thus far." He sat back and waited until he had Cromag's full attention.

"The first victim was a 30-year-old male by the name of Manuel (or "Manny") Osorio. He was found at his home in Shadow Hills, California by your patrolman Jenkins, who had answered a complaint from a neighbor about the stereo blaring loudly all night long."

Cromag, mustering all the sarcasm he could, said "Oh boy, Space Cop, I'm impressed! Anybody could've gotten that right off the blotter—that's public record now."

Hunter continued, unfazed by Cromag's sarcasm. "He was found lying on his back, with his reproductive organs severed and nowhere to be found. He suffered a loss of blood which alone would have been sufficient to cause his demise, but in addition he had been administered a chemical agent that caused immediate paralysis. That is why there were no outward signs of struggle or any indication that the killer moved his body on to the bed after killing him in so brutal a fashion."

That stopped Cromag in his tracks. *Whoa... how the fuck did he know that?* Cromag's curiosity was now more than piqued. *How could this stranger know details about the homicide that were kept private from everybody but the Medical Examiner? Who is this guy?*

The stranger saw the look of shocked disbelief on Cromag's face, knew he was making progress, and went on.

"Allow me to continue," said Hunter. "This was the first of seven homicides that you are investigating with no success. All the victims died in the same manner and were found in similar settings—and all were killed within days of each other. The second murder occurred the very next day in La Crescenta—the victim's name was Clifford Shaw; the third victim was Rodney Culbertson, killed at his home in Tujunga; the fourth was a university student named Colton Drummond; the fifth victim was murdered in a parking lot at Muscle Beach; the sixth murder was David Shulman, but his roommate witnessed the killer and was able to provide you with enough information for a sketch; and the seventh victim…"

He stopped momentarily because he knew he was about to rip a scab off Cromag's heart. "… Was your own brother, I am sorry to say. But in each case—and what remains the most incredible thing that links all these murders—is that there was no DNA evidence at any of the crime scenes other than that of the victims."

That clinched it! This last fact—about the murder scenes being sterile and devoid of any DNA other than the victim's—was the most baffling circumstance of all, and so inexplicable it had not been shared with anybody other than the investigative team. Everybody had been sworn to secrecy, to prevent a leak that was capable of causing a public panic. This revelation made Cromag silent. *I don't know how he learned all this … but I will find out.* His aspect softened; he had no choice but to hear out this "Hunter" and get to the bottom of it.

"Okay," said Cromag, "You're starting to log some cred with me. Since you know so much, maybe you can explain to me the 'DNA vacuum' that characterizes these murders. I've investigated a zillion homicides, and if there's one thing I've learned it's that there's always evidence left at a crime scene. When a murder occurs, there's a trail of clues left behind—and it may take a lab full of scientists to interpret it, but it eventually leads to the perp. It's one of the laws of the homicide universe: There's always trace evidence when human beings kill each other. How do you explain its absence here?"

"Because the killer is not human, Connor Cromag."

CHAPTER 44

JUST WHEN CROMAG HAD DECIDED TO GIVE THE GUY A CHANCE, the stranger had clobbered him with another unbelievable claim. *Oh boy, you just keep piling on, don't you?* Cromag thought. He decided to be polite and proceed rationally.

"Okay, Hunter—put yourself in my position. First you tell me you're from outer space—and you expect me to believe that—and now you mention that 'oh by the way,' the killer isn't human, either. Is she 'not of this earth' as well?"

"Everything you have just said is correct, Connor Cromag."

Cromag blanched at the implications of what Hunter had just revealed. Pondering it made him wobbly. If the killer were indeed alien, it would explain so many things that just didn't add up in the investigation.

Cromag just stood there, a mute spectator to his internal struggle. His rational mind, refusing to accept Hunter's story, was now battling against the inescapable, devastating truth of it. *It all made sense now. What other explanation could there be?*

Hunter could see Cromag's doubt putting up a valiant fight.

"I see you need a little more convincing," said Hunter. "Follow me outside—and bring your service firearm with you."

Cromag followed, too curious to resist. They walked out through the back door and found themselves in an alley that was dark and uninhabited, except for a feral cat or two.

"Show me your weapon, Connor Cromag, and describe it."

liked the place and would come here to converse with his demons or drown them, as circumstances required.

Everything looked and smelled the same as it always had. Booths upholstered in red vinyl. Freakishly ugly wallpaper. The stink of beer and cigarettes. The familiarity comforted him. He ordered two shots of whiskey and threw them down immediately. The bartender was unfazed; this was routine behavior for most of those who sat at his bar. Cromag ordered two more and dispatched them just as quickly.

Connor ordered another pair, and took them over to a booth in the darkest part of the bar. As a not-so-subtle deterrent to interaction with anybody who might wander near, he laid his Glock and detective shield on the table in front of him. Only an idiot would fail to get the message. Only fools approach rattlesnakes whose tails are vibrating.

He was sipping his Jameson's, when lo and behold—it looked like someone was about to ignore his silent warning. Yes, someone was approaching the booth. He ignored it, and pounded the first shot. Surely, this moron would sense that he didn't want company, right? Cromag did not want to engage; he just wanted to be left alone.

Finally, the person was standing right next to the edge of the booth.

"Connor Cromag," the stranger said, and waited in silence to be acknowledged.

Oh, Christ—he knows my name? Who the fuck is this? Connor had no choice but to look up. The guy had deep-set eyes, smoky-green in color, very unusual. "Yeah…who are you?"

And then he said it:

"I… am the only one who can help you catch your brother's killer."

"My Glock G45, the latest 9mm firearm from Glock, designed and developed with enhancements specifically for law enforcement. Lightweight, powerful."

"But very primitive," Hunter said. "This is mine." He reached inside his garment and withdrew what looked like a drum stick, only slightly shorter and a little fatter.

"What do you think a projectile from your Glock G45 would do to that object sitting there?" He had pointed to an inverted bucket near a dumpster.

"Well, one shot would make it dance quite nicely, and there would be two big holes in it afterwards—one at the point of entry, and the other where the bullet exited. And it would make a hell of a lot of noise in this narrow alley."

"Precisely," said Hunter. "Allow me."

He aimed the drum stick at the bucket and pressed a small button on the shaft. A flash of light emitted from the end of it—blinding, like a magnesium flare—and the bucket was gone instantly. It had been vaporized, with no more noise than a slight crackle. No smoke, no residue, no nothing. Cromag gaped. *What kind of weapon was that?* Though he was truly amazed, he decided to continue playing the Devil's advocate, just for grins.

"Not bad, Hunter. Is that all you got? How do I know you didn't steal it from some secret military project? I know they're always working on developing new weapons." But as the words left his mouth, he knew they were bullshit; his resistance was crumbling.

"Very well then, Connor Cromag. I must resort to using my amulet. Please excuse me for what I am about to do. I promise I will not harm you."

"What? What are you talking about?"

The words had no sooner left Cromag's mouth than Hunter reached one hand up to the amulet encircling his neck and aimed it at him. Cromag was instantly bathed in a canopy of brilliant green light. What happened next finally made him a true believer.

Hunter turned the bezel ring that encircled the amulet and Cromag began to rise, in the grip of the eerie green beam that was emanating from the bright crystal. Hunter tilted the amulet, and Cromag rose higher, and higher still, until he was floating hundreds of feet above the bar.

Cromag was hyperventilating now, his pulse sprinting, his eyes bulging with a combination of fear and astonishment. He was helpless, suspended in some weird type of tractor beam, way above street level. He was so high he could see the skyline of downtown Los Angeles. He managed somehow to squeak out a plea to Hunter, who was watching, emotionless, on the ground far below. He prayed that the guy could hear him.

"O-o-okay! Okay! I believe you now! I believe you! P-p-please... bring me back down."

Cromag shut his eyes, like a kid on his first roller coaster ride, hoping and praying it would be over soon. His eyelids were welded shut, his heart pounding. Was he finally descending? He dared not open his eyes. The Hunter let him down gently in the alley, and the amulet stopped emitting its green light.

Cromag struggled to catch his breath, now broken equally into gasps of amazement and sighs of relief. He stopped fighting it. Like a spectator watching a master illusionist perform, Cromag suspended his disbelief and accepted what at first seemed unacceptable. Cromag, who'd been trained to seek out evidence and believe what it said, could not find any facts to dispute this stranger's story. In light of everything he'd seen and heard and experienced in the last fifteen minutes, Cromag had no evidence to support any other conclusion. He had little choice but *to believe*.

"Okay," said Cromag. "One cop to another: Who is this perp, and how do we bring her to justice? You do know that we think she's female, right?"

"Yes," Hunter said. "But to be precise, she is a female *Biosynth*, one of the most advanced models ever created."

CHAPTER 45

"A BIO-*WHAT*?" CROMAG ASKED, SQUINTING HIS EYES AND TILT-ing his ear towards Hunter.

"A Bio*synth*."

"What the hell is that?"

Hunter paused for a moment, then proceeded to spill the backstory that linked the sudden appearance of the killer to the string of homicides. Cromag resigned himself to listening. He would judge later.

Hunter told Cromag about his home world, with its green Sunstar, and the dreaded Destroyers, who had created the Biosynth and sent it on its mission. He said he had pursued the Biosynth across space. He had tracked her and observed her in secret, learning more about her actions and waiting for an opportunity to confront her.

During Hunter's narrative, Cromag felt helpless, trapped by his ignorance. All he could do was continue listening. He interrupted periodically when he had questions.

"But why did they create this Biosynth to begin with?"

"Connor Cromag, there is a balance in the universe, and it very often exerts its influence accompanied by irony. All the intelligence, technology and ruthless armies of the Destroyers were no match for a primitive organism that cannot even be seen by the naked eye."

Hunter then explained that the Destroyers were dying of a deadly micro-bial virus for which they had been unable to find a cure. The microbe not only caused a fatal illness, but rendered any survivors sterile and unable to reproduce.

"In desperation, the Destroyers sent exploratory probes to the furthest reaches of the universe, searching for something—*anything*—that could offer some hope in saving their race from extinction."

"And what became of those searches?" Cromag asked.

"After much exploration, on the verge of giving up their last fragment of hope, they found what they needed. It was a vast distance from their home world, but it was the only place in the universe where the substance could be found."

"Where was that?" asked Cromag.

"Here on planet Earth."

The Stranger paused. He knew that Cromag's doubt and suspicion were now at saturation level. He had accosted this unsuspecting Earthling and had convinced him to listen to his narrative, to understand many strange new things—and even more difficult—to accept them without resistance.

To an Earthling detective, whose entire function revolved around verifiable evidence, hearing all of which Hunter had spoken, and being asked to believe it blindly, was a gargantuan leap of faith. But Hunter knew that time was running out, and he needed an ally—a human ally—to fulfill his mission. He persisted.

"So," he continued, "They created the Biosynth to obtain the necessary material as quickly as possible."

"But I don't understand," said Cromag. "What is the substance and why did they have to create a super-amped female assassin to obtain it?"

"Because of where the substance is found."

Cromag didn't have a clue, and his face said so. He was bewildered, but had no choice other than to ask more questions.

"But you already said the substance is found on Earth. Where on Earth?"

Hunter sighed, paused, and then spoke.

"In the reproductive organs of human males."

CHAPTER 46

CROMAG'S FACE LOOKED LIKE IT HAD BEEN WHITEWASHED with quicklime. He started to put the pieces of the puzzle together. He didn't like what he was beginning to see. *Whoa… he thought, no pun intended, but this is worlds away from a typical serial killer's profile…*

"So … help me understand this," Cromag said. "She isn't killing these guys to get her jollies or some other type of demented gratification that serials get from killing?"

"Correct," said Hunter. "She does not kill because of some uncontrollable psychopathic impulse or sexual deviation, or perverse desire for gratification, but only because it makes her mission easier. There is no personal or psychological motive involved. She is here for one reason—and one reason only."

"And what is that?" asked Cromag, his body starting to tremble in anticipation of Hunter's answer. He was beginning to acquire a frightening understanding of Eve Nouveaux's *modus operandi*.

The Stranger looked into Cromag's eyes with a piercing intensity that made Cromag feel even more uncomfortable.

"She is here to harvest."

"To *harvest?*"

"Yes, Connor Cromag. Her harvesting operation involves obtaining the male reproductive organs of selected specimens. When she has completed her harvesting, she will return to those who created her."

To hear Eve's MO characterized in so clinical a manner made Cromag sick to his stomach. The brutal murders of all those guys—including his brother—had been perpetrated by an inhuman entity totally detached from the significance of taking a human life. Not one shred of remorse. Murdering and mutilating her victims meant no more to her than picking lettuce would mean to some migrant worker. Realizing this made Cromag nauseous, but at the same time renewed his fervor to catch her—and kill her.

"Why does she seek out a particular type of victim—in this case, young athletic guys?"

"Because the material she seeks has qualities that have to do with human genetics. Those males with more pronounced masculine character-istics of muscular size and strength have a proportionately higher concen-tration of the substance than the regular population."

Cromag was beginning to get it. It all made sense now. Eve chose Exceleron Fitness because it was a fertile location for the specimens she was seeking. A no-brainer. There would be a much higher proportion of studs in gyms than bars. And it followed that the Destroyers—as diabol-ically clever as they obviously were—took everything into account when designing this *femme fatale* from Hell.

"And I guess it's no accident that Eve is extremely attractive, right?"

"Correct, Connor Cromag. If you are utilizing bait, you want the bait to be as attractive as possible to your quarry, do you not?"

"Yes, of course," said Cromag. Eve's creators had overlooked nothing.

"To that end, the Destroyers devoted vast amounts of research in devel-oping a 'perfect human female' copy whose charms no human male could resist. Her beauty and attractiveness are no accident. They are the result of painstaking experimentation and development. Her physical form, her appearance, her mannerisms, her gait, all those things that contribute to her appeal, were exhaustively researched. Their quest was to create some-thing that would represent the apex of sexual desirability to a human male. They succeeded—she is beyond perfect. And she is virtually indistinguish-able from a human female except under the most stringent scrutiny. She is anatomically correct in every detail."

"Speaking of which—her 'anatomy,' I mean—how does she…?" Cromag felt awkward inquiring about that brutal part of the killing that had earned Eve the moniker "Jewel Thief."

"She has a specially designed apparatus in her 'vagina,' I believe you call it—that enables her to inject her victims with a paralyzing nerve agent, and then sever their organs quite rapidly, completing the act of harvesting in a matter of seconds. The apparatus is not visible to casual inspection, but is put into operation at the precise moment when needed."

Wow! That takes the concept of 'bad sex' to a whole new level, thought Cromag. *That is pure evil. How fiendish can you get?*

"Aside from the obvious urgency of stopping a killer who murders a new victim every other day, there is another time constraint which affects her, and which exerts a profound influence on her harvesting operation," Hunter said.

"What do you mean?" asked Cromag.

"Our Thinkers have made calculations based on the current rate of infection among the Destroyer population. They have estimated when the microbe will achieve a 100% infection level, dooming them to extinction. But the Destroyers are not stupid, either—they have made the same calculations. That is why they dispatched Eve so urgently. It is also why she must complete her harvesting and return while their window of opportunity remains open."

Cromag was having trouble following and needed to have the whole theory dumbed down just a bit. "In English please, Hunter? In Earthling homicide detective language—so I can understand it, okay?"

"I will use Earth time measurements to explain," said Hunter. "The journey from the Nebula took two weeks of your Earth time. The return journey will take just as long. That is four weeks—one month—already gone from her timeline, just for traveling. She has been here nearly three weeks. When I left, our Thinkers had estimated that the plague would reach saturation level and result in the extinction of the Destroyers in six weeks' time. Allowing for even a small margin of error in the projections, the Biosynth must leave Earth with what she has harvested, *within seven of your Earth days.*"

Cromag was silent, and spent a good minute just looking at Hunter, mulling over what he'd said. Then he spoke.

"You're confident that we can find her and destroy her within this time?"

"Yes, Connor Cromag, I am sure."

"You better be."

CHAPTER 47

CROMAG HAD TO MAKE SOME CRITICAL DECISIONS—AND HE had to make them quickly. He'd already taken a big leap by believing Hunter's story and trusting him. But what choice did he have? All the resources of law enforcement had failed to apprehend Eve. Now that he knew who she really was, it became even more imperative that she be stopped. He simply *had* to put his trust in Hunter. And that meant teaming up with him.

Yes, the two of them would have to partner if they hoped for any chance of bringing Eve Nouveaux down. They needed each other. But that presented another dilemma. He just couldn't introduce Hunter to the rest of his team, or even to Linda. The chances of his entire team believing Hunter's story were nil. Instead, they'd probably conclude that Cromag had finally lost his marbles in response to the trauma of his brother's death. And they would take him off the case. He could not allow that to happen.

So, he decided on another route. He would hide Hunter, not say a thing about him, and work with him covertly to track down Eve and kill her. He had four days of his bereavement leave remaining, during which time none of the squad would be contacting him, out of respect. A lot could get accomplished in four days. He'd have Hunter stay at his place and they would combine their know-how to bring the Biosynth to justice.

As they drove back to his house, Cromag pondered the whole concept of the Biosynth, and how devastating she was. To the Destroyers, she was nothing more than a tool they had built to get a job done. But to her victims, the innocent young men who had died not even knowing what their killer's true motivation was, she was the embodiment of pure evil. She was using male sexual desire as a weapon against the very men she had chosen, and they were being led to slaughter like so many unsuspecting lambs.

And the way she did it! A woman's vagina, which any man would agree was one of the most wonderful things in God's creation, was instead something unimaginably evil, in Eve's synthetic body. Cromag shuddered at the scope of it. Of all the dangers in a man's path, what could be more treacherous than one that he was unable to resist, one that he was naturally hard-wired to succumb to? To a young man with healthy hormones, what could possibly be deadlier than beauty?

CHAPTER 48

.: ":.: .'

HE HAD AN ALLY! THE ISOLATION AND DESPERATION THE Hunter had felt since his arrival here were gone, thanks to the cooperation of the Earthling, "Connor Cromag." He had studied the Earthling and weighed his decision carefully before he took the bold step of approaching him.

He had been left with no choice. The Biosynth had arrived on Earth, had assimilated perfectly, and had begun the merciless process of harvesting. She had already taken the lives of so many Earthling males that he felt he had no alternative but to seek the support of an Earthling, or his mission would fail horribly.

After studying the methods Earthlings used to communicate, he quickly learned to follow the informational feeds they called "news," that were transmitted to special viewing devices the Earthlings kept in their homes, and on their persons. It was by studying these transmissions that he learned of Connor Cromag. He was the leader of the Earthling Hunters pursuing the Biosynth, though they knew nothing of her true identity. The Hunters on Earth were known as "police," and they had the same function as Hunters on his home world: they were trained to enforce the laws, pursue wrong-doers, and capture or destroy them as the situation demanded.

He knew that if he could establish an alliance with this Connor Cromag, they could share information and combine their resources to destroy the Biosynth. The fact that the Earthling had so recently lost his own brother to the Biosynth was unfortunate, but helped in the Hunter's quest to enlist his aid. He felt pain about Connor Cromag's loss, and regretted having to seek him out when he was in mourning. But it had all been necessary.

He had the highest regard for this Earthling—for his willingness to suspend his disbelief and accept the Hunter's explanation of his mission. It pained him to think what might have transpired, had he not gained his confidence. Not only had Connor Cromag accepted him, but he had welcomed him into his dwelling like a brother.

With the next appearance of Earth's yellow Sunstar, he and Connor Cromag would begin their pursuit in earnest. He knew he must rest in preparation. He looked out at the nocturnal sky and was overwhelmed. It was almost identical to a view of the night sky from his own home world. Billions of Sunstars glimmering from the farthest reaches of space. The universe was so vast! Although he knew it to be a flight of fantasy, he imagined that one in particular was the Sunstar of his home world. As he lay down, he focused on it and made a silent promise that he would return victorious.

CHAPTER 49

. : "..: ."

CROMAG WOKE UP EARLY AND FOUND HIS NEW PARTNER sitting on the front porch, looking out at his beautiful lawn and garden. Flamboyant red hibiscus flanked the entrance to the house. Brilliant petunias, snapdragons and other annuals filled the flowerbeds, bursting with all the colors of the spectrum. The bougainvillea that Cromag had planted years ago was now fully grown and laden with gorgeous magenta blossoms. Junipers and leafy philodendrons complemented the lush array. The air was heavy with the fecund aroma of earth and flowers.

"Good morning, Hunter."

Hunter was contemplative, and paused before responding.

"There are no colorful life-forms on my planet, Connor Cromag. There are no colors at all. It is dry and barren, much like the "desert" region of your Earth, but even more so. You have a magnificent planet, and I hope that you are thankful for it. I am captivated by the beauty of your dwelling, and am implanting this vision of it in my memory, so I can summon it when I am back on my home world and surrounded by arid brown rock."

Cromag nodded his head in silence. He couldn't imagine life without green grass and flowers. Maybe freeways, smog, and earthquakes were a small price to pay after all. They went inside the house.

The night before, when Cromag had been trying to fall asleep, he had reviewed the logistics of working with Hunter. Since his arrival on Earth, Hunter had been hanging around in shadows, dressed in dark clothing, and maintaining a profile so low it bordered on subterranean. Now, if he was going to assist Cromag, which meant being out in public, Hunter was going to have to blend in better—a whole lot better.

In an effort to make him less conspicuous, Cromag took Hunter to the mall. There was a Men's Wearhouse there. He got Hunter outfitted with casual wear that made him look like a So Cal native instead of an undercover cop from the Morbiddon Nebula. Hunter got a makeover from head to toe. A fade haircut at Sportclips; some T-shirts and jeans; tennis shoes; and the finishing touch: a pair of Oakley wraparounds.

Hunter really liked the sunglasses. He put them on and kept admiring his reflection in the mirror.

"They claim 'thermonuclear protection,' Connor Cromag. I am eager to return to my home world and see how protective they are of the rays from my planet's Sunstar."

Ooookay… thought Cromag, wondering if the Oakleys would really provide the protection claimed in their ad slogan. *I'm sure Hunter will eventually find out one way or the other…*

In looking over the "after" version of Hunter in the dressing room, one thing still bothered Cromag: that damned pendant, or amulet—or whatever you wanted to call it. It was the one thing that still shouted, *"I am not from around here."* He had noticed how the salesperson at the Men's Wearhouse had looked at the thing, then looked at Cromag, and then back at Hunter, with an expression on his face that seemed to say *Really? A grown man wearing a superhero charm?* Cromag had to do something about that amulet, but how to do it tactfully and not offend Hunter?

"Well, you look good, Hunter," said Cromag. "You really blend in now; we can work together without arousing suspicion. But there's just one thing…"

"Yes?" said Hunter.

"I wish there were something we could do to camouflage that Happy Meal pendant you insist on wearing."

"Happy Meal?" asked Hunter. "I do not understand. How can a meal have emotions?"

Cromag laughed out loud. To a foreigner—or *alien*, in Hunter's case—the idiosyncrasies of the English language must have seemed bewildering. Seeing this as a perfect opportunity to acquaint Hunter with more Earth culture, he said, "I'll show you what a Happy Meal is," and they got into his car and were off to the nearest McDonald's.

"Two Happy Meals, please."

The girl at the counter looked at them, noted the absence of children, and said, "You sure? They're made for kids and the portions are pretty small. I don't know how hungry you guys are…"

"Understood, we want the Happy Meals. Thank you."

They sat down near the play area. "Here you go," said Cromag. "It's designed to make children happy. That's why they call it a Happy Meal."

Hunter seemed to grasp it at first, but then looked confused again. "What has that to do with my amulet?"

"I made the reference because these meals always include something flashy that a child would enjoy, like a fake weapon, an action figure, or some costume accessory — *like a magical pendant*, for example …"

"Aha," Hunter said, catching Cromag's inflection and sarcasm about the amulet. "I understand now. I am, as the Earth expression says, 'A quick study.' I can keep my amulet hidden beneath my outer clothing, if you like."

"I think that would be a good idea. Make you less conspicuous…"

"But what is this?" Hunter asked, as he pulled a small object from the meal box. It was a Star Wars action figure: the character Chewbacca.

Cromag laughed again. "It comes with the Happy Meal." He reached in and retrieved the action figure from his own meal. It was Star Wars, too: Han Solo.

"These two are best buds, Hunter … hang on to both of them as a souvenir of your visit to Earth." He handed his action figure to Hunter.

"Best Buds?" Hunter's face was a portrait of confusion.

"Yeah…close friends—partners."

"Understood," Hunter said. "These fried potatoes are quite delicious, but why do they call them French Fries? Do they ship them here from France?"

Cromag withheld his laughter but rolled his eyes. *It was going to be a long day…*

CHAPTER 50

THEY RETURNED TO CROMAG'S HOUSE AND GOT DOWN TO BUSI-
ness. Cromag said, "How do we determine where she's gonna strike next?"

Hunter had been expecting the question. He used his amulet to project
a holographic map of Southern California onto Cromag's dining room table.
At first Cromag was surprised, almost shocked, but then he remembered he
was dealing with a space alien. "So that's what your amulet is for," he said.

"Oh, this is just a mere hint of its capabilities, Connor Cromag." He held
his gaze, as if to say, *"you don't know the half of it…"*

The image of California was like a detailed topographical map. Cities
and freeways were identified, but muted, in a lighter color so as not to be a
distraction. The names were quite readable. Suddenly, red dots appeared on
the map. They were scattered across the state, but very concentrated within
Los Angeles and the San Fernando Valley.

"Do you know what those red dots represent?" asked Hunter. Now it was
his turn to be teacher.

Cromag took a guess. "Are they the Exceleron Fitness locations throughout the state?"

"Very good, Connor Cromag," Hunter said. Suddenly, a blue aura engulfed
some of the red dots. "And these…are the locations where Eve has snared a
victim for harvesting."

The red dots with blue auras seemed to be dispersed and random. Cromag groaned. "I'm not seeing a pattern here, Hunter. How can we predict where she'll strike next?"

"But there *is* a pattern, Connor Cromag. See this location—Shadow Hills—where she secured her first victim? Did you know it was the first Exceleron Fitness gym built in Southern California, back in your Earth year 1987?"

"No, I didn't know that."

"And the location where she sourced her second harvest is here, in La Crescenta," he said. "It was constructed in 1988. And where was the third location?" he asked. Hunter already knew, but enjoyed playing teacher.

"Right here," Cromag said, pointing to the dot representing Tujunga.

"Erected in 1989," said Hunter. "Are you beginning to see the pattern now?"

The revelation hit Cromag like a blindside punch. It was so clear and obvious—and simple. "She's picking out the locations in chronological order, based on when they were built!"

"That is correct, Connor Cromag. What appears to be random and unplanned, is actually not."

"But what about Muscle Beach?" asked Cromag. "That wasn't even an Exceleron Fitness location."

"Yes, but I believe the Biosynth chose it to reinforce the appearance of randomness. I believe that now, since she has very little time left, she will resume her original pattern in choosing the next harvest location."

"Okay, when was the next club built?"

"In 1990, right here." He pointed to the map. It was the Canoga Park location.

"What are we waiting for?" said Cromag. "Let's get moving."

"Not yet, Connor Cromag. Recall that the Biosynth—"Eve"—has lured and murdered all her victims in the morning hours, before mid-day."

"Yeah, that's right."

"She needs a certain amount of time each day to recharge her energy stores. She does so in the afternoon and evening. This ensures that she will be powerful and strong in the morning. I think we must plan to be at the Canoga Park facility when it opens tomorrow morning. We will conduct a 'stake out,' as you call it. Is that correct?"

Cromag smiled at Hunter's police slang. "Yes, Hunter—a stake out."

CHAPTER 51

CROMAG AND HUNTER GOT UP EARLY THE NEXT MORNING AND left for Canoga Park. It would be about a twenty-minute drive on surface streets. They took Sherman Way—the main artery that bisects the San Fernando Valley into north and south. The streets were pretty open but starting to thicken as morning rush hour got cooking.

As they drove west on Sherman Way, Cromag reflected on the Valley's history. In its early days, it had been little more than a sprawl of citrus orchards and olive groves, a beautiful, pastoral paradise just over the hill from the clamor and clang of Los Angeles. Being so close to the metropolis, but with a beautiful laid-back vibe, the San Fernando Valley's destiny soon became clear: to become the largest suburb in post-war California. After World War Two, they began building residential communities in earnest. The orchards and olive groves were soon replaced by tracts of single-family homes, malls and schools.

Now, there were still pockets of peaceful rural existence here and there, but they were disappearing quickly. Nonstop population growth saw to that. Over time, the quantity of people and cars doubled and tripled, but the infrastructure hadn't kept pace. The roads were now woefully inadequate for a population approaching one million.

The midway point was the town of Reseda. Once known as "The Hub of the Valley," Reseda for years had been an idyllic middle-class town and a great place to raise a family. But this ideal place to cultivate the American Dream gradually changed under the relentless influx of immigrants.

Here now, years later, Reseda was very different. The streets where Connor and Clay used to ride their bicycles looked like they had been transplanted from a border town. Taco stands. Dollar stores. Places that sold crap furniture. Once a community morphed like this it never recovered. The Reseda of Cromag's youth was gone forever. It was sad.

They continued to drive west and soon reached the outskirts of Canoga Park. They turned on De Soto Avenue and drove half a block to the Exceleron Fitness complex. They parked under an oak tree that provided a fair amount of cover. They didn't want to attract any undue attention.

When they had parked, Hunter spoke. "The radioactive isotopes that power the Biosynth emit a stream of detectable radiation. It is harmless, but strong enough to produce a recognizable signature. I am able to discern that signature. Not at any great distance, but within reason. I can tell when she is approaching."

It was just about seven o'clock. Members had already crowded around the door, waiting for the club to open. There was a knot of perhaps two dozen men and women. Cromag wouldn't have been able to pick Eve out unless she had a neon sign on her back that flashed "Biosynth."

"You picking up anything yet, Hunter?"

"No, Connor Cromag—not yet."

A couple of hours went by. Cromag looked at his watch. "This is the way it is on a stake-out sometimes, Hunter. I can remember being on all-night stake outs that lasted into the next day. One even lasted thirty-two hours. We pissed into paper cups and lived on coffee and donuts. But we eventually got our perp."

More time went by. Cromag almost started to nod off when he felt Hunter shaking his arm. "Connor Cromag! I have picked up her signature. She is approaching."

Cromag snapped to alertness. He looked at the entrance, and then around the parking lot. There wasn't a soul in sight. The only thing that was moving was a sleek black convertible, polished to a mirror finish. It was a brand-new Maserati.

"The signal is getting stronger," Hunter said. "She is in that automobile."

"How do you know the signal is getting stronger? How can you tell?"

"I feel it in my"…he hesitated, anticipating an irritated response from Cromag. "I feel it in my amulet. It is throbbing."

Cromag groaned. "I might have known."

They waited in silence. The driver's door opened and she stepped out—all six magnificent feet of her. At that moment, Cromag had another déjà vu experience, similar to the one he had felt when he had first examined the photo of Eve in the forensics lab. He had seen her before; he could swear it. But where?

"Let's let her go in and troll for a bit," said Cromag. "You're sure you'll be alerted when she comes out, right?"

"Sure as shit, bro!" Hunter said.

Hunter's unexpected use of Earth slang made Cromag crack up. "Been studying up, huh?" He grinned. If they hadn't been pursuing the most dangerous killer on Earth, they might have had a good laugh. But this was no time for levity. They continued to wait.

It didn't take long. In about fifteen minutes, Hunter snapped his head up and focused on the entrance. "She is coming out…"

There she was, sidled up to a young guy who was just a little taller than her. They were smiling and laughing as they walked out into the parking lot. She leaned over and whispered something in his ear, and they split up. The guy got into a pickup truck, and Eve got into her Maserati. The guy led the way, followed by Eve, then Cromag and Hunter, following from a distance.

"Is this what is known as 'tailing a suspect,' Connor Cromag?"

"Yes, it is. Just make sure you don't lose her radioactive stink. I have no idea where they're going."

The answer came quick enough. The guy nosed his truck into the lot of the Canoga Meadows Motel. Cromag slowed, but didn't stop; he didn't want to tip them that they were being tailed.

"Not wasting any time, are they? They're gonna do it here instead of going to his place. He's in a rush."

The truck pulled into a spot and the Maserati parked next to it. The guy got out and went to the motel office to get a room. Cromag parked his car on the other side of the lot and they waited.

The guy returned shortly, dangling a room key at Eve and flashing a shit-eating grin. Eve got out of her car and they walked together to the room. As soon as they shut the door, Cromag and Hunter went live.

"Okay, Hunter, I'll go in through the front and I want you to circle behind the building to the back, just in case Eve tries to escape through a window."

Cromag knew he had to time his entrance perfectly. He couldn't wait too long. Eve didn't waste time; when she had a victim, she did her thing as quickly as possible. Cromag approached the motel room on the silent toes of a ninja.

CHAPTER 52

INSIDE THE MOTEL ROOM, DAVE KITTRIDGE WAS HAPPIER THAN a pig in shit. He'd never gotten lucky at the gym before, and never, ever with a babe as hot as this one. He kept pinching himself to make sure he wasn't dreaming.

Then he realized he was lacking something. He had some weed in his truck. The thought of fucking this chick while he was stoned got him even more excited. He could feel the lumber truck making a delivery in his trousers.

"Hey, lady, uh—I didn't catch your name…"

"It's Eve."

"Hi, Eve. My name is Dave. I forgot something in my truck. I'll be right back."

"Okay. I'll be waiting." She smiled, and a Ponderosa Pine sprouted between Dave's legs.

He catapulted from the room, nearly tripping in his haste. Halfway back to his truck he collided with Cromag. Cromag flashed his badge and ordered him to freeze.

The guy thought it was a prostitution sting. *That hot bitch is an undercover cop? No way…* He got frantic and pleaded with Cromag. "No, no, it's not what you think, officer. It's totally consensual. She was the one who hit on *me*…"

"It's not about that," said Cromag. "That woman is a fugitive from justice, and I'm about to arrest her. Consider yourself lucky—she's bad news. Now get into your truck and don't look back. Forget this ever happened. Understand?"

"Y-Yes, sir!" He blurted, stumbling to his truck. He burned rubber all the way out of the lot.

Cromag resumed his original trajectory. He reached for his Glock instinctively. "Dammit," he said to himself, "I should have asked Hunter if a couple of nine-millimeter hollow points would be enough to bring her down."

He approached the door like a creeping shadow. It was unlocked. He opened it slowly. The guy had splurged. The room was actually a suite, equipped with a bar, TV, and an adjoining room where the fun took place. He could hear someone in there. He tiptoed silently to the entrance—and then he saw her.

She had her back to him and was primping next to the bed, using a compact mirror from her purse. She couldn't see him, but he could see her. She arranged her hair and applied red lipstick to her full, sensuous lips. She was gorgeous—and what a spectacular figure! All courtesy of the Destroyer scientists. She was wearing the wispiest of lingerie: a lace bra and crotchless panties. She looked like she had stepped out of a Victoria's Secret catalog—the intergalactic edition.

Cromag ran his eyes over her perfect ass, covered scantily by the delicate silk. And yes, there was the tattoo of the black widow spider, splayed across her upper buttocks. He saw her large, pendulant breasts in profile as she turned slightly. The bra had cutouts for her nipples, and they were protruding tantalizingly from the fabric, firm and upright. *Omigod, she's perfect, just perfect...* Cromag almost went into an erotic trance, but caught himself and remembered why he was there.

He thundered into the room, raising his pistol. "Los Angeles Police Department! Raise your hands above your head and get down on your knees!"

But Eve had no intention of doing either one of those things. She turned and faced Cromag, and at that moment he remembered where he'd seen her before. It was that day in the gym, weeks ago, when she'd shown up and had all the men drooling. That was before she'd even claimed her first victim.

He realized how beautiful she was. The features of a Michelangelo sculpture, framed in luxuriant cascades of shimmering black hair. At first, she smiled at Cromag, but then her face morphed into a hideous, demonic visage and she snarled like a cornered wolverine.

Her eyes lit up like emeralds aflame. It was a startling thing to behold. She leaped across the room and pounced on Cromag, so fast and so hard he lost his grip on his pistol. He saw it clatter to the floor and spin under the bed. She grabbed his throat and began to strangle him.

Cromag gagged, trying to draw breath. Her strength was astounding. His throat was in a bear trap, his esophagus about to be crushed. He couldn't breathe, and he began to feel terror. *This can't be happening to me…I can't let her get the best of me…*

He started to weaken, but miraculously, an image of his brother Clayton flooded his mind. It gave him the determination to continue fighting. He summoned all his strength and put his hands around her throat. *I'll give you a taste of your own medicine, you fucking bitch …!*

Years of weight training had given Cromag arms like tree trunks, and a grip that could crush walnuts. He locked his fingers around Eve's neck and funneled all his strength into a death-grip. He wanted to crush her throat and snap her spine.

But his supreme exertion was fruitless. Instead of submitting and letting go, she *smiled* at him, her eyes sparkling with fury. He had never seen eyes like that—brilliant, verdant—a startling, isotopic green that seemed backlit from deep within.

She renewed her choke-hold with a new surge of power. Then, incredibly, she picked him off the ground until his feet were dangling a foot off the floor. *Holy fuck! Is this for real? How can she be this strong?* All two hundred and ten pounds of Cromag were helpless, held aloft in her grip.

Her strength seemed limitless. He felt himself starting to slip away. He was starting to lose consciousness. *No, no, this can't be how it all ends…I have to avenge my brother's death… I have to get out of this…I must beat her…but how?*

The room started to blur; a flurry of white dots clouded his vision. He knew this was a precursor to blacking out. He would soon lose consciousness. It felt like they were engaged in a mixed martial arts bout, and Eve had him in a deadly submission hold. But the difference was, he wouldn't be able to "tap out" and have the referee end the match. No, there were no refs here…just him and the Biosynth—and it was a fight to the death.

He heard a buzzing in his ears—another harbinger of losing consciousness. He remembered the last time he had heard buzzing like that. He had been just a kid, getting his tonsils taken out. When he breathed in the anesthetic, he heard the buzzing—and was soon asleep. This time, the buzzing meant that he was about to go to sleep, but he would not be waking up…ever.

He fought the realization. He thought of Linda, of how they'd just met and embarked on a journey of love together. Now it was all going to be cut short. He felt remorse. He had kindled a relationship, and now it would all be taken away, leaving her with senseless grief. She would be another victim of the Jewel Thief—collateral damage. Now that he had precious few seconds of life remaining, thoughts began to race through his mind. *They say your whole life flashes before your eyes right before you die …*

He started to slip away. Despite his courage, his strength was sapped. His grip on Eve's windpipe involuntarily began to loosen. She responded by increasing her grip on his. He saw her evil smile widen even further, when she realized she was about to vanquish him. He looked into her eyes one more time, and saw only the darkness of death.

Just as he was about to die, the Biosynth stiffened and abruptly relaxed her grip. *But why?* As Cromag fell to the floor, he saw that Eve was standing motionless, bathed in an eerie green light. *What was that?* Cromag lay flat on his back and gulped in deep breaths of air, the first ones he'd been able to take since their battle began. He opened his eyes and saw someone standing opposite Eve. It was Hunter!

He had his amulet between his fingers and was manipulating it in a strange way. Blinding flashes of green light were pulsating from it, aimed at Eve's eyes. Cromag was hyperventilating and attempting to speak. "Hunter…" he gasped, "wh- where were you…?" but before he could hear Hunter's response, the room spun like a vortex, and everything went black…

CHAPTER 53

.: ":.: .'

"CONNOR CROMAG? ARE YOU OKAY, 'BRO?'"

Cromag could hear a voice somewhere, muffled and indistinct. It gradually got louder and clearer. He felt like he had come out of surgery and was in a recovery room. The voice was Hunter's. Hearing the word "bro" coming from Hunter was an endearing welcome back. His vision returned next. He looked up and saw Hunter crouched over him. "Wha—what happened?" Cromag said, still groggy.

"I was able to overcome the Biosynth and terminate her function," Hunter said.

Cromag looked to his side and saw the motionless body of Eve Nouveaux, aka "The Biosynth," aka "The Jewel Thief Killer," lying on the floor. Never would she murder and mutilate another man.

Cromag regained his composure and contemplated the aftermath. For obvious reasons, it was impossible to handle Eve's corpse like any other criminal who'd chosen to die rather than surrender. Cromag shuddered to think how the ME would react, performing an autopsy on this demonic creation. They couldn't bury her, either. They couldn't take the chance that someday her body might accidentally be unearthed. Nobody could ever be allowed to find Eve's body—*ever*.

He voiced his concerns to Hunter about getting rid of the evidence. "Not a problem," said Hunter. "I will do a molecular deconstruction."

"What? How're you gonna do that?"

"How do you think, Connor Cromag?" Hunter smiled like an imp and fingered his amulet.

"I might have known," said Cromag, "That fucking amulet again. Jeezis…"

"Please stand back, Connor Cromag—and shield your eyes."

Hunter turned the ring that encircled the stone and the amulet blazed brilliant green. He aimed the beam at Eve's lifeless body. Slowly, the image of Eve started to get fuzzy, indistinct. Cromag rubbed his eyes. Was he really seeing this? Eve's shape continued to lose its definition and became a blur of dark and light shades, like an impressionist painting.

Suddenly, the image disintegrated into pixels, spreading out like a gaseous cloud in the room. Cromag gasped. The image became less and less discernible as the cloud dispersed. *Holy shit! Am I really seeing this?*

Within a couple of heartbeats, no trace was left of Eve, not even one speck. She had vaporized into the ether. *Ashes to ashes, dust to dust,* thought Cromag, but then felt ashamed for having used a biblical reference. Eve Nouveaux was as far away from God and all things holy, as something could possibly be.

Afterwards, tidying up the room, Cromag saw something on the night table next to the bed. "Well, whaddya know," he said, holding up a shiny object that glimmered in the light. "I've always wanted to see what one of these babies can do…"

It was the key fob to Eve's Maserati. They left the room, but on their way to the parking space, Cromag had a change of heart about his intended joyride. What if something went wrong? What if he got stopped for a routine check? How would he explain why he was driving a car registered to the number one suspect in his investigation? He wouldn't be able to. He would be fucked, plain and simple. He put the keys in the ignition and locked all the doors. Hunter looked at him.

"Someone will eventually call it in as an abandoned car and their attempts to contact the registered owner will prove fruitless, since she never existed. The car will eventually be sold at public auction. It leaves us clean. Let's get out of here—it's Miller time."

"Miller time?" Hunter asked.

Cromag laughed. "It's time for another tutorial on the colloquialisms of our language, and what 'Miller Time' means. Get in." They left the motel and roared down Sherman Way, heading back to his house in Mission Hills.

As they drove, Cromag mentally reviewed what would happen now. There would be no new victims. The public would slowly begin to relax again. Time would pass. People would forget. Memories and details would get blurry. Soon enough, the Jewel Thief mystery would pass into history along with so many others. The murders would become cold cases and join the other mildewed files in the basement at Division headquarters. It was sad to cheat the victims' families out of any closure they might have gotten from knowing who the murderer was, but there was no other way. He had no other choice. How could he ever explain who—or *what*—Eve was? Especially since there was no body anymore. It was best to forget it and move on.

CHAPTER 54

.: ":.! ."

AFTER THEY PULLED UP AT CROMAG'S HOUSE, HE SHUT OFF THE engine and grew somber. He turned to Hunter, with a sincerity he didn't often display to people, and looked him in the eyes.

"Hey, partner. You saved my life back there. Thank you."

"No biggie, bro'—I got your six," said Hunter, with the driest delivery imaginable.

Cromag burst out laughing. "You been watching cop shows on TV or something? Where do you keep coming up with this street talk?"

"I took immersion training in your language before my departure. But I still have much to learn. I wish I could stay, but I must return to my planet to report the success of my mission."

"I know, I couldn't have done it without you. The whole planet owes you a debt of gratitude. Too bad they'll never be able to express it." Cromag was going to miss this guy, no doubt about that. But this wasn't the time to dwell on sad things like good-byes. It was time to celebrate.

They got in the car and drove to The Hilltop, where they had met each other for the first time just days ago.

"Two Millers," said Cromag to the bartender. He returned with two chilled bottles of Miller High Life beer.

Cromag explained "Miller Time" to Hunter. "It was an advertising slogan that became very popular. There is a time to reward oneself for a job well done, and 'Miller Time' became synonymous with it. We've earned our 'Miller Time,' thanks to you and that amulet. I gotta admit, I thought the amulet was a little hokey at first, but that sucker has grown on me in the last few days."

Hunter was grinning, and Cromag realized it was the first time he had seen an "I told you so" expression on his face.

"I told you it had many functions besides being a form of identification, Connor Cromag."

"I'd like to get me one," Cromag said, "But I'm gonna bet they don't carry them at Big Five Sporting Goods."

"You are correct, Connor Cromag. It is a Helionite crystal—extremely rare. The Sunstar around which my planet revolves experiences periodic surface storms, just like Earth's Sunstar. During these storms, it casts off molten particles—similar to what your Thinkers call 'meteorites.' They travel at great speed into our atmosphere and crash on our planet's surface. As they cool, they crystallize and are referred to as 'Helionite.' The crystals are endowed with energy from the Sunstar, and our Thinkers have learned how to channel that energy and utilize it. The crystal amulet has great power."

"I'll say," said Cromag. "I saw it with my own eyes—how you used it to send Eve down for her dirt nap."

"Dirt nap?" asked Hunter.

"It's an expression, based on our practice of burying our dead in the earth. It became popular among gangsters who frequently kill people. It's crude and tasteless, but Eve certainly wasn't deserving of any politically correct euphemisms."

"I see," said Hunter. "I wish I had more time to absorb the many-faceted nuances of your language," Hunter said.

"I'll try as best I can to keep you informed," said Cromag. They finished their beers and Cromag ordered two shooters of Cuervo 1800 tequila. "Time for your graduate studies in unwinding, Hunter," he said, as he pushed the shot glass over to him. "Do as I do." He raised the shot to his lips, threw it back, and slammed the inverted glass on the counter. Hunter followed suit. They smiled at each other.

Cromag ordered another round, and then another. Hunter matched him, slam for slam, like an old drinking buddy.

After five rounds, Cromag had to say something. "Hey man, I thought you'd be shit-faced by now. Are you sure this is your first time drinking this stuff? Do they have Tequila on your planet? I thought you'd be under the table after three shots."

Hunter opened his mouth as if to say something, but paused to think before speaking. He said, "I guess I don't react to this beverage the way an Earthling does…"

"Yeah," Cromag said. "I guess you Hunters are built differently."

"Yes, Connor Cromag."

If only you knew, thought Hunter.

CHAPTER 55

THOUGH IT WOULD BE IMPOSSIBLE FOR CROMAG TO EVER forget what had happened, the media and the public started to do so, and faster than might have been expected. After going a week with no new homicides, the public exhaled, finally. Graffiti and headlines barked, "Where is the Jewel Thief?'—with the subliminal wish being, *"We hope she is gone forever..."* But those familiar with serial killers were hesitant to join in the collective sigh of relief. Hadn't history shown that many serials go dormant for a while, and then return with a vengeance?

Cromag pushed these concerns from his mind. He knew the truth: that Eve Nouveaux would never again terrorize the male population of Earth. But knowing that truth and keeping it secret would forever demand his undying resolve to keep it that way. The world must never know.

Ironically, Hunter's departure was delayed. He had said his goodbyes to Cromag and was prepared for the journey back to his 'hood in a far corner of the universe. But after making some last-minute calculations, he learned that a major meteor shower was about to cross his flightpath. He would be grounded on Earth for a few more days. Cromag told him to watch the house and feed his cat. He and Linda had planned a getaway to Lake Arrowhead.

He had a friend who owned a cabin up there. Cromag had always had a standing invitation to take advantage of it, but he was always buried in work, and had no reason that would trump his dedication to his job. Until now. Events had reached a lull; but more importantly, he was in serious love—and could think of no better place to spend private time with Linda than an idyllic forest retreat far away from Los Angeles.

He met Linda at her apartment in Studio City, threw her things in the trunk, and they were off. As they left the city behind, Cromag mused on the old saying that cited the benefits of California: "Where else can you go to the desert, the mountains, or the ocean, all within a two-hour drive? California has it all…" *Yeah,* thought Cromag. Including the highest tax rates; the highest population of homeless people; the highest prices for housing; and the worst metro traffic. *Need I say more?*

Despite its shortcomings, Cromag loved California. What wasn't to love about the state that had produced Linda Evans? She was California born-and-raised, and he felt supremely blessed that their paths had crossed. As they left town, he looked over at Linda periodically, his heart smiling so hard he thought his chest would split.

"What are you looking at?" She asked, when she caught him staring.

"The woman I'm head over heels in love with," he answered, stroking her cheek softly. She responded like a purring kitten, offering herself to his caress. She could never have too much of Connor's affection.

"I love you too," she said, "more than you'll ever know."

They headed East on the 210 Freeway. It was hopelessly congested through Pasadena and Monrovia, two notorious bottlenecks. Cromag kept the image of a secluded log cabin foremost in his mind, and the traffic's sting was lessened. As they passed through Rancho Cucamonga on their way to San Bernardino, traffic started thinning out. When they reached the turnoff for Highway 18, Cromag knew they were well on their way. He allowed himself to start feeling excited.

They turned north on Highway 18 into the Angeles National Forest. The welcoming, verdant peace of the forest cradled Lake Arrowhead in a bower of tree-covered mountains. It was light years away from the concrete and freeways of metro L.A. The wooded topography and clean mountain air of Lake Arrowhead made it a choice getaway spot for sweltering Angelenos who might have forgotten what a cool summer night felt like, or what snow looked like during the winter. Arrowhead was an accessible paradise for jaded city-dwellers. There were conifers and evergreens, a beautiful body of water, and none of the frenetic feel of Los Angeles.

They continued gaining elevation until they reached The Rim of The World Highway, with its majestic views and eye-popping drop-offs into the canyons that flanked it. They continued through the little hamlet of Rimforest and turned on to Highway 173, which would take them into Lake Arrowhead Village.

Lake Arrowhead was the highest reservoir in the state. The man-made lake had undergone a makeover in the 1920s, when it was taken over by developers and became an R&R destination for Southern Californians. There were hiking trails, swimming, boating and fishing, with plenty of trout and largemouth bass to lure anglers. With a resident population that perpetually hovered at a little over twelve-thousand people, it still had a mom-and-pop feel. No big resorts. Lots of small cabins and private homes moonlighting as bed-and-breakfasts. A perfect getaway.

They reached the cabin and Cromag located the key underneath a juniper stump near the woodpile. It was an A-frame log cabin, cozy and intimate, and their hearts melted when they realized they would be spending time together here, alone.

Cromag got a fire going as soon as they had unpacked. They had eaten at a small restaurant in the village upon arriving, and had picked up a couple of bottles of wine. They got comfortable and sipped Chardonnay on the leather couch as the flames worked that singular magic that fires have.

They kissed deeply, and moved to the bearskin rug in front of the fireplace. They got naked and made love for hours. Cromag had not felt such peace and joy in a long, long time.

They had mutually vowed to shut off their cellphones during their stay. Before retiring, they agreed to wake up "whenever"—whether that coincided with the morning sun peeking through the pines, or hours later.

They'd just eaten breakfast when Cromag felt compelled to reboot his cellphone and check in. Force of habit. Luckily, there were no messages and no texts. *No news is good news,* thought Cromag. He had no clue that his utopian reverie was about to be shattered within the next few moments.

CHAPTER 56

. : "..! ."

LINDA WENT INTO THE BATHROOM TO SHOWER. CROMAG finished cleaning the kitchenette and washed the dishes. He was wiping down the table when his phone rang. He saw the caller ID: it was Bennett. *Uh-oh…* he thought, *he's not calling me to say hello, that's for sure…*

"Hello. This is Cromag."

"Sarge… you know I wouldn't bother you unless it was important. Are you sitting down?"

"Spit it out, Bennett. What is it?"

"It looks like she's back…"

"What? Like *who's* back?"

"There's been a homicide at some estate in Pasadena. It's got Jewel Thief written all over it."

Cromag blanched. His voice came out in a coarse whisper, as if Eve were choking him all over again.

"Are you sure?"

"Identical to all the others, Sarge. No evidence, no clues."

Cromag's heart plummeted. He inhaled deeply. "Okay, Bennett. I'm on my way."

Cromag hung up, stunned.

No. Fucking. Way.

CHAPTER 57

AS SOON AS LINDA CAME OUT OF THE BATHROOM, SHE COULD tell something was wrong. Cromag looked like he'd just been diagnosed with a fatal disease.

"Connor, what is it? What's wrong?"

Cromag had always been known for keeping close counsel. With anybody else, he would have manned up, held it inside, and took care of business silently. But this wasn't anybody else. This was *Linda*.

"There's been another homicide."

"The Jewel Thief?" she asked, her face a map of horror.

"Same MO," said Cromag. He was vague on purpose. He wouldn't confirm that it was Eve Nouveaux. *How could he?* Hunter had turned Eve Nouveaux into space dust. He had seen it with his own eyes. *How the fuck could this be?*

They embraced. "I've got to get back. The murder was committed in Pasadena. You can stay here and I'll come back and get you."

"Oh no, Connor—I'm coming back with you. I might be needed if there is any forensic work to be done."

They were out of the cabin in five minutes. On the ride back, Cromag was silent, too shaken to say anything. Linda reached over and took his hand in hers. She could feel the tension in his body. Explosive energy straining for release, like a cocked crossbow.

The drive back took half the time the drive up had taken. Cromag was speeding the whole way, bordering on being reckless. He was obsessed now with an inexplicable mystery. The desire to know the truth fueled him, like madness fuels the actions of a psychopath.

Although he'd never used his law enforcement creds to beat a traffic ticket, he was prepared to do so now, if need be. He played the scenario out in his head. State trooper camped out on the roadside. Cromag passes at supersonic speed. Trooper lights 'em up and there's a short pursuit. Cromag presents his license and registration. The trooper finds out he's a detective, gives him a polite admonishment to slow down, then lets him go.

The scenario he imagined never came to pass. He made it back into the metro crunch without incident. He dropped Linda off and jetted over to Mission Hills. Hunter was sitting in his backyard, playing with the cat.

Hunter looked at him strangely. "Did I lose track of the time, Connor Cromag? You were not expected to return until the day after tomorrow."

"We've got a problem, Hunter—a *real* problem."

He related the news and Hunter was silent. He appeared to be in deep thought. "I have a theory about this, Connor Cromag, but I must be in proximity to the crime scene to verify my suspicions."

Cromag thought for a moment. Same dilemma. *How am I gonna get Hunter close to that crime scene without opening a can of worms?*

He decided he would take Hunter with him. They would go in Cromag's personal car, to maintain some undercover anonymity. He would park as close as possible to the scene and leave Hunter in the car to conduct his analysis while he went inside and examined the crime scene. It was the best they could do. It would have to suffice.

CHAPTER 58

.:.":..

CROMAG WAS THREADING LANES ON THE 210 FREEWAY LIKE A drunk driver. Hunter was expressionless, but Cromag noticed he looked over at the speedometer a couple of times to gauge their speed. Here he was again, breaking the law, but he had no choice. Since he was in his civvy car, he couldn't just prop a bubble on the roof and siren-blast a path through traffic. He had to risk getting caught speeding. *Just please don't have them ask Hunter for ID if we get stopped.* That would be all he needed right now.

They exited on Colorado Boulevard and headed for the pricey hillside neighborhoods north of the freeway. The homes morphed from "nice" to "wow" to "spectacular" in just a few blocks. Cromag wondered what it would take to own a home up here. *More than a detective's salary, that's for damn sure...*

Cromag knew they were getting close. From a quarter-mile off, he saw yellow tape and patrol cars. They parked way down the street.

"Will this be close enough for you?" he asked Hunter.

Hunter was toying with his amulet, manipulating it and turning it. Funny how that amulet had gone from an object of ridicule in Cromag's eyes, to an absolutely essential piece of gear, in just a week. Never again would he shit-mouth that amulet.

"Yes, Connor Cromag. I am picking up evidence of residual isotopic radiation... the unmistakable signature of a Biosynth."

"But how can that be?" Cromag asked. "We killed her a few days ago. How could she come back to life?" He had a look on his face like a little boy who'd just been told his dog had been run over by a car.

Hunter felt his anguish. "To use a police expression that you are familiar with, they sent back-up."

They sent back-up? Are you fucking kidding me? Cromag went limp, like his skeleton had been sucked out of his body and his flesh and organs had puddled on the floor. It took him a minute to recover.

"You mean another Biosynth?"

"Yes, Connor Cromag. It appears so."

Cromag was dopey with shock. "Omigod…this is a nightmare. I've gotta get inside and check out the crime scene. Wait here until I come back."

Cromag could have done the walk-through blindfolded. After seeing eight examples of Biosynth handiwork, he could recite the details by heart. Missing genitals, a dead vic, no evidence. Just blood, blood, blood.

The disappointment among the CSI team was palpable. Just when the city had let loose a major sigh of relief, here we go again. When would there be an end to this?

Cromag approached Bennett for additional details, more out of habit than genuine curiosity. There was nothing new. Just a new location and a new victim.

"Give me a call if anything turns up." Then he left. He returned to Hunter waiting in his car, and they sped off.

CHAPTER 59

AS THEY WERE DRIVING BACK ON THE 210 FREEWAY, CROMAG'S phone rang. It was Bennett.

"Yes, Bennett—go ahead."

"We lucked out, Sarge. Lester Gordon, the victim, was the owner of a security company that supplies high-end video surveillance equipment to businesses. He had his whole house on camera—every room, every window, every entrance. We've got footage of the vic and suspect entering the house together."

"That's good news. Get the tape over to Linda ASAP. I'll meet you back at Division in about forty-five minutes." Cromag felt somewhat better. Here was an encouraging zephyr of fresh air amidst the suffocating fumes of frustration.

Cromag dropped Hunter off at his house, and then drove to Division. He parked, and leaped up the stairway, taking the steps two at a time. He passed the Captain on his way up. There were fresh furrows of disappointment in his brow. He'd obviously been told about this new killing. They looked at each other momentarily, but neither man said a word. What could they say?

Cromag went to his office and checked his correspondence and emails, just going through the motions. His mind was on the video grab from the latest crime scene and he was waiting for a call from Linda.

It came within seconds—the console light flashing, announcing an intercom call from forensics. He pushed the speaker button. "I left five minutes ago...I'll be there in a flash." He didn't even wait for a response from Linda. He vaulted down the stairway and took the hallway turn on two wheels.

He skidded to a stop outside the lab, almost getting into a head-on with Bennett. They went in. Everybody skipped the cordialities, and they followed Linda to a monitor.

She loaded the tape. The front door video cam had been optimally positioned. It gave a panoramic view of the entrance and anything within twenty feet of it. A couple approached the doorway. Linda zoomed in on the face of the woman.

"I'll be damned," said Bennett. "She dyed her hair."

Sure enough, that brooding, sexy brunette they'd gotten used to was nowhere to be seen. Instead, there was a tall, gorgeous blonde. Same height, same build, just different coloring. Cromag wasn't surprised. The Destroyers had a basic model they could accessorize any way they wanted. *The fuckers.*

Though Cromag knew the truth about the killer he kept silent. What could he possibly say? *It's just too incredible to believe; I can hardly believe it myself.*

Luckily, the appearance of the blonde provided a simple explanation the police and public would buy: she had taken a short break but was still around, and had changed her appearance in an effort to avoid detection. Only Cromag knew this was actually another killer, a "Sister Synth" fresh on the scene, who had come to finish the job that Eve Nouveaux had started. His stomach churned at the thought.

He asked Linda to print close-ups of the woman's face and had Bennett go through the drill: circulate the updated photo to all agencies and double-down on the investigative effort. He took a copy of the blonde's headshot and returned to his house.

Hunter was waiting, eager for an update. Cromag showed him the photograph, and they planned their attack with tactical precision. Based on the projected path of the original Biosynth's trail of murder, they targeted the next two probable Exceleron Fitness locations where the Blonde Synth would go to harvest. They made plans to stake out *both* locations at the same time: Cromag would cover one, and Hunter the other. Cromag outfitted Hunter with a walkie-talkie so they could maintain constant communication.

"Connor Cromag," Hunter began, "Nothing has changed as far as the time constraint faced by the Destroyers. The replacement Biosynth is aware of the deadline she must meet, and I am sure she will relax her normal vigilance and suspend caution to accomplish her goals. She has less than seventy-two Earth hours to complete harvesting and return to the Destroyers, or they will perish."

"Okay," said Cromag. "We'll plan on being onsite at the clubs at opening time, just like we did on our last stake-out. You'll be stationed at Verdugo Hills and I'll be at Monrovia. The clubs are very close to each other—that's good. We'll stay in touch with the two-way radios." He showed Hunter how to transmit and receive.

"Copy that, partner," said Hunter. "This thin blue line has two ends: yours and mine."

Cromag rolled his eyes. *Fucking Hunter ... just can't resist an opportunity to slip in some cop jargon, can you?* He realized that Hunter wasn't trying to be humorous, he was just trying to "assimilate." But he'd better make sure that Hunter understood some basics about the operation they were about to undertake.

"One more thing, Hunter. Very important. Keep me in the loop at all times. If you see her, don't try to be a hero and confront her yourself. You're not gonna do something crazy like that, are you?"

"No worries, CC—that ain't how I roll."

Hunter's attempt at humor was intentional this time. He had hoped his glide into 'hood slang would put a smile on Cromag's face, but no smile was forthcoming. Cromag couldn't muster even a grin right now. Truth was, though he wouldn't admit it to Hunter, he was scared shitless.

CHAPTER 60

. : ⦙.: .⦙

THEY GOT UP THE NEXT MORNING, LONG BEFORE THE SUN would start peeking over the mountains that rimmed the northeast Valley. They said very little as they checked and double-checked their gear and reviewed the logistics of their plan. Hunter used his amulet to bring up the map again, and Cromag pointed out how close the two locations were.

See?" Cromag said. "If she shows up at your spot, I can get there in about five minutes. You call me the minute you make an ID. If she shows up at Monrovia instead, I'll bark loud and clear."

They loaded their gear. Cromag gave Hunter the keys to his Dodge Charger. He'd given Hunter a behind-the-wheel test the day before, to make sure the guy could drive the damn thing. He had performed incredibly well, enough to calm Cromag's nerves and make him start believing they might just pull this off.

Cromag got into his unmarked cruiser and fired it up. They made a sound-check on their walkie talkies. He gave a thumbs-up to Hunter as they pulled out of the driveway. All systems go.

They drove in single file on the 210 Freeway, Hunter first, followed by Cromag. The exit for Verdugo Hills was looming, a half-mile away. "You got this, Hunter?" Cromag asked.

"I do, Connor Cromag. I will call you when I have arrived at my destination."

Cromag watched as Hunter took the offramp. He was going to take the very next exit. It was all in the hands of God now…

Just as Cromag pulled into the lot at the Monrovia gym, his walkie-talkie squawked.

"Connor Cromag, do you copy?"

"Loud and clear, partner," said Cromag.

The doors of both gyms opened on schedule and the early-arriving members filed in. Now came the fun part: the waiting game.

Hunter had been making some adjustments to his amulet when he noticed an eye-catching ride drive into the lot at Verdugo Hills. It was a red Ferrari—just the kind of car a Biosynth would drive. The car parked, and a leggy blonde got out. Hunter's amulet was flashing like a July 4th sparkler. Her isotopic signature registered a strong reading. Positive ID—it was her! He tapped Cromag on the squawker.

"Connor Cromag, I have the suspect in sight. She is entering the building."

"Okay, Hunter. I'll be there in five minutes. Don't take your eyes off that entrance. As soon as she finds a victim she'll be leaving."

Cromag got back on the freeway and roared towards Verdugo Hills. He got there and looked around for his Charger. Nowhere to be found. *Shit.*

He called Hunter. "Hunter! Do you copy?"

"Yes, Connor Cromag."

"Where the fuck are you? I told you to wait for me."

"I could not, Connor Cromag. She came out almost immediately. I did not want to lose her trail."

Cromag forced himself to remain calm. "Okay, Hunter. Where are you headed?"

"We are heading West on the 210 Freeway. We have just passed the Sierra Madre exit."

"Got it. I'm on my way. Stay with them."

Cromag punched the cruiser and it leaped forward like a hungry leopard. He smoked his tires all the way out of the lot and headed for the freeway onramp. By his estimation, he was about eight minutes behind Hunter.

He needed an update. "Hunter. Where are you right now?"

"We have exited on Lowell Avenue and are driving up the hill."

The area was familiar to Cromag, and it gave him a hunch. There were a lot of cheap motels on Foothill in that part of town. The blonde Biosynth was in a hurry and had probably talked her intended victim into a quickie at the nearest motel. The way she looked, it wouldn't have taken much convincing.

"Connor Cromag, we are pulling into the 'Good Knight Inn'. It is just past the intersection of Pennsylvania Avenue and Foothill Blvd."

"Yeah, I know where it is. I'm about seven minutes out. Wait for me."

There was no response from Hunter, but it didn't matter. Cromag was on a trajectory headed for the Good Knight Inn. He passed a flurry of mom-and-pop shops that dotted both sides of Foothill Boulevard. They had been there forever, some changing their names, some changing ownership, but always a familiar feature. Dry cleaners, flower shops, convenience stores, bakeries.

On the right he saw the sign for the Good Knight Inn. It was corny, in keeping with the advertising trends that were popular during its heyday. It featured a knight in armor, holding a jousting lance, atop an ornately-costumed horse.

As he pulled into the lot, he was startled by something he did not expect to see: a young, well-built guy, running at top speed on the sidewalk. And he was stark naked.

As if that weren't startling enough, a red Ferrari roared out of the parking lot, fishtailing, with tires screaming as it rocketed on to Foothill Boulevard and sped off in the opposite direction.

Uh-oh, thought Cromag. He started to feel anxious. What would await him when he got there? He pulled into the lot and screeched to a stop. His car, the one Hunter had been driving, was parked there, but Hunter was nowhere to be found. *Dammit, Hunter, I told you to wait for me…*

He looked up at the veranda on the second floor and saw one of the doors gaping open. He catapulted up the stairs, instinctively drawing his Glock. His heartbeat was manic.

He approached the doorway slowly. Not a sound. He got closer, crouching down on his knees. Very slowly now. He peeked around the side of the doorjamb. The room was empty. The window in the bathroom was open and a breeze was playing with the curtain, making it dance like a flag in the wind. Everything was dark and silent. Scary silent.

He let his eyes adjust for a moment and that's when he saw a body lying on the floor. It was Hunter.

CHAPTER 61

.: ":.: ."

CROMAG RAN OVER TO HIM. WHEN HUNTER NOTICED CROMAG he attempted to roll over and change position. He looked like he was hurt, in pain.

"Hunter! What's the matter, bro'?" Connor asked. "You OK?"

Hunter muttered something, and Cromag could see that things were not okay. Hunter had his hands clasped over his abdomen.

"You're hurt! Let me see …"

"No—no… it's fine…it's n-n-nothing," Hunter stammered.

"Bullshit." Let me get a look at it." He leaned in and pried Hunter's hands apart, then froze.

There, instead of seeping blood and the entry wound he was expecting to see, was a mass of wires and glowing connectors. He looked into Hunter's eyes, then back to the wound, then back at Hunter. Cromag wanted desperately to say something, but his mouth was locked in the rigor of shock.

"You're…you're…" Connor babbled, like a drooling imbecile. His tongue was useless, like a dead fish in his mouth. He couldn't form the words to describe his horror. Hunter spoke slowly, in pain as much from what he had to say, as he was from his wounds.

"Yes, Connor Cromag—I am a biomimetic."

Cromag was a statue carved from the stone of bewilderment. Emotions, questions, and confusion all flooded his mind, washing away any semblance of solid ground where his reason could establish footing. He was trying to understand it all, in the manner that a child would react to the sudden loss of a beloved companion.

"No. No way. *No fucking way!*" Cromag bellowed, clutching at denial despite a whirlwind of realization that was shattering the beliefs he had held about Hunter since first meeting him. He had accepted that Hunter was another life form, but not *this*—not some fucking *machine!*

"I am sorry, Connor Cromag."

"Wha-why-why didn't you tell me?" asked Cromag. A kid learning the truth about Santa Claus couldn't have felt more betrayed.

"I needed to gain your confidence and trust. I was afraid that if I revealed my true identity you would not help me."

Cromag was on the verge of tears, but gathered his composure quickly as a new emotion fueled his aspect: rage.

"*She* did this to you. Didn't she?" he hissed, arteries bulging in his neck like the roots of an oak.

Hunter nodded his head. His green amulet was still glowing, but with much less intensity now. It began to flicker.

The same sickening feeling of loss on the horizon, of grief about to cross his threshold, began to well up in Cromag as it had when Clay had been killed. He had come to like Hunter and felt a camaraderie with him. In the most basic, uncomplicated analysis of their relationship, they had been two cops working together. True, they were separated by a universe of time and space, of different origins—but they were partners, nonetheless—and he had felt the bond between them.

He felt alone and helpless, the same way he had felt when he had lost Clayton. Here he was, losing another brother.

"What do you want me to do?" asked Cromag in anguish. If Hunter had been a human partner, he would have called it in, asked for backup and paramedics. But since his partner was a robot from outer space, standard procedure went out the window. There would be more questions and more problems than he could deal with. He felt helpless and looked imploringly at Hunter.

As if reading his mind, Hunter said, "There is nothing that can be done, Connor Cromag. She has wounded me—and fatally, I am afraid. But I have also wounded her quite seriously. She has lost the use of her right arm and her right leg is severely injured. She will walk with a limp for the remainder of her existence. I also gave her a 'shiner' on her right eye. But her wounds will not prevent her from continuing her mission, I am sorry to say."

"That's okay, partner. You did great—more than I would have been able to do." He wanted to scream at the top of his lungs. He was angry at Hunter, for not having waited for him. But what good would anger do now? He looked down at Hunter. His breathing was shallow.

"I don't have much longer," Hunter said feebly. "My energy pulse is dwindling and cannot be restored."

"So, what do I do?" asked Cromag. He was now hyperventilating, and fearful.

"You must carry out our plan by yourself. You alone must destroy the Biosynth before she completes her harvesting and returns to her creators. The future of your species depends on it."

"By myself? Without your help?" Cromag began to fall apart, almost whimpering as he struggled to hold back tears. The gravity of Hunter's request had encased him in a suffocating wrap of realization.

Cromag was pinned down by fear and doubt. But he realized he had only one choice. Like so many others who'd suddenly been summoned to action in the face of a formidable challenge, he would have to respond as a great man would respond. Cromag thought of all these things as he pondered his future, and reflected on his past.

His life in law enforcement fast-forwarded before his eyes: his days as a rookie, investigating his first homicide; all the killers he had outwitted; all the psychopaths he had sent to the electric chair or life imprisonment; and especially—the ones he had killed on the spot because they refused to surrender. But his last memory was the most poignant, the most painful—and would end up being the one he would bolt his resolve to.

It was an image of his brother—his beloved, sweet little kid brother Clayton—who was innocent and loving, and had been murdered and mutilated without a shred of remorse by some cyber-whore assassin from another world. His veins pulsed with lava. He would not allow such injustice to go unpunished. He took a deep breath and faced Hunter, armed with new determination.

"What do I need to do?"

CHAPTER 62

HUNTER STRUGGLED TO SPEAK. HE WAS BECOMING FEEBLER BY the minute. His amulet was flickering with just a soft glow now.

"When I wounded her, I was able to get close enough to make a complete wave-mapping of her isotopic signature, and attune my amulet to its pulse. Now she can be tracked, not just within twenty-five yards or so, but from many miles away. Let me show you."

He aimed his amulet and projected a map of Southern California on the wall. There, in the southbound lanes of the 405 Freeway, was a green dot, moving rapidly.

"That is her," he said. "You can summon this information any time you want to get an accurate reading on her location. She was driving a new red Ferrari—not the most common car around. That should be of some help."

He went on to explain that there would only be the briefest of opportunities to surprise the Blonde Biosynth and do what was necessary to defeat her. He reminded Cromag that, though the Biosynth was wounded, she was nonetheless a formidable adversary. Cromag didn't need convincing. Hadn't he almost died at the hands of the original Biosynth, Eve Nouveaux? If Blondie was even half as tough—with a crippled arm and leg—she would be more than a handful.

Hunter's support and encouragement as he lay dying were admirable, but Cromag had to face an inescapable truth: He had to confront her—and defeat her—*alone*. Cromag would have to set a trap—with himself as the bait.

Hunter's movements were sloth-like now. His breathing was labored as he wrapped up the loose ends with Cromag. He instructed him in the use of the Helionite amulet. It alone could disable the Biosynth and render it inoperative.

"Turn the ring that surrounds the crystal counter-clockwise," said Hunter. "It will activate the pulse-beam and you can use it to disable the Biosynth."

Cromag took the amulet and held it, got the feel of it. There was a smaller, faceted crystal mounted on the ring. He turned the ring and the amulet became brilliant. He aimed the crystal at the wall and pressed the smaller stone. The room was bathed in green light as an intense beam of pulsing energy fired from the crystal and cast a pinpoint on the distant wall.

"That's it, Connor Cromag. You must activate the beam in that fashion and aim it at the remaining functional eye of the Biosynth—her left eye. It will disable her."

Cromag nodded. "How do I make her dissolve?" he asked.

"You can initiate a molecular deconstruction by turning the ring *clockwise* and then pressing *this* crystal," Hunter said, indicating a second gem on the ring framing the stone.

"Do you understand its function now?" Hunter asked, his voice but a whisper now.

"Yes," said Cromag.

"Good. There is just one thing left to do. It is time for me to leave you now, Connor Cromag. You must 'dissolve' me as well, as soon as my function ceases."

"No, no…" said Cromag, in tears. He was a child being told it was time to go to bed at the end of an emotion-filled day.

Hunter grabbed his arm. "I'm counting on you, brother…here…" From his pocket he extracted the Star Wars action figures of Han Solo and Chewbacca, the ones he had been carrying ever since their Happy Meal so many days ago. He handed them to Cromag.

"Best buds…partners…" Hunter said, and then he said no more.

The amulet flickered one last time and became dark.

CHAPTER 63

.: "..: .

CROMAG WEPT UNABASHEDLY. THERE WAS ONLY ONE OTHER guy he'd ever had a bond so strong with: his brother Clayton. Drawing on the memory of Clayton for strength, he committed himself to playing out the endgame with the Biosynth according to the plan he and Hunter had crafted. She would not get away with this.

He held up the amulet, turned its bezel-ring clockwise, pressed the gemstone, and bathed Hunter's body in eerie green light. His form began to appear fuzzy and indistinct. The image became pixelated and started to disperse in the room. Within seconds, the cloud that had once been Hunter spread into the atmosphere, never to return. Cromag bowed his head in silent tribute to the intergalactic cop who had become a partner and friend in such a short time.

He left the room key on the dresser, turned out the light, and shut the door on the dark secrets the motel room would hold silent forever. He returned home.

The house was silent when he entered. He had been making plans here with Hunter just hours ago. But there was no time for nostalgia. It was time to trigger the last phase of the plan. He projected the holographic map of the Exceleron Fitness locations on to his kitchen table. The next predicted target of the Biosynth was the location in Studio City.

He called Linda. He told her that he was about to launch a sting operation on a dangerous fugitive. Although he hated lying to her, he had no other choice. How could he possibly tell her the truth? Maybe, someday.

When he was finished, he said "I love you, Linda," with all the sincerity his heart could muster.

Something in Connor's tone alerted her, gave her pause. She could sense something ominous lurking, but kept silent. *This is what it means to love a cop.*

"I love you too, Connor. Please call me as soon as you can."

"I will. Good-bye."

Connor lay awake in bed that night. Knowing what was on his agenda the next day made any possibility of sleep a delusion. He got up well before dawn, had some coffee and gathered his tactical kit: his Glock, fully loaded and with back-up clips; his K-Bar knife, which he strapped to his ankle; and of course, Hunter's amulet. He gripped it tightly. He forced himself to overcome his doubts and believe in its power. It would help him overcome the most menacing adversary he'd ever faced.

He stood before the bathroom mirror, naked from the waist up. He knew that he was a few years older than a typical candidate on the Biosynth's "preferred" list, but he didn't let that discourage him. He was still in great shape. He was thankful at that moment for every minute he'd ever spent in a gym. If he had looked anything less than fully buffed, he'd have a snowball's chance in Hell of luring the Biosynth and taking her out.

He went to his garage, where he kept a set of dumbbells, and pumped iron for twenty minutes, flushing his muscles with blood and getting them ready for the confrontation. He wanted "the bait" to be as attractive as possible for the Biosynth bitch. He put on a tank top that hugged his chest tightly and displayed his shoulders and huge guns in proper form. It was showtime.

He got into his Charger as the sun was rising and headed for Studio City. He was one of the first to arrive in the lot. He parked under a tree, out of the way, but with a good view of the parking lot and the club entrance. He activated the amulet and set it on the center console. He was prepared to hang loose for as long as he needed to.

He didn't even have to wait ten minutes.

The amulet lit up and began flashing. A red Ferrari showed up to his right and cruised through the lot, slow and sinister, like a shark in a coral reef. The frequency of the flashes increased as the car got closer. Cromag was tense, nervous. *You can do this. Do it for Clay, for Hunter.*

The Ferrari parked and a spectacular blonde exited. She had legs up to her neck. She tossed her hair to one side and headed for the entrance. She was limping. Cromag's heart almost went into fibrillation when he realized this was his quarry. But he needed to make sure.

As discreetly as he could, he got out of his car and headed for the entrance. He maintained the stealth of a ninja assassin, cautious not to arouse suspicion. He pulled up casually, right alongside her, and then opened the door like a gentleman. He flashed his best smile and said, "Hi."

She turned to face him and returned his smile. Her beauty was stunning, but to Cromag, the most wonderful thing about her was that she had a shiner on her right eye. *Yes! The legacy of her encounter with Hunter. Identity confirmed.*

He accompanied her into the main exercise room. Predictably, all the males in the room turned to get an eyeful. He couldn't blame them; she was truly exceptional. Weights were clanging and the musical soundtrack was cranked, so he had to raise his voice a little.

"My name's Connor. What's yours?"

"I'm Dawn."

What he wanted to do most was to grab an Olympic plate, and send all forty-five pounds of it crashing into her skull. But he had to restrain himself. This was his only shot. Win or go home. And where would home be if the universe were doomed? He dialed his facial expression to its "horny guy on the make" setting and locked it in place.

"Do you come here a lot?" he asked.

"No, I'm just here for a little while vacationing, and wanted to exercise. How about you?" She was so honestly attractive that Cromag felt a renewed awe for the malevolent alien intelligence that had crafted her.

"I'm also on vacation—but I have some time to kill today," Cromag said, keeping his expression as deadpan as possible. He froze momentarily, fearful that his unintentional double-entendre of "time to kill" might trigger a literal interpretation on the part of the Biosynth and blow his cover. But that didn't happen. She just smiled at him, licking her lips in an exaggerated gesture.

"Since we already have something in common, maybe we should work out together," he said.

"I would like that," she said.

Bait taken. All I have to do now is set the hook.

He wanted to push the conversation in the direction it needed to go, so he started pulling pick-up lines from the Clayton Cromag playbook in an attempt to steer and accelerate the outcome. His brother had been a pro at speed-scoring and had shared his knowledge and lexicon with Connor.

Cromag's gut ached at the corny lines he was spewing, but "Dawn" was eating it up. It took all his discipline to maintain the ruse. He just wanted to gut this bitch, not fuck her! But she could not be allowed to have even the slightest inkling of his true feelings. He would have to maintain his façade of deception to the very end.

He dug deep into Clayton's bag and opted for heavy artillery. He had very little to lose at this point. He came right out and told her he wanted to have sex with her and that he knew of a motel right down the street. Was she interested? He waited and held his breath.

She lit up like a pinball machine.

"Yes," she purred, "I would *love* to fuck you. Let's go."

They left the club together. He pointed to his Charger. "That's my car. Follow me. The motel is just down the block."

They exited the lot and pulled up at the Motel Six on Ventura Boulevard. Cromag went to the desk and got a room. He walked out, jangling the keys aloft to get her attention. He smiled, even though he was holding back the urge to projectile-vomit his guts out. *Be patient. All the work and preparation has culminated in this moment. Don't blow it.*

She followed Cromag into the room and as soon as the door was closed, she locked lips with him, thrusting her tongue into his mouth as she pulled his tank-top off over his head. Then she took off her sweats and unharnessed her breasts, full and pendulous, as they tumbled into view. Her large nipples were erect and pink, inviting like some exotic, deadly fruit.

Connor knew that everything depended on what he would do in the next few minutes. *Everything.*

"I've got a surprise for you," he said.

"Oooh, I love surprises," she cooed.

"Just give me a minute to use the bathroom and I'll show you what it is…"

He went into the bathroom and took off his pants, leaving himself naked. He reached into the pocket and withdrew Hunter's amulet. He turned the bezel-ring counter-clockwise and readied it for action. He came out of the door and said, "You have to close your eyes. No peeking."

She squealed like a schoolgirl. Had the Destroyers actually built in this adolescent reaction as part of her menu of programmed responses? It didn't matter now. He approached her on tiptoe, on her right side, which he knew to be blind. He held the amulet up at the level of her eyes. Hunter had been right; she couldn't see out of that eye.

"Turn around. Here it is..."

She wheeled around, just as Cromag pressed the activating button on the amulet's ring. A beam of pure, green Helionite energy shot from the center of the crystal and drilled into the pupil of her left eye. For a brief moment she became aware of what was happening to her, and a look of horror manifested itself on her face. That look was replaced with one of sheer animal rage as she snarled and looked directly into Cromag's eyes.

But it was already too late. She wobbled momentarily and then crashed to the floor, lifeless.

Cromag remembered the life-and-death struggle he'd had with her predecessor, Eve, and he was relieved, but also suspicious of the fact that taking out the Blonde version had been so easy. He kept the amulet's beam trained on her eye, ready to fire another pulse, but after another minute he realized it wouldn't be necessary. He kicked her body a couple of times like it was roadkill—and finally exhaled. He hadn't realized how hard he had been shaking.

Under other circumstances, even with a deadly criminal, Cromag might have sat on the bed to relax for a minute, but not in this case. He aimed the amulet at the voluptuous corpse, turned the ring, and bathed her in a wash of emerald death.

She started to fragment as the molecular deconstruction took place. The beautiful body that had been designed to inspire lust in countless men, turned into a repulsive, amorphous blob, before dissolving completely in a vapor of white and pink pixels.

"What a waste," he said out loud. The room was empty and quiet, devoid of anything other than the dark truth of what had just transpired—a truth that would remain forever unshared. Cromag dressed, gathered his things, and left the room. He shut the door and didn't look back.

EPILOGUE

. : "•.: .•

CROMAG RETURNED TO REGULAR DUTY TWO DAYS AFTER HIS encounter with the Blonde Biosynth. His co-workers were glad to have him back. Over the course of the next week, the daily routine resumed without further incident. On the weekend, he and Linda went out to the desert to recharge. Being together in the expanse and silence of the Mojave gave them peace, and the opportunity to re-discover why they loved each other so much.

It soon became two weeks since the Jewel Thief had taken her last victim; those two weeks became a month; and that month grew to three months. In the city, there was a growing sense of freedom from the oppressive aware-ness of a killer's threat, and the feeling of relief became palpable. The media began to embrace the possibility that the Jewel Thief was an ugly and tragic phenomenon from the past, that everyone was now safe once more. Feature articles and broadcast coverage combined a dark remembrance with a bright hope that the killer had gone into hiding, or disappeared, or stopped for some other mysterious reason. People were less concerned with *why* the killings had stopped; they were just glad that they *had* stopped.

After nine months of declining attention, the Jewel Thief murders were assigned "cold case" status, and the files were relegated to a storage area in the basement of Division.

Cromag was home alone on the morning he picked up the newspaper and learned it was the one-year anniversary of the day the first victim had been discovered. He paused and reflected for a moment, then went to the gun safe he kept in his den.

It was a special model that had been custom-constructed to his specifications, built to be impervious to anything short of a nuclear detonation. It featured advanced security safeguards as well. Gaining access required a retinal scan and fingerprint confirmations before the concrete-and-steel door would allow itself to be opened.

Cromag opened the safe and reached deep within the vault for a strongbox resting on a shelf. He opened it, removed an object, and held it up to the sunlight. It was Hunter's amulet. The Helionite crystal refracted the rays and cast prismatic green shadows on his face. He remembered Hunter and was silent. Then he placed the amulet back in the strongbox, ever respectful of the awesome power it held.

He locked the gun safe. In closing its massive door, he was closing a door on the past and its frightening secrets. He alone would be the only person to understand what had really happened during the time of the Jewel Thief Killer, and how close humankind had come to eradication. No one on Earth would ever know. No one—except Connor Cromag.

THE END

ABOUT THE AUTHOR

Raoul Edmund lives in Cave Creek, Arizona with his soulmate, Shirley, and their two cats. He has a degree in Psychology and was an advertising copy-writer for many years before trying his hand at fiction. He loves the desert, motorcycles, cats, and his woman---but not necessarily in that order. You can contact him at **RaoulEdmund.com**